HIGH SEASON

Also by Jon Loomis

Vanitas Motel
The Pleasure Principle

HIGH SEASON

Jon Loomis

St. Martin's Minotaur ✤ New York

www.minotaurbooks.com

Library of Congress Cataloging-in-Publication Data

Loomis, Jon.
  High season / Jon Loomis.—1st ed.
     p. cm.
  ISBN-13: 978-0-312-36769-5
  ISBN-10: 0-312-36769-4
  1. Sheriffs—Fiction. 2. Murder—Investigation—Fiction. 3. Cape Cod (Mass.)—Fiction. I. Title.

PS3562.O593H54   2007
813'.54—dc22

                                  2007018141

First Edition: September 2007

10 9 8 7 6 5 4 3 2

For Porkchop

Author's Note

This book is a work of the imagination set in a real but "fictionalized" place. Some of the locations are actual; many are inventions, adaptations, or amalgamations. All of the characters are fictitious: Any resemblance to real persons, living or dead, is entirely a matter of coincidence. The portrayals of governing and law enforcement bodies are not intended to be factual; I have intentionally played fast and loose with such things as the structure of the state and local governments and the size, organization, history, and operations of Provincetown's police department. I've taken liberties, too, with elements of Provincetown's history, politics, and economy—which aren't as simple as I've made them out to be—for the sake of getting on with the story.

As for the interior of the inhabitants
I am still in the dark about it.

Thoreau, Cape Cod
(Chapter X, "Provincetown")

HIGH SEASON

Chapter 1

Frank Coffin's office was windowless and cramped, hidden away in the darkest corner of the Town Hall basement, next to the boiler room. A fat sewage pipe ran the width of the ceiling; now and then a drop or two of ominous fluid plunked onto whatever paperwork lay strewn across Coffin's desktop: condensation, he hoped.

In the old days, when his uncle Rudy was chief of police, Coffin's office had been on the third floor. Small but sunlit, the upstairs office had high ceilings and two tall windows that looked out on the harbor. Then Rudy was forced to resign amid allegations of bribery and extortion, and when the new chief, Preston Boyle, arrived in May, his first official act had been to move Coffin into the basement. *Nothing personal*, Boyle had said. Coffin had been a cop for a long time: fourteen years in the Baltimore City Police Department—including nine in the homicide division—and eight years as Provincetown's first and only police detective. He knew what was personal. Losing the upstairs office amounted to a demotion.

Coffin's intercom buzzed. It was Jeff Skillings, the day's desk officer. "Lady to see you, Frank. Says her husband's missing."

Melinda Merkin was a small woman with an unusually large head. She wore a lime green pantsuit. A diamond of at least two carats sparked on her left hand. Her hair was brown with frosted highlights and wispy bangs—a style, Coffin thought, directly out of the early eighties. She wore black sunglasses, which she took off as soon as she sat down. Her eyes were dark and tired and bulged like a terrier's. Her eyebrows appeared to have been painted on. Skillings handed Coffin a manila folder as he showed her in.

"Good gravy, what a mess," she said, when Skillings was gone. She dabbed at her eyes and nose with a shredded Kleenex. "If this gets in the papers, it'll just be the end of us."

"What do you mean, the end of us?" Coffin said. He wrote the word *Merkin* on the manila folder, then circled it. He looked inside. It contained a photograph of a man dressed in a blue suit, a small gold cross pinned to one lapel. A banner hung against a wall in the background. It read 1999 BIBLE BAPTIST CONV————. The rest of the word was out of the frame.

"My husband is *Ron* Merkin," the woman said. "The *Reverend* Ron Merkin. We're on TV in thirty-seven states. If this gets out, the show's over, Rover."

Coffin leaned back in his chair. He'd seen Reverend Ron on TV once or twice while channel-surfing; he remembered a sweaty, angry man with white froth in the corners of his mouth. Merkin had built a large national following by showing up at gay bars, pride rallies, even the funerals of AIDS victims, followers in tow, chanting antigay slogans and brandishing crudely lettered signs that read like fourth-grade hate mail. Coffin suddenly felt angry and a little claustrophobic, trapped in his office with this odd woman and her accompanying cloud of perfume: lily of the valley, maybe; something floral and heavy.

"Reverend Ron," he said, tapping his pencil on the desk. "He's the God Hates Fags guy, right?"

"Lord, no—Ronnie's thing is God Hates *Homos.* God Hates *Fags* belongs to someone else—it's trademarked. We'd be drowning in deep doo-doo if we tried to use that."

Coffin opened the folder, took out the photo, and placed it on his desk.

"So, if you don't mind my asking," Coffin said, "what's your business in Provincetown? Performing a little missionary work among the heathen?"

"Look, Detective—" She stopped, hesitated for a moment. "I collect ceramic figurines."

Coffin tried to interrupt, but she held up a shushing finger.

"Dog figurines, Detective. Mostly porcelain and china. Every shape and size, every breed, from every country and period you can think of. I've been collecting them for thirty years. Everywhere you look in my house, you're looking at dog figurines. I mean, I've got thousands, literally. I couldn't stop collecting now if I tried, and even if I *could* stop collecting them, I wouldn't want to, you know what I mean?" She held up the finger again. "My husband, bless his heart, does not understand my thing for dog figurines. I'm sure there are moments when he wishes every surface in his house did not have a half-dozen china pooches sitting on it. I'm sure, Detective, that there are times when that poor man is sick to death of the whole shooting match. But does he criticize? Does he complain? Not very blessed much, I'm here to tell you. We all have our stuff, Detective. I've got mine, he's got his; dollars to doughnuts you've got yours."

She opened her bag, extracted a second photograph, and placed it on the desk in front of Coffin. It showed the same beefy man, standing in what looked like a motel room. He wore beige pumps—big ones—and a calf-length navy blue dress with a white Peter Pan collar.

Coffin couldn't suppress a sharp bark of laughter. He looked up at Mrs. Merkin. "Sorry," he said.

"That was taken last winter," she said. "Key West."

Coffin looked at the picture again. The big man seemed to be trying to straighten his wig, which was greenish-blond and looked as rumpled and forlorn as road kill.

Drag queens he could understand, sort of; there was something tongue-in-cheek about the whole thing, all that glitter and flash, a kind of burlesque-on/homage-to the whole idea of glamour in all its blowzy, tittering goofiness. The straight cross-dressers were harder to figure out—the just plain transvestites everyone in town called tall ships. The tall ships tended to be large men who strode up and down Commercial Street in plus-sized tweed skirts, support hose, and pumpkin-colored lipstick; craggy-faced and lonely-looking men with dispirited wigs and five o'clock shadows poking through pancake makeup. Sometimes they had their wives, even their kids in tow. They reminded Coffin of his Aunt Connie after she'd been through several rounds of chemotherapy.

"So, can you tell me what happened last night?" Coffin asked.

She nodded. "He got all fixed up and said he was going out to walk around, don't wait up. That was around ten o'clock. I woke up a few times in the night, expecting him to be there, but he wasn't."

"He got dressed up and went out to walk around by himself?"

"As far as I know, yes."

"Was that unusual?"

Melinda Merkin smiled a little with the left side of her mouth. "Well, not for Ronnie. He likes to be seen, without people knowing who he is. He likes that a lot."

"Does your husband drink?" Coffin asked.

"He gave it up years ago. God told him to."

"Any drug use that you know of?"

"No. He's never messed with any of that stuff."

Coffin hesitated. "Does your husband have affairs? One-night stands?"

Melinda Merkin furrowed her painted brows; deciding how much of the truth to tell, Coffin guessed.

"I guess a lot of men struggle with the lust thing at some point in their lives," she said, "but Ronnie's mellowed out in the last few years. He wasn't exactly Casanova to begin with."

Coffin placed the two photos side by side and looked at them closely. "Does your husband sleep with men, Mrs. Merkin?"

"No! Good Lord. Just because a man likes to wear a dress every now and then doesn't make him queer."

Coffin raised his eyebrows. "Did you two have an argument or anything last night, before he . . . ?"

She dabbed at her eyes again; the Kleenex was smeared with mascara. "I am too daggone tired out by all this business to fight about much of anything anymore, Detective. I'm not exactly jumping for joy, but I'm doing my best to deal with it, because I love my husband."

Coffin slid the photos into the manila folder, along with his notes. "Mrs. Merkin," he said, "odds are your husband will turn up in the next few days. We get one or two cases like this every year—it's easy for out-of-towners to get swept up in things around here—but we haven't permanently lost a husband yet."

Mrs. Merkin looked him straight in the eye. "He's a good man, you know. He takes good care of me and our children. He's not some pervert—he's a good, steady, God-fearing man, except for this one thing."

"Yes, ma'am," Coffin said. "No one's suggesting otherwise." He waited a beat. "We'll ask around as discreetly as we can. He'll turn up."

"Can I have my picture back? The one in the dress?"

"Maybe we'd better hold on to it for now, if this is how he's likely to appear. We'll keep it safe."

Mrs. Merkin sighed. "It's his sisters' fault," she said. "They used to dress him up like Tinker Bell when he was little."

Later, briefing the night shift in the cramped squad room, Coffin handed out color Xeroxes of both photos of Ron Merkin. Jeff Skillings, Lola Winters, and Coffin's cousin Tony were full-time, year-round officers; four part-time summer cops were also present. Everyone chuckled at the picture of the big man in the blue dress.

"What's that on his head?" Tony said.

"I think it's a marmot," said one of the summer cops.

"Please keep an eye out for this gentleman," Coffin said. "His name is Ron Merkin. He didn't come home last night, and his wife would like him back."

Skillings was grinning. "Ron Merkin?" he said. "Not the *Reverend* Ron Merkin?"

"That's right," Coffin said. "Do *not* discuss Mr. Merkin's appearance in this photo with anyone outside the department, especially the news media. No matter how tempting it might be."

Then Chief Boyle took over the meeting. He was small and red-faced and wore his hair combed over a speckled bald spot. Four months ago, Boyle had been deputy police chief in Ashtabula, Ohio. He was, according to the Ashtabula PD, an excellent administrator, scrupulously honest, a man who believed in doing things under budget and by the book. In a press release, Provincetown's Board of Selectmen had described him as "the perfect candidate." He was the exact opposite of Coffin's uncle Rudy.

"For the past several years," he began, eyebrows bristling, "the PPD has turned a blind eye to drug use and public indecency among the gay community."

This was essentially true, Coffin knew. Police did not patrol the gay clubs hoping to bust ecstasy dealers, nor did they harass the men who frequented the darker shadows of the town beach at night. Coffin's uncle Rudy had believed that there was no percentage in pissing off the gay community, a stand with which the selectpersons, most of whom were merchants or bar owners or guest-house proprietors or owners of significant real estate or otherwise invested in the town's economic health, wholeheartedly agreed.

"Starting tonight," Boyle continued, "that's going to change. Tonight, at 0230 hours, we will conduct a raid on Havemeyer's Wharf."

Coffin groaned. His cousin Tony turned to one of the summer cops. "The dick dock," he whispered loudly.

Boyle held up a warning forefinger. "Residents have complained. The situation has gotten out of control. I was hired to keep the peace and ensure public safety, and that's what I intend to do."

The dick dock poked into the harbor like a crooked finger, warted along its length with rickety cottages. It was one of Provincetown's busiest late-night trysting places; during the peak summer months, on warm nights, dozens of gay men gathered on the beach beneath the spindly pier, where many indulged in anonymous sex, paired off or in groups. Even a year or two ago, Coffin could not have imagined the residents of those cottages objecting; in the "old" days, people had rented there precisely because they wanted to be part of the scene. Now that the Havemeyer cottages had all been condoized and were selling for ten times Coffin's annual salary, the new, wealthy residents were apparently not amused by the dick dock's nocturnal mating ritual.

Boyle waved a handful of plastic handcuffs. "Everyone make

sure you've got plenty of twisties. Make sure you wear gloves. Watch out for needles, in the sand and in pockets. And be aware that drug possession counts on this one: If they're holding, they're busted."

Coffin raised his hand.

"What is it, Coffin?"

"Tomorrow's women-only hot tub night at the Spinnaker Inn," he said. "Are we planning to raid them, too?"

Boyle's brows bristled and twitched. "We're talking about public indecency, Coffin," he said. "Lewd conduct. You can't just go down to the beach and do the funky monkey anytime you want. No particular group of people in this town is above the law. No matter what your uncle the shakedown artist thought."

"Good for us, sir," said Jeff Skillings, face completely deadpan. Skillings had been on the force for fifteen years and had lived openly with his partner, Mark, a manager at Fishermen's Bank, for five.

"What's that, Skillings?" Boyle said.

"Stamping out indecency and all, sir—it's about time."

One of the summer cops squirmed in his seat. "Uh, Chief?" he said, raising his hand.

"What is it, Pinsky?"

"What's the policy on using force—like, if somebody resists arrest? Just nightsticks? Or can we take the tasers along, just in case?"

"Too bad we don't have bullwhips," Skillings said, still straight-faced.

The summer cops nodded. Coffin laughed.

"You got something else to say, Coffin?"

"Just laughing, Chief," Coffin said.

"Well, stop it."

Coffin's shift was over; when he got home, he would make a couple of calls. News of the impending raid would travel fast.

Chapter 2

What Valley View Nursing Home had a view of, mostly, was the town cemetery, its lush grass and lichened tombstones, some of them over two centuries old, carved death's heads and epitaphs half scoured away by rain and blowing sand and salt air. Coffin's grandparents and great-grandparents were buried there. Not his father, of course. His father had been lost at sea.

At first, Coffin's mother had made sour jokes about the graveyard's proximity: *At least they won't have far to take me; they can roll me over there in a wheelbarrow.* In the past few months, though, she had lost interest in anything outside her room; she was too busy jerking the staff around, Coffin thought, too thoroughly amused with torturing those sturdy Cape Cod ladies, with their baggy scrubs and determined smiles.

Her door was open. She was sitting up beside the bed. A female aide with muscular forearms was trying to spoon-feed her something from a plastic cup. Mashed potatoes? Tapioca?

"Come on now, Sarah," the aide said, making a little yummy sound. "Just try a bite."

Like a movie star, Coffin's father had always said, when he'd had a couple of drinks and was feeling affectionate. She had been, too, even through her sixties. Coffin thought she was still beautiful, though the Alzheimer's had aged her, given her a tight-lipped, furtive look. Her ancestors were Portuguese; they had come from the Azores in the 1840s, picked up and brought home to Cape Cod by Yankee whaling ships in need of good sailors, which the Azoreans, living as they did on tiny islands in the middle of the Atlantic, most decidedly were. She had their dark eyes and olive skin. Her hair kept its jet-black gloss until she was almost seventy but had, in the last year, turned the dull gray of galvanized steel.

"Get that slop away from me," she said. "How many times do I have to tell you fat bitches?"

"Hi, Ma," Coffin said from the doorway.

She looked up, eyes cunning and bright as a crow's.

"Who the hell are *you?*" she said. Alzheimer's had made her foul-mouthed, irascible. Sometimes she cracked Coffin up; sometimes he wanted to slap her, tell her to snap out of it, be her old self again. Her old self, the doctors assured him, was gone forever.

"It's me, Ma. Frankie."

"Frankie's dead," she said, turning away as if the subject were closed.

Coffin sighed. "I'm the only one who isn't dead, Ma."

The aide gave him a little frown. "We've decided we don't want to eat," she said. "We refused our breakfast and our lunch."

"Who the hell is *we,* fatso?" Coffin's mother said.

Coffin leaned against the door frame. "Any sore throat or upset stomach?"

"We don't seem to be having any physical problems, no," the aide said.

"So what's up with this not eating deal, Ma?"

"None of your stinking beeswax." The eyes again, hard as glass.

"You have to eat, Ma."

"I don't have to do a goddamn thing except sit here in this shit hole till I croak."

Coffin sat on the side of the bed. "Okay, fine. Don't eat. It just means I'll get your money that much sooner."

She looked away. "If I had any money, would I be stuck in a dump like this? And what makes you think I'd leave anything to a wet fart like you?"

"I've got power of attorney, Ma. Remember? Over your whole estate. The only way I don't get your money is if you outlive me." In truth, her modest savings had evaporated by the end of her second year at Valley View. Now well into her third, she was living on Medicare and Social Security and whatever Coffin could spare after paying alimony and the mortgage on the Baltimore row house still occupied by his ex-wife. The only thing of value Coffin's mother still owned was the house in which he lived. Sooner or later, that, too, would have to be sold—the property taxes were already straining Coffin's meager checking account. He had decided not to tell her; it was the kind of news that would leave her agitated, withdrawn. Until she forgot it. What was the point?

"You little turd," she said, picking up the remote control and turning on the TV. "I never liked you, you know." She changed channels rapidly, stopping when the television was tuned to *Wheel of Fortune.*

The aide shrugged and stood up. "We'll try again later. I guess we'll eat when we're hungry enough." She left the room.

Coffin's mother smiled wickedly. *Like the Grinch,* he thought.

"Vanna's getting as fat as chubbo there," she said, tilting her head toward the door. "And all that plastic surgery—she looks like some kind of puppet."

"She looks pretty good to me, Ma," Coffin said.

She shot him a foxy look. Her eyes were bright and empty. "Anything with tits looks good to you. You're just like *him.*"

"Who's him?"

"Your father's sister's husband, you moron. He'll fuck anything that walks."

Coffin considered this: could philandering be added to the list of his uncle Rudy's moral failings? It seemed more likely than not. "He's not so young anymore, Ma."

"He was here the other night," Coffin's mother said, staring at the TV.

"Rudy's in Key West. You know that."

She glared at him. "He was *here*. Sitting right where you are. Moron."

"Mom—"

"He says he's got something for you," his mother said, raising the remote and flipping rapidly through the channels.

"What?"

"Can't you see I'm trying to watch the goddamn television? Dumb-ass."

At the desk, Coffin asked to see the visitor's log.

"What exactly are we looking for?" the nurse said, a note of suspicion in her voice.

Questions from family members are not encouraged, Coffin thought. She was young and plump. Her name tag said NATALIE.

"I'm just curious if anyone's been to see my mother in the past few days. Any men."

She flipped through the logbook. "He wants to know if Mom's got a boyfriend," she said, as if Coffin weren't standing there. "Mr. Kotowski last Tuesday. Mrs. Campo day before yesterday. Other than that, just you."

"No Rudy Santos?"

"Nope."

"Any chance somebody could get in without signing the log?"

"No, sir. Not here at Valley View. We run a tight ship."

Coffin thanked her and went out to the parking lot. He drove a sagging Dodge sedan that was still registered to his mother. The fenders were lacy with rust; the door seals leaked; the interior smelled like low tide. He would have junked it in a minute, but he couldn't afford to replace it. He sat in the Dodge, smoked a cigarette, and listened to a talk show on WOMR, the local all-volunteer FM station, about discrimination against transgendered persons within the gay/lesbian community. Apparently it was rampant.

He thought about the night Rudy had called his apartment in Baltimore, after his breakdown. Coffin had been collecting disability, but it was about to run out. His wife had left him.

"What the fuck are you doing down there?" Rudy had said. "Come on home. I'll set you up. Easy job, no stress." Big, jocular Rudy. Rudy the loose cannon, the bad cop who knew about every drug deal, crooked poker game, and boy prostitute in town, and who made sure he took a cut from each of them.

When Coffin finished the cigarette, he got out of the car and climbed the sloping sidewalk back to Valley View's front door. Standing just outside, he had a clear view of the nurse's desk. He waited two or three minutes until the plump nurse, Natalie, picked up the phone, spoke into it briefly, then gathered up her clipboard and walked away, disappearing down one of the nursing home's four main corridors. Coffin went in—the automatic doors swooshing open—and ambled past the desk and down his mother's corridor, all the way to the end. He went back to the desk; no one was there. He went down another corridor. He peeked into the day room. Everywhere, old people sat parked in their wheelchairs—most of them strapped in like fighter pilots. They stared at him. He left, feeling their eyes on his back as he walked away.

Coffin lived in a two-story cottage, cedar shakes weathered silver-gray. It had a postage-stamp yard, where a tangle of rose devoured a cockeyed trellis. The rooms were cramped and low-ceilinged, crowded with dark Victorian furniture: glass-fronted cabinets brimming with blue-and-white china; ornate tables; strict chairs skullcapped with lace doilies. The doorways were narrow, the stairs steep and tight. Worn Persian rugs covered the floors. A red overstuffed chair dominated the living room. Coffin's father had sat there, winter evenings—smoking and drinking scotch, talking back to the television set. A taxidermied goat's head glared from above the fireplace, dust in its long beard. It was his mother's house; sometimes Coffin felt her presence there, as if she were hiding in a closet or under the bed, eyes bright and malicious.

Jamie arrived twenty minutes late, parking her old blue Volvo wagon across the street. She was a yoga instructor, slim-hipped and sinewy, dressed in a long batik skirt, blue tank top and hand-beaded necklace. Her full name was Jameson Lynnelle Culpepper; she was the daughter and granddaughter of army colonels from South Carolina and a descendant of Pierre Gustave Toutant Beauregard, the Confederate general who fired on Fort Sumter in 1861. Seventeen years ago, while her ancestors twirled in their graves, she'd refused to apply to Duke or Virginia, insisting instead on going to Sarah Lawrence. She'd been living up north ever since. She opened the Volvo's hatchback and took out a bag of groceries. Coffin kissed her at the door.

"The perfect woman," he said. "Smart, good-looking, brings food."

"Hello, handsome," she said.

Coffin smiled. "Smart, blind, good-looking, brings food," he said. "It doesn't get any better."

In the kitchen, Jamie unloaded the groceries. "What we have here is two *beautiful* tuna steaks," she said, producing them with a flourish. "Two bottles of pinot grigio, very nice, on sale. Fresh asparagus. And, for an appetizer, mussels gathered by *moi*, mere moments ago, along the breakwater."

There were lemons and a jar of capers, too, and a tube of wasabi paste so strong that when Coffin tasted it his sinuses seemed to explode, which was oddly exhilarating, and his nose began to run, which wasn't. He and Jamie cooked together: She steamed the mussels in white wine and garlic; he seared the tuna steaks in a very hot pan with just a faint slick of olive oil and served them rare with capers, sliced scallions, and the fiery wasabi. Jamie put together a salad—artichoke hearts, romaine, spinach, her own invented miso dressing. Coffin sautéed the asparagus in sesame oil.

They had been together almost a year. They saw each other three or four times a week, went to a movie, made dinner, took a walk. Conversation was easy, and the physical part was terrific—better than in Coffin's past relationships. Sex was just sex, unfreighted by commitment angst or a long menu of old resentments. It was the perfect relationship: just enough intimacy, just enough space. Coffin thought it was probably too good to last.

They ate slowly, piling the empty mussel shells into a white bowl. Ella Fitzgerald sang blues from the old-fashioned record player. After dinner, Coffin opened the second bottle of wine and sat next to Jamie on the sofa. Jamie lit a cigarette, and they listened to the small yearning of crickets outside. She leaned into him, her warm weight on his chest. Coffin felt a surge of something like contentment, mixed with desire. He kissed Jamie on the top of her head and she made a soft purring noise in her throat. She had a great voice, low and a little scratchy. He kissed her again and she arched her back, a kind of invitation to touch, which he did, gently cupping her breasts through her top. Her breasts were small and still firm; Jamie had never had children, and perhaps that made a difference.

In the bedroom, Jamie lit one of the small votive candles on the nightstand and took off her clothes. She looked good in the candle-light, Coffin thought; all that yoga kept her lean and flexible. He felt lucky and grateful for that luck, and a little self-conscious about his own body, which was no longer anything to write home about. He took off his clothes anyway and lay down, and Jamie put her hand on his chest. It seemed to Coffin like a long time since they'd made love, even though it had only been a few days. Coffin turned toward her, slid his thigh between hers. He kissed her on the mouth. Jamie tasted of cigarettes and garlic and white wine. She pulled away, then raised herself on an elbow, lifting a breast to Coffin's mouth. The nipple was hard, the size of a fingertip.

"Not bad, for an old woman in her thirties," she said.

Coffin smiled. "Not bad at all," he said.

Later, they lay in the wavering candlelight. It was warm. A stuffed seagull stared from the top of the hulking mahogany dresser, glass eyes glinting.

Jamie sat up and lit a cigarette. "So I've been thinking, Frank," she said, exhaling a blue stream. She smoked an all-natural, or-ganic brand that wasn't supposed to kill you as fast.

"Thinking is good," Coffin said, nuzzling the ridge of her pelvis. Her skin tasted like bread.

"We've been getting along pretty well lately, don't you think?"

"Just fine," Coffin said, a slight sinking feeling in his gut.

"We're fond of each other, and all that."

"True. Very."

"So what's stopping us from having a baby?"

"Ortho Tri-Cyclen," Coffin said.

Jamie thumped his chest with her fist.

"Ow."

"Don't be a dope. Did you know that a woman is only half as fertile at thirty-five as she is at twenty?"

"So . . ."

"So it's now or never, buddy. Put up or shut up. Shit or get off the pot—"

Coffin held up a hand. "I get it," he said.

"Smart boy," Jamie said. "I knew you would."

"So you're thinking—"

"Now. Well, not *right* now." She nudged his wilted penis with her big toe. "But pretty damn soon. I'm officially off the pill in three days."

"Wow," Coffin said, sitting up.

Jamie narrowed her eyes. "That's a very noncommittal wow."

"Well, what if I'm not ready to have a baby?"

"Oh come on, Frank. You're forty-four years old—"

"Forty-three."

"Whatever. You're not getting any younger. How many more chances are you going to get, realistically speaking? Besides, it's not like I want to marry you."

"You don't?"

"Nope." Jamie put her cigarette out and kissed Coffin on the top of his head. "I figured you'd need a day or two to think it over," she said. "Did you know you're getting a little bald spot back here? It's very cute."

Coffin touched the spot she'd kissed. "Bald spot? You're kidding."

Jamie looked into his eyes. "I wouldn't kid you, buddy boy."

Chapter 3

Baltimore: *the streets clotted with gray slush. A dull sleet falls, icing the windshield except for a football-sized hole the defroster has made.*

He's with his partner, Rashid, responding to a call on Herndon Street, in a district of liquor stores, check-cashing shops, and rundown row houses. The front of one of the buildings is cordoned with yellow tape; a pair of street cops are out on the stoop, smoking cigarettes. The top floor apartment, Coffin knows, contains five bodies: a woman, three children, and an unidentified adult male.

They park across the street and slog through the rutted slush. Coffin's feet are cold. Some of the frigid glop has slopped into the collar of his left boot, melted into his sock. The building's front steps are crumbling, half demolished as if a truck had crashed into them. Rashid stops to bum a cigarette from one of the cops.

"Fucking Parliaments," Rashid says, lighting up. "What's the point?"

Inside, in the vestibule, the floor is crazed with muddy footprints. There's a mingled smell of Pine-Sol and old steam radiators and fried onions. The brass doors of the mailboxes have all been pried open. The stairs seem unnaturally steep. After they've climbed two flights, Coffin starts to feel light-headed. He stops to catch his breath. Things are happening to his vision—the dim stairway wrinkles and swims.

"I don't know," Coffin says. He puts his hand on the greasy banister, takes it off, wipes it on his pants leg.

"What don't you know?"

"I don't think I want to go up there."

"Me either," Rashid says. "Fuck it. Let's go get some breakfast."

"I'm serious. I'm not going up there."

Rashid looks at him, then looks at him again. "Okay," he says slowly. "You don't have to. You don't look so good. Go out and get some air."

Coffin takes a deep breath. The stairway is hot, and suddenly he's sweating—his T-shirt is soaked. It happens all the time, he knows: Cops wake up one day and just can't do it anymore, can't deal with the meanness, the pointless violence, the squalid truth about death. In Baltimore, the cops call it hitting the wall, and sometimes you get over it and go back to work, but mostly you don't; you end up as a security guard at a mall or running an all-night convenience store. He has a wife and a mortgage; his mother is ill. I have to, *he thinks.* I have to go in there.

"I'm okay," he says. He shivers. "Sorry. Let's go."

The apartment door is open. A few neighbors are gathered outside. There's a uniformed cop there, too, guarding the crime scene, arms folded across his chest. Another uniform's waiting inside. "Two in the bedroom," he says, pointing. "Two in the kitchen. One in the bathroom. Fucking hillbillies."

Coffin groped for the shrill noise of the phone in the dark, found the handset, dropped it, knocked over the plastic bottle of spring water beside the bed. The digital clock glowed 6:03.

Jamie rolled over and said, "What's going on?"

"Go back to sleep," Coffin said, patting the swell of her hip through the covers. He picked up the phone and pushed the TALK button.

"Hello?" he said, swinging his legs out from under the sheets.

Still half asleep, Jamie said " 'Lo?" and grabbed him by the firming handle of his penis, gently pulling him back into the warm bed—which was where he suddenly, desperately wanted to stay.

"Frank?" It was Lola Winters, one of Provincetown's full-time police officers. "Sorry to bother you, Frank—but something's happened. A guy found a body out at Herring Cove."

"A body?" Coffin said, gently detaching himself from Jamie's warm hand; embarrassing, somehow, talking on the phone when someone was holding your penis. "You mean dead? What's it doing out there?"

"Don't know, but it's a definite homicide. The guy was strangled with a scarf. The Park Service is there now; the state police and the coroner are on their way."

"Okay," Coffin said, suddenly breathless. "Okay, I'll be right there." The phone bleeped softly when he pushed its glowing OFF button.

He felt light-headed; the space in the room seemed weirdly flat. There had been a total of two murders in Provincetown in the last eight years. He had hoped to retire before investigating another one.

Jamie rolled over, mumbled something, then began to snore softly. Coffin dressed as quietly as he could in the near dark: chinos, hiking boots, blue flannel shirt, and a jacket—it would be windy and cold out at Herring Cove this early in the day.

Still groggy, Coffin shut the front door and trudged down the short concrete walk to his car. The sidewalk was laced with the small, shiny trails left by last night's slow migration of slugs.

In the eight months after his uncle Rudy had been forced to resign, when Coffin had been acting chief, he'd driven one of the department's two gleaming, unmarked Crown Victorias. Now, with Boyle running the department, he was stuck with the Dodge. He wrenched open the door and squeezed his tall, stooped frame behind the wheel. When he turned the key, the Dodge coughed once, weakly, and died.

"Christ," he said, hating the car more than ever. He turned the key again and the Dodge sputtered to life, its perforated muffler rumbling. He tried to turn the radio on, but the knob came off in his fingers.

He didn't notice the blue Chevy pickup parked across the street, or the man inside, slumped down in the driver's seat, smoking a cigarette.

It was early, and there was no traffic on Commercial Street except for delivery vehicles: beer trucks unloading kegs, Sysco refrigerated food trucks delivering everything from steaks to frozen broccoli to the tourist restaurants. The Dodge chugged past the town center and the Coast Guard station, with its volleyball net and long pier fingering into the bay.

Coffin was drawn to Commercial Street's west end. He often found himself driving past his great-grandfather's house with its cupola and mansard roof and the ornate front door framed by two enormous stone lions the old sea captain had brought back from China in the 1880s. Ephraim Coffin built the house near the end of the whaling era; not long after, when the sperm whales had grown scarce and the demand for whale oil was dwindling, he sank his considerable fortune into the China trade—losing everything when all three of his tall-masted merchant ships sank in a Hong Kong typhoon the next year. Ruined, believing he was jinxed, he hanged himself in the house's central cupola, with its perfect view of the harbor.

The Coffin jinx. It started in 1820 when Owen Coffin, whose young wife was pregnant with Ephraim's father, signed onto the Nantucket whaler *Essex* as harpooner. Eight months later, in the South Pacific, the *Essex* was rammed and sunk by a rogue sperm whale—an incident so freakish and so notorious that it became the factual model for *Moby-Dick*. Most of the crew survived the wreck. They sailed away in small boats, steering for South America, though they were only a few hundred miles from the Sandwich Islands—*there be cannibals*. Days later, starving on the open sea, they drew straws; for fear of cannibals, they would become cannibals themselves. Owen lost. He was the first to be eaten.

The jinx had struck every generation of Coffins since. Big Bill, Coffin's grandfather, had been killed running a boatload of Prohibition scotch into Herring Cove in 1929. Coffin's father had simply vanished into the sea; the Coast Guard found his boat the *Nora Jean* drifting empty in 1978, near Great Island. And his brother Ed, who joined the navy and served on a Swift boat in Vietnam, had disappeared into the jungle two weeks shy of shipping back to the States. Coffin had become a policeman, like his uncle Rudy. Any job, he'd said, that didn't involve boats.

Behind the Dodge, a giant Cadillac SUV blew its horn, and Coffin sped up, climbing a short, steep hill with the blue harbor visible between the houses on his left. He passed the Red Inn, then a cluster of older summer cottages, then his friend Kotowski's ramshackle house beside the stone breakwater that ran all the way out to Wood End. At the end of Commercial, he swung right onto Route 6A, past the still-skeletal condo development called the Moors. All he could get on the radio was WOMR. Two women were discussing the possible cancer risks associated with jelly sex toys. He switched the radio off, twisting the knobless metal post;

the Dodge clattered and chugged and threatened to stall. Thin columns of mist still rose from the tidal salt marsh that marked the extreme east end of Herring Cove beach. A few hundred yards to the northwest, the salt marsh devolved into scrubby woods.

When he reached a cluster of police and emergency vehicles parked on the sandy shoulder, Coffin pulled the Dodge in behind them, turned off the engine, and got out. There was a path between the trees. The woods quickly dwindled into high dunes, spiked with silver-gray beach grass. The sandy trail between the dunes was much marked by foot traffic. With the tide almost entirely out, Coffin still had no choice but to splash through occasional tidal pools.

During the summer months, Herring Cove beach was oddly segregated: There was a section, farthest from town, where families seemed to settle; the lesbian beach lay a bit to the south of them. This end, farthest south and closest to Commercial Street, was the gay men's beach. Usually packed from late morning until sunset, it was deserted at 6:30 A.M.

The path rose to the top of a last row of dunes, and Coffin could see that in the middle distance, to his right, the beach was busy with official-looking people, vehicles, and screaming, swooping gulls. A uniformed state police officer stopped him thirty paces from the crime scene perimeter, maybe a hundred square yards of sand cordoned by a skewed rectangle of yellow police tape. The tape lay on the ground, held in place with rocks at each corner. The unweighted sections fibrillated in the bay breeze.

"Whoa there, bud," the trooper said, putting his hand on Coffin's chest. He wore puttees and tall black boots. The short black brim of his peaked hat was pulled down, almost covering his eyes. "Where do you think *you're* going?"

Coffin dug in his pocket for his shield and held it up in front of the trooper's face.

"Oh, sorry, De*tec*tive," the trooper smirked. "Try to keep out of the way, all right?"

The dunes were cluttered with vehicles and webbed with boot and tire tracks. A couple of Park Service rangers—a man and a woman—waited greenly next to their pickup truck, trying, Coffin guessed, not to look at the dead guy. Park Service rangers spent most of their time handing out citations for beer-drinking, skinny-dipping, and the endless variety of sandy couplings performed out in the dunes—not investigating murders. A man with a golden retriever stood beside them, pale and shrunken in his expensive blue sweater.

Coffin watched as a shiny black Suburban drove slowly through the sand, almost bogging down in a slough before stopping just outside the cordoned area. Four troopers piled out and started unloading dogs from their plastic crates. Lola Winters and Coffin's cousin Tony hovered near the PPD's only 4x4 vehicle, an aging Jeep.

The dead guy lay in a slough between two dunes, surrounded by a low midden of sand. The coroner was already there, snapping Polaroids. He was a funeral director from Chatham, a thin, sleepy-eyed man named Sherman; Provincetown was too small to have a coroner of its own. His assistant leaned on his shovel, smoking a cigarette. A tall, bulky state police detective in a brown suit shot videotape, pointing his camcorder at the dead man, the gulls, the crisscross of tire tracks in the sand, even his own footprints. Vincent Mancini, the Cape and Islands district attorney, stood with his back to the body, watching the small waves slop one after the other onto the sand. The water was silvery, almost dead calm; it seemed as dense as mercury.

"Merkin," Coffin said. He felt dizzy; his legs seemed unnaturally long—a sensation he remembered from Baltimore, near the end, when things were starting to go bad. The late reverend wore a pink and yellow floral muumuu and one size-twelve dove gray pump with a sensible heel. His other foot was bare, the toenails painted crimson.

His face was swollen and discolored, almost black. His tongue stuck out. A long raspberry-colored taffeta scarf was knotted around his neck so tightly it dug into the flesh. The wind ruffled his wig, which looked like a glum woodchuck in the morning light.

"You know this guy?" said Mancini, turning around. He was close to Coffin's age but slimmer. His hair was glossy and dark, gelled into an artful rumple. He wore pressed jeans and a suede bomber jacket. His designer sunglasses had oval frames and blue mirrored lenses.

The state police detective pointed his camera at Coffin.

"His name's Ron Merkin," Coffin said. "His wife reported him missing yesterday."

Mancini took a silver pen out of his pocket, clicked it, and wrote the name down in a small notebook. "Well, the good news is, he's not missing anymore," Mancini said.

"The bad news," said the coroner's assistant, exhaling a stream of smoke, "is that scarf definitely doesn't go with those shoes."

The coroner grinned and snapped a picture. "Maybe what you got here is a crime of fashion," he said. His camera whirred, and a blue square of paper squirted out of its plastic slot.

"*The* Ron Merkin?" the detective in the brown suit asked, zooming in on Merkin's face. "The one on TV? My sister sends him money." A green crab clambered out of Merkin's open mouth and stilted off in the direction of the water.

"Jesus." Coffin's head swam; his palms felt tingly and moist. "Did you see that?"

The four men looked at him. Merkin's muumuu ruffled in the salt breeze. "See what?" said the coroner.

"Provincetown," the state policeman said, pointing the camcorder at Coffin again. "What a freak show."

Lola stood with her hands on her hips, watching the K-9 crew work outward from Merkin's corpse, dividing the surrounding dunes into quadrants, little regions of smell. Officer Lola—that's what the year-rounders called her—had been Coffin's first and only hire during his brief, uncomfortable tenure as acting chief. Smart, fearless, and well-trained, she was a former army MP, a crack shot, a black belt in this and that. Coffin felt old and out of shape whenever he saw her.

"Why the K-9 unit?" she said.

Coffin squinted into the wind. "Because it's there."

"You all right, Frank?" Lola said. "You're a little pale."

"I'll be okay," Coffin said. He pointed his chin at the man with the golden retriever. "Who's the gent with the dog?"

"He found the body," Lola said. "Or the dog did, I guess."

The man with the golden retriever sidled up to Lola.

"Is anybody going to take my statement, Officer?" he said. "The rangers said I'd have to give a statement to the police, but I'm not feeling very well, and my partner's going to wonder what happened to me." The golden retriever settled onto its haunches, eyes fixed on the dogs from the K-9 unit.

The man was slender, around fifty years old, and deeply tanned; his hair was dyed blond. His blue sweater shimmered in the gray morning light.

Lola took out her notebook. "We can do that," she said. "I'm Officer Winters, and this is Detective Coffin."

"Coffin?" said the man. "How weird is that?"

"Pretty weird," said Coffin. "And your name is?"

"Pfeffer. Paul Pfeffer—with a silent *p*. And this is Molly." He patted the retriever on the head. She leaned against his leg, tongue lolling, long and pink.

"Hi, Molly," Lola said.

"So you were out walking with Molly," Coffin said, "and she found the body?"

Pfeffer nodded. "It was awful. She ran ahead of me, and I lost sight of her for a few minutes. I came over the crest of a dune, and she was pulling at something in the sand."

"Not nice," said Coffin.

"Not nice at *all*," said Pfeffer. "At first I thought it was a dead gull or a seal or something. Then I saw she was pulling on a piece of fabric—you know, this bright print *fabric,* and I thought, you know, *curtains.* But then I realized a second later it was a skirt or a dress—and then of course his foot popped out of the sand, and I said, *Oh my God, it's a person. . . .*"

He stopped and put a hand over his mouth for a long moment. Then he shook his head rapidly back and forth a couple of times, as though he were trying to erase the memory of the dead man's foot and its polished nails.

Coffin scratched Molly behind the ear, and she looked up at him with a panting, doggy smile.

Pfeffer took a deep breath. "I had the dickens of a time getting Molly away from there, and then of course we went lickety-split right straight to the ranger station, and I've been out here ever since."

Lola's pen paused above the notebook. "Any idea what time it was when you found the body, Mr. Pfeffer?"

"About five thirty," Pfeffer said. He pushed back his sleeve and showed them his watch. It was a big watch, with a chunky gold bracelet.

"Kind of early to be out for a walk," Coffin said.

"I don't sleep very well," Pfeffer said. He shuddered visibly. "After this, I won't be surprised if I never sleep again."

———

"Hey, Frank," Coffin's cousin Tony said, a slick of olive oil on his chin. "What the fuck, right?" Tony was possibly the worst cop on the planet. He was leaning against the Jeep's front fender, eating a sandwich. At forty-one, Tony was the longest-serving year-round member of the force. He had only been promoted once, by Coffin, then promptly demoted again two weeks later, also by Coffin, for roughing up a tourist from Wisconsin.

"Is that linguiça?" Coffin asked. "At 7:00 A.M.?" The smell of the fatty orange sausage made him feel suddenly nauseated.

"Doris packed my lunch," Tony said, taking a bite of the sandwich. Tony's wife was a small, frowning woman who walked without moving her hips. "I got wicked hungry, all this walking around in the dunes."

"You drove," said Coffin.

"There was walking," Tony said, sounding hurt. "I walked all over the freaking place out here." He poured coffee from his thermos into its little plastic cup. "So what's the deal on this guy? Crazy, right?"

"Right," said Coffin. "Crazy."

"So what's he doing out here in the dunes?" Tony said, through another bite of sandwich.

"I guess that's the $64,000 question. Tony?"

"Ha?"

"Not a word about this to anybody, right? Especially the newspeople—they're going to be all over us."

"Gotcha."

"I mean it, Tony."

"I'm not as dumb as you think I am, cousin," Tony said, wiping his hands on his uniform shirt. His brow furrowed. "Know what I think?"

"Shoot."

"Whoever did this? That 'God hates fags' deal really pissed 'em off."

By noon, the crime scene investigation had run out of gas. The dogs were loaded by their handlers back into their plastic crates, which were lifted into the back of the black Suburban. The coroner's men zipped the body into a rubber bag and heaved it into a Park Service Jeep, which drove slowly over the dunes to the parking lot, where the bag was transferred to an ambulance. The coroner and his helper jumped into their van and took off; then the ambulance drove away, no siren, no lights flashing, no hurry— Ron Merkin was as dead as a human being could get.

The ambulance would drive the body fifty-odd miles down Route 6 to Cape Cod Hospital in Hyannis, where the attending physician would write up a death certificate. Then Merkin's remains would go to the county medical examiner's office in Pocasset, where they would be stored in a cold drawer until an autopsy could be performed. The ME, or his assistant, a pale young woman named Shelley Block, would weigh the body and take its core temperature by inserting a large thermometer into its colon. They would photograph any wounds and anything else on the body that might seem noteworthy: scrapes, bruises, scars, or tattoos. The degree of rigor would be noted, and the extent to which the corpse had been visited by insects and scavengers. Because Ron Merkin was a cross-dresser, he would be checked for possible sexual assault—his sexual organs examined, a long swab inserted into his rectum, then smeared onto a petrie dish. The coarse hair on his pubis and around his anus would be combed out into a baggie, then examined under a microscope—the ME looking for any hairs that didn't match. Then Ron Merkin would be scalpeled across the upper chest from shoulder to shoulder, and all the way down the torso from sternum to pubis. His ribs would be split (*like a lobster,* Coffin couldn't help thinking, as he drove to the Tip Top Diner), his heart and lungs and liver and everything else pulled out, examined, and weighed, the contents of his stomach cataloged. The residue under his nails would be scraped, and the scrapings checked for fibers or skin. The ME would make an incision from ear to ear across the top of the head, then flop Merkin's scalp forward over his face, remove the fore-crown of his skull with a special trepanning saw, lift out the brain, and place it on a metal tray for examination and weighing. Ron Merkin's blood would be tested for alcohol, toxins, and drugs. His clothing—the muumuu—would be FedExed to the gorgeous new state police forensics lab in Sudbury. What remained of Ron Merkin would then be picked up by an employee of a Boston funeral home, at the widow's request, and driven directly to a crematorium where it would be incinerated, the ashes and chunks of bone pulverized together into dark gray powder, which Ron Merkin's wife would take home in an elaborate bronze urn, to be placed on the mantelpiece among a large number of frolicsome porcelain dogs.

Chapter 4

Coffin and Lola sat in a booth at the Tip Top Diner, eating breakfast. The Tip Top's booths were upholstered in orange vinyl. Fishing nets and plastic lobsters hung from the walls. It was Provincetown's last good greasy spoon—a fragile, unpretentious island in a sea of trendy cafés that charged ten dollars for a cheese omelet. Coffin's scrambled eggs contained no Boursin; his bacon was pig meat, not turkey or soy. His toast was just toast, white bread—neither sourdough nor cracked wheat—which he smeared with butter from a small foil packet.

"No way the wife did it," Lola said. She set her coffee cup down and made a sour face, as though she'd swallowed a bug. "This coffee tastes like mop water."

Coffin bit his toast. "Real coffee's *supposed* to taste like mop water," he said, through a mouthful of crumbs. "Why no way?"

"Not strong enough. Merkin was a big guy. Linebacker sized. He'd put up a hell of a fight."

Coffin grunted, shrugged. "Maybe," he said. "Maybe she cracked him over the head with a ball bat first. Or drugged him. Or hired someone to kill him." He took a bite of scrambled egg. "I mean, his cross-dressing thing put them in a pretty vulnerable position. If it ever got out, good-bye television ministry. They'd end up on some reality TV show or making John Waters movies."

The waitress appeared at Coffin's elbow, holding a chrome coffeepot. She was a neighbor of Coffin's, a stout, pink-faced woman named Dot. "I saw John Waters the other day," she said, refilling their cups. "Coming out of the A&P. He had bags and bags of celery. Don't ask, I says to myself." Dot shook her head and padded off.

"If Melinda Merkin wanted to avoid scandal," Lola said, glancing over her shoulder to make sure Dot was gone, "would she kill her husband in a gay resort town and dump him on a public beach in drag? And you can stop playing devil's advocate now. I'm not an idiot."

Coffin smirked, pushed a slice of bacon into his mouth. "Sorry," he said. "Anyway, it's all academic. It's not our case."

"State police."

"And the Cape and Islands DA. Standard procedure. We hand out the parking tickets, they investigate the homicides."

Lola picked a speck of fuzz from her hat, which sat beside her in the booth. "Doesn't that piss you off, a little?"

"Are you kidding? You're kidding, right?"

"Of the last five murders on the outer Cape, how many have they actually solved?"

Coffin thought for a minute, pursing his lips and squinting a little. "One, maybe. The woman out in Truro. Hasn't gone to trial yet."

"That's what I thought. Not exactly an inspiring track record."

"Well, no. I guess not."

Lola fiddled with the salt shaker, sliding it back and forth in a small pool of water. A bright rectangle of sunshine lay across the table, backlighting the fine hairs on her forearm. "Do you ever miss it, Frank? Being a homicide cop in a big town like Baltimore? The excitement?"

Coffin shivered, suddenly cold. "Excitement's overrated."

Lola raised her orange juice in a mock toast. "To the quiet life."

"Besides," Coffin said, "somebody's got to handle the drunks, speeders, and bicycle thieves." He stuffed another strip of bacon into his mouth and took a slurp of coffee.

Lola squinted at Coffin's plate. "Should you be eating that? How's your cholesterol?"

"You sound like Jamie," Coffin said.

For a while they didn't talk. Lola piled scrambled eggs onto a slice of toast and ate them. "So how *is* the yoga lady these days?" she said finally.

"She wants to have a baby."

"Wow."

"That's what *I* said."

Lola leaned back in the booth, giving her plate a little backhand wave good-bye. "That's pretty serious, Frank. Marriage. Spawning."

"She doesn't want to get married. She just wants to have a baby."

"Very progressive." Lola raised her eyebrows. "So?"

Coffin frowned into his coffee cup. "I don't know. I haven't decided yet."

"She give you a deadline?"

"A week."

Lola grinned. "The lady doesn't mess around. What if you say no?"

"We didn't talk about that." Coffin wiped a hand across his eyes. He was tired. His head had begun to throb. He wanted to lie down in the booth and take a short nap. "God. Why do relationships have to be so complicated?"

"You're asking the wrong person. I haven't had a date in months."

Coffin's brows went up. *Too bad she only likes girls,* he thought, and then felt instantly stupid for thinking it, as he always did—it sounded like something Tony would say. If Lola were straight, after all, she probably wouldn't be in Provincetown. If she were straight, she'd still be just as far out of his league—practically a different species. "Really?" he said. "That's kind of hard to believe."

"Mostly I get asked out by girls who miss their daddies," Lola said. "Or who want to get revenge on their daddies. Or both. There's also the occasional cop groupie. A guy with your experience would know all about that."

"Yeah," Coffin said. He'd heard about cop groupies but had never met one. "Right."

Outside, a steady stream of traffic was heading out to the beaches: BMWs, Porsches, big SUVs. Men on bicycles wavered past in twos and threes.

"What was Merkin doing at Herring Cove, do you think?" Lola said.

Coffin buttered his last wedge of toast. "What does anyone do at Herring Cove, besides go swimming?"

"Watch the sunset?"

Coffin raised an eyebrow. "Besides that," he said.

Lola put a hand to her mouth, as if she were shocked. "But he was a *Baptist.*"

"Even a Baptist likes to get a blow job," Coffin said.

"Some even like to give them. But the wife said he didn't fool around."

"My shrink used to say that everybody's got three lives. A public life, which is how you present yourself to the world; a private life, which is what your family knows about you; and a secret life—the stuff only *you* know about you."

"So if you're a homophobic TV preacher in your public life,"

Lola said, "and wear support hose and a muumuu in your private life . . ."

"God only knows what goes on in your secret life." Coffin stood and put a ten-dollar bill and two quarters on the table. "But like I said—"

"I know." Lola straightened her hat. "It's not our case."

Coffin pushed open the door. It was almost hot in the sunlight. One gleaming SUV after another whooshed past. A small squadron of gulls was hang-gliding serenely overhead.

"Frank?" Lola said. Her eyes were very blue. "What about you? Do you have a secret life?"

"I wish," Coffin said. "I'd be a lot more interesting if I did."

Chapter 5

Coffin sat in the small, rickety chair in Chief Boyle's office, watching Boyle sip coffee at his desk. The town manager, Louie Silva—Coffin's second cousin—slumped in a leather armchair next to Coffin, short legs stretched out. Just behind him hovered Brandon Phipps, the newly hired destination marketing consultant.

Louie was plump, sleek, and fretful. He wore a big pinky ring and a gold chain around his neck. He looked like a nervous, affluent duck.

"A murder is one thing," Louie said, passing a hand through his glossy black hair, "but a high profile deal like this? Could be very, very bad for business."

"That's what would keep *me* up at night," Coffin said.

Phipps raised his right eyebrow a quarter of an inch. "What Mr. Silva means to say is that we must consider the effects of an incident such as this on the town's media image, on both the regional and national levels—and its impacting of long- and short-term visitorship trends. It's most urgent that this matter be resolved as expeditiously as possible. For all concerned."

Phipps was handsome in the uncomplicated, dimple-chinned way that television actors are often handsome. He had subtle blond highlights in his hair, and the muscles under his tailored shirt were the kind you get from working out in a well-appointed gym, with a well-appointed personal trainer.

"Thanks for the clarification," Coffin said.

"You're quite welcome," Phipps said, his enunciation as crisp as the creases in his gabardine trousers.

Boyle was even more red-faced than usual. He shot Coffin a warning look. "We're all on the same team here, Coffin."

Louie mopped his face with a handkerchief. "Brandon's right," he said. "A killing like this could make people extremely nervous. It's bigger than just tourism."

"Investors hate uncertainty, Detective," Phipps said. "Certain investment-driven opportunity dynamics can only be optimized in a safe and predictable business environment."

"Naturally," Coffin said.

"So," Boyle said, "we want you to conduct a parallel investigation. Quietly. Just in case the state police miss anything."

Coffin frowned. "That would be a serious breach of protocol. Definitely an ethics violation—maybe enough to bring me up on criminal charges, depending. You'd be putting me in an extremely vulnerable position."

"Let's just say we don't have a lot of confidence in the state police," Boyle said, propping his chin on his fist. "Their track record stinks."

"What are you talking about?" Coffin said. "They just got the guy who murdered the heiress out in Truro."

"It took four *years!*" Louie said. "Four fucking years! They DNA tested the entire goddamn *town*. The guy was so fucking dumb, he voluntarily gave up his DNA and then waited around for a year for the results to come in! That's the only reason they got him. This Merkin thing is like a suicide bombing at Disneyland. We can't wait four years for the state police to figure it out."

Boyle scowled. He swiveled his chair around and looked out the window. "The whole setup irks my gonads. What can they do that we can't?"

"Basic crime scene investigation. Interrogation. Polygraphing. Forensics. They've got the big new crime lab down in Sudbury."

"Ha!" Boyle said, over his shoulder. "They're underfunded, understaffed, and unfamiliar with the territory." He swiveled around and pointed a stubby finger at Coffin's heart. "You know damn well the crime lab's budget has been slashed; they're backlogged like you wouldn't believe. That's why it took so long to get the Truro DNA results."

"Sure, but they're still better trained and more experienced than we are."

Louie gazed at Coffin, drumming his fingers on the arm of his chair. "Who the hell is *we* exactly, Frankie?"

"Look, Louie—"

"*You're* experienced in homicide investigation, Frank. You're a regular Dick fucking Tracy. Commendations from the governor of Maryland, no less."

"That's over," Coffin said. "I don't do homicide anymore. Dead people freak me out."

"Dead people freak *every*body out, Coffin." Boyle rolled his eyes back in his head and stuck his tongue out. "I mean, they're dead, right?"

Coffin said nothing.

"It would just be an informal investigation," Louie said. "A couple of days at the most. No big deal. As a favor to me."

"If I wanted to investigate homicides, I'd go back to Baltimore. They pay better."

"For Christ's sake, Coffin," Boyle said. "Are you refusing a direct order?"

"A second ago, it was a favor."

Louie squinted. "A second ago I thought you'd say yes."

"You'll get your unmarked car back," Boyle said. "And if you get results, we'll talk about your office."

"Forget it," Coffin said.

"Look, Frankie," Louie said, "we're family, right? I don't want to play hardball with you. I'm a big fan of yours, you know that."

"If you say no, you're fired," Boyle said.

Coffin took a breath, let it out. His eyes felt gritty; he had a slight tickle in his throat. "I'll need Officer Winters pretty much full-time. I'll need office support. I'll need relief from the rest of my caseload. And you can stick the car up your asses."

"You're doing the right thing, Frankie," Louie said. "This protocol deal with the state is all bullshit, anyway."

"You can mention that to Mancini," Coffin said. "When he indicts me."

The phone buzzed. It was Arlene, Boyle's secretary. "Chief?" she said through the intercom. "Channel Five News is on line one."

Boyle's eyebrows shot up. Then he sighed. "Tell them we can't comment at this time. Tell them to refer all questions to the state police or the Cape and Islands district attorney's office."

"Okeydokey," Arlene said.

"Funny thing," Boyle said after he'd switched off the intercom. "The raid last night on the dick dock? No one was there. Like they knew we were coming."

"Funny thing," Coffin said, opening the door.

———

Coffin found Lola on the ground floor, talking on the pay phone outside the squad room. He waited just out of earshot until she hung up. She was frowning.

"Everything okay?" Coffin said.

"Struck out again," Lola said. "What am I, radioactive or something?"

"Sorry," Coffin said.

Lola waved a hand. "Same old same old," she said. "No big deal."

"You got your wish," Coffin said. "Boyle wants us to investigate the Merkin homicide. Off the books."

"Wow. Why?"

"Boyle owes his job to the powers that be, and the powers that be are very nervous."

"About Merkin? How come?"

"Good question. I asked our fine town manager the same thing. Apparently it's bad for the business climate."

"I'm moved," she said, "by the depth of their concern for the deceased. When do we get started?"

"Tonight," Coffin said. "We're going to a drag show at the Crown."

Chapter 6

Coffin trotted down the wide, stone steps in front of Town Hall and stepped out into the slanting light of a Cape Cod afternoon in August. The air was cooling after the noontime heat; the breeze had turned and was blowing off the bay, rich with the smell of the incoming tide.

Beautiful as it was, summer was still Coffin's least favorite season in Provincetown, August his least favorite month. From a midwinter population of around three thousand, the town swelled to as many as sixty thousand shopping, whale-watching, partying, cruising, beach-going souls in the high season. All of them had to eat, drink, sleep, and park; all of them were determined to have fun, the meaning of which varied wildly from one out-of-towner to the next. True, the tourists brought a huge influx of cash, the town's economic lifeblood, a necessary evil now that the fishery was all but dead. But like most year-rounders, Coffin resented the sweating press of them—their pink skin and bovine progress down Commercial Street, camcorders whirring. Every summer, by mid-July, he found himself longing for winter, wishing the tourists would all go away and never come back, wishing they would just send the money without bringing their dogs and strollers and RVs and most especially their dumb-ass tourist selves.

On the sidewalk, Coffin shouldered through a knot of stout retirees in matching T-shirts. They had gathered to watch a Boston television news crew setting up in front of Town Hall. The sound man, cameraman, and producer all huddled near a serpentine tangle of cable. The hair-sprayed reporter straightened his tie, which he wore with a sport coat, sky blue shirt, and khaki shorts. The TV remote van was parked illegally along Commercial Street, big antenna unfurled from its roof like an alien sunflower.

A black Lexus sedan sat idling in the narrow parking lot, blocking Coffin's Dodge. The driver's side window slid silently down. Mancini and the brown-suited state police detective were inside. A younger detective in a gray suit sat in the back.

"Got a minute, Coffin?" Mancini said from behind his blue mirrored lenses.

The Lexus's rear door swung open. Coffin climbed in next to the younger detective; he had high cheekbones and surprisingly long eyelashes. The interior of the car was cold, the air conditioner blasting a small nor'easter.

"Let's take a ride," said Mancini, "and have a little chat. Have you met Detectives Pilchard and Treadway? Treadway's just started with us. Shut the door, Treadway."

The young detective—Treadway—reached across and pulled the door shut. The Lexus slid into traffic on Bradford Street.

"I've been telling the boys here about your credentials," Mancini said. "Top of your class in the Baltimore Police Academy. Perfect score on the detective exam. Star of the homicide division. Commendations from the governor. Blah, blah, blah. Very impressive."

"That was a long time ago," Coffin said.

"Still, the old instincts don't just disappear."

"Like riding a bicycle," Pilchard said over his shoulder.

Mancini turned on Alden, which was blocked by a UPS truck making deliveries. He looked at Coffin in the rearview mirror. "I'm curious about your take on the Merkin killing."

"I don't know enough yet to have a take."

The older detective turned around in his seat and smirked at Coffin. "I figure the wife did it," he said. "Got some help from a boyfriend, maybe."

"Maybe," Coffin said. "Maybe it's a hate crime. Maybe it's a robbery, or a drug thing. Could even be accidental."

Pilchard snorted. "An accident? You saw the body, right? Didn't look to me like he got caught in a piece of freaking farm equipment."

"Erotic asphyxiation," Mancini said. "That what you're thinking? Whoever was doing the scarf work got carried away?"

Coffin shrugged. "Stranger things have happened."

"Interesting theory," Mancini said, glancing at Coffin in the mirror with his blue sunglasses.

"It's not a theory," Coffin said, "but it's possible, given what we know."

"The wife's got motive," Pilchard said.

"Have you talked to her?" Coffin said.

"Tried to take her statement an hour ago," Pilchard said. "Couldn't get much out of her."

"She was crying a lot," said the younger detective.

"Could have been play-acting," Pilchard said. "Putting on a big blubber-fest."

"Maybe," Coffin said.

The UPS driver climbed back into his truck and turned onto Commercial Street. Mancini followed him. The line of traffic was dense and moving very slowly.

"So tell me something, Detective," Pilchard said after a few moments of silence. "How'd a stud homicide guy like you get stuck here in Outer Queeristan?"

"I grew up here. I've still got family in the area."

"The detective's mother is in the local nursing home," Mancini said.

"You do your homework," Coffin said.

"I try."

"Okay," Pilchard said. "Grew up here. So you moved to Baltimore and became a cop? How come? Why not be a fisherman, or sell cheap crap to tourists like everybody else?"

"I never liked boats," Coffin said, the thought of them making him feel slightly queasy. "My ex-wife got accepted into Johns Hopkins, pre med—so off we went."

"But why a cop? Why not a cabdriver or an accountant or a doorman?"

"My uncle was a cop. It seemed like an interesting job."

"It was," Mancini said. "The way he did it."

Pilchard scowled. "So you ace the academy in Baltimore, get kicked up to homicide, then come back to this godforsaken freak show to do what—write speeding tickets? Because of your sick mother? Talk about dropping a bomb on your career."

"Maybe he missed the local flavor," Mancini said, as five heavyset men in jean shorts, flannel shirts with cutoff sleeves, and work boots ambled across the street in front of them.

"Family comes first," Coffin said. "A good Republican like you should appreciate that."

"Hey now," said Pilchard.

"A word to the wise, Coffin," Mancini said, blue sunglasses in the rearview mirror. "Just in case your curiosity threatens to get the best of you. We're not in Baltimore, and this is not your investigation. Hear what I'm saying?"

"You're the boss," Coffin said.

"If it was just some local yokel, I wouldn't mind," Mancini said, "but this one's big. You know how it is."

"Someday, the White House," Coffin said.

"Governor first," Mancini said. "After that, who knows?"

There was another long silence. Mancini navigated slowly down Commercial Street. Tourists packed the narrow sidewalks; drag queens strolled past, statuesque in platform heels and enormous bee-hive wigs, handing out flyers for that night's show at the Crown. Three muscular men on Rollerblades swooshed in and out of traffic, dressed only in rainbow-striped thongs, tanned bodies glistening.

"You're from here, right?" Pilchard said.

"Right."

"So what's up with all the homos? What is it about this place?"

Coffin shrugged. "Turns out, gay people like going to the beach."

"Lots of places have nice beaches," Pilchard said.

"Two things," Mancini said. "Artists and sailors. P'town's been a hangout for artists since the early 1900s. Wife-swappers, alco-holics, and drug addicts, mostly." He made quote marks with his fingers. "'Free thinkers.' Where artists go, homosexuals follow— like fleas on a dog. It never fails."

What a bunch of dicks, Coffin thought. The air-conditioning was giving him a headache.

Treadway, the young detective with the long eyelashes, gazed out at the glittering water as the Lexus rolled past MacMillan Wharf. "I don't see any sailors," he said.

Mancini smirked. "You're looking at one of the best natural harbors in the northeastern U.S. Most of the North Atlantic fleet was parked here in both world wars. Anyplace there's a lot of sailors, you get homosexual men looking for a little rough trade."

Pilchard scowled. "I got my own theory," he said. "I think it's got something to do with obelisks."

"Obelisks?" Coffin said.

"Yeah, obelisks. Stone towers. Everywhere you got a lot of ho-mos, you got a big-ass obelisk. P'town's got the Pilgrim Monument. San Francisco's got the Coit Tower. Lots of queers in D.C.—most of 'em living a mile or two from the Washington Monument. New York's full of big tall towers. Paris has the Eiffel Tower. London's got the whatsis monument—Lord Nelson or whatever. It's like wherever you put up a giant stone schlong, homos flock to it."

"For Christ's sake," Coffin said, his head throbbing.

"The Eiffel Tower's metal," Treadway said.

"Whatever," said Pilchard. "You get my point."

Traffic was stalled at a particularly narrow place along Commercial Street, a block from the post office. The driver of a battered van had stopped to chat with a pedestrian—a very old woman wearing a broad-brimmed hat from which pink and purple Christmas ornaments dangled. The line of cars waited patiently.

"This fucking town," Mancini said, lips pressed into a tight line. "How the fuck does anybody ever get anything done?"

"They don't," Coffin said. "That's the whole idea."

It was one o'clock, and Jamie's advanced class had just ended. Soothing sitar music drifted from the wall-mounted speakers. The students were rolling up their purple yoga mats, putting on their shoes, filing out in twos and threes—almost all women, dressed in their bright spandex crop tops and stretch yoga pants, hair pulled back in ponytails. Several stopped to thank Jamie on their way out. The aerobics studio was hot, and Jamie had worked hard, putting them through their sun salutations, abdominals, and inversions. Her tank top was drenched with sweat.

She turned to leave, but a last, solitary student was blocking the door. It was Duffy Plotz, the town's recycling engineer—one of only two men in her advanced class. He was tall and lean, with big hands and long, spidery fingers. His head seemed slightly too small for his body, floating above his shoulders on the long stalk of his neck. Standing there in the doorway, he looked to Jamie like a big, awkward bird.

"Can I help you, Duffy?" Jamie said, her heart sinking a little. Plotz had asked her out—and been rejected—four times in the last three months. *More than three and you're a stalker,* she thought.

"Well, I was wondering," Plotz said, licking his lips and looking down, "if maybe you'd like to meet for lunch sometime this week. No big deal—just grab a sandwich or something."

"Duffy," Jamie said, crossing her arms. "What did I say the last four times you asked me out?"

"You're in a relationship and you don't date your students," Plotz said. "But this isn't a *date.* It's just lunch. Friends having lunch."

Jamie sighed. She felt a little sorry for Plotz. It had to be lonely, being a single, straight man in Provincetown—especially if you were socially awkward. "I don't think it's a good idea, Duffy," she said. "I'm sorry, but I just don't."

"Okay," Plotz said. "No problem." He smiled. His teeth were small and incredibly white, as if they'd just been bleached. "Can't blame a guy for trying!"

Back in the Town Hall parking lot, Coffin cast a longing glance at Boyle's Crown Vic, then wrestled open the Dodge's sagging door and ducked inside. He turned the key and the engine cranked and died, cranked and died. Finally, on the fourth try, it roared to life, a cloud of oily blue smoke spewing from the tailpipe. Three teenage boys on skateboards gave him dirty looks—*polluter!*

After waiting a minute or two for a gap in traffic, he backed onto Bradford Street, goosed the Dodge up the hill, passed the un-deniably phallic jut of Pilgrim Monument, and turned right on Shank Painter Road, the Dodge's front end shuddering. He passed Conwell Marsh and the A&P, finally pulling into the parking lot of Billy's Oyster Shack.

From the outside, Billy's was not encouraging: potholed parking lot, green Dumpster wild with gulls. The paint peeled; cigarette smoke had yellowed the windows. Step through the sprung screen door, though, and you found yourself in an agreeable time warp. Billy's hadn't changed much in the last thirty years: torn red vinyl booths and mother-of-toilet-seat formica tables, stand-up raw bar, jukebox full of blues and Motown. When people who didn't know better talked about Billy's, they said it was "retro." "Retro" was a made-up thing, Coffin believed—an interior decorator's word ("inferior defecators," his father had called them), a self-conscious attempt to mimic the past—but only the chrome and cow-shaped creamer part of the past, the polished and disinfected surface, not the inside of the past, the grit between the floorboards, the flypa-per hung in the windows like bunting. Not the past's unlikely business plan, either: fresh oysters, cheap beer, hold the phony ambience.

Billy's *was* the past, and as such, Coffin knew, it was doomed. One day it just wouldn't open, killed by property taxes and its shrinking clientele, and in the long off-season would reincarnate itself into something he hated: Chez Whatever, purveyors of small food on big plates; a new dance club; another place selling T-shirts and plastic lobsters and postcards that said "Sun Your Buns in Provincetown" above photos of muscular men in thong bathing suits.

Billy was short, stocky, and slope-shouldered. He walked with a hard limp and always seemed to be leaning a bit, head cocked, as though he were listening to a neighbor's conversation through a wall. He'd been a fisherman until the mid seventies—had fished with Coffin's father in all weathers for almost fifteen years. Then a winch line had snapped and a net full of cod and trash fish had fallen on Billy, crushing him like a bug, breaking his pelvis and his back. Coffin's father had helped him with his medical bills and "loaned" him the money for the restaurant when he'd recovered. Coffin knew his father had never let Billy repay a dime.

Coffin stood at the raw bar, watching Billy expertly shuck the dozen oysters he'd ordered—*zip zip zip,* and there they were on their beautiful half shells, pinkish gray, essence of low tide.

"How's Captain Nickerson doing?" Coffin asked, squeezing a thick lemon wedge over the paper plate full of oysters. Billy's parrot sidled nervously on its little swing. The bird had belonged to Coffin's father; it was found aboard his fishing boat, the *Nora Jean,* when the Coast Guard discovered the vessel drifting and empty, back in 1978.

"He's old, ugly, and highly inappropriate," Billy said. "Just like me. That's why I like having him around. Plus, he reminds me of your old man."

"Dad loved that bird. He used to let him out of his cage so he could fly around the house. Drove my mother crazy."

"He was a good man, your pop," Billy said. "I know you two didn't get along so good, but he was all right."

"He had his moments," Coffin said.

Captain Nickerson eyeballed Coffin, tilting his green head. "Show us your tits!" he said.

Coffin ate the oysters slowly, slurping them from their carbuncled shells, savoring the rubbery pulp between sips of beer. They were the local variety, small, firm, and very briny, and he ate them plain except for the squeeze of lemon juice to discourage any lingering bacteria. He did not believe in burying good oysters under cocktail sauce.

"So—any leads?" Billy asked, leaning against the counter, wiping his broad hands on a bar towel. Billy was a scanner junkie, Coffin knew, one of those odd men who spent their free time listening to hour after hour of mindless police and fire department chatter, just in case something "good" happened—which, until now, had meant a break-in or bicycle theft or DUI.

Coffin shook his head, mouth full of oyster and beer. He chewed deliberately and swallowed. "I thought Kathleen smashed your scanner with a ball bat," he said.

"Got a new one." Billy grinned, showing big yellow teeth. "On sale at Radio Shack, down in Orleans."

"We don't know squat," Coffin said. Anything he told Billy would be broadcast all over town in ten minutes flat. "Not our case, so nobody's telling us anything." He sucked another oyster into his mouth.

Billy rolled his eyes. "Oh, that's great," he said. "State police, then. Couple of brown suits from off-Cape interrogating the tourists. Can't be good for business."

"The hell do you care?" Coffin said. "Last time a tourist came in here was three months ago. You threw him out because he was wearing a Yankees cap."

"Eat me!" said Captain Nickerson. "Eat me!"

Billy smirked. "I taught him that. Pretty good, huh?"

"You're a genius."

"So, I got a theory," Billy said, leaning close.

"Good for you." Coffin sipped his beer, then dabbed the foam from his mustache with a paper napkin.

"I figure it's a hate crime."

"Anything's possible."

"Yeah," Billy grinned. "I figure the wife hated the son of a bitch so much, she wasted him." He cackled, then coughed.

"Thar she blows!" said Captain Nickerson.

"Delightful," Coffin said, frowning at the parrot. "You teach him that, too?"

"Nope. I figure your pop's responsible for that little nugget." Billy leaned an elbow on the bar. "The Merkin guy—is it true?"

"Is what true?"

Billy lowered his voice to a hoarse whisper. "He only had one ball."

Coffin frowned. "You hear that on your scanner, too?"

Billy leaned close. His breath smelled like cigarettes and whiskey and something else, a sour whiff of decay. "I heard some other stuff, too."

Coffin finished his beer. "Like what?" he said.

"I heard maybe your uncle Rudy's in town. Or was, anyway."

"Who told you that?"

Billy's eyes were slightly yellow, like a goat's. *Liver problems,* Coffin thought. *Cirrhosis, maybe.*

"Ticky. Said he saw Rudy yesterday at the Little Store, buying rolling papers."

Ticky was a retired fisherman with a neurological disorder that made his face twitch and jump in unpredictable ways. For the past ten years, he'd spent most of his time and most of his monthly disability check at Billy's.

Coffin's face felt hot. Rudy the loose cannon; Rudy who had something for him. "You believe anything Ticky says, you're dumber than I thought."

Billy grinned. "The way things are going," he said, "I don't know *what* to believe anymore."

Coffin had been waiting in Dr. Branstool's office for almost ten minutes. The big bay window had a fine view of the town cemetery, the graves of all those fishermen, their wives and children.

There were the recent graves, too, so many in the eighties and early nineties, as the AIDS epidemic raged unchecked.

Dr. Branstool's office was brightly lit, with walls the color of buttercups. His desk was neat, the blotter and telephone and pictures of his children at precise angles. Coffin had the urge to rifle the file cabinet but sat still instead. Someone knocked discreetly at the door, and Branstool stepped in.

He wore a white lab coat over starched chinos and a pale blue shirt. His tie was raw silk, unpatterned, with a blueish gray sheen. His hair was short, not quite brown but not quite gray, his face placid, recently shaved. Branstool was a bit of a cipher, Coffin thought. He appeared neither stupid nor smart, outgoing nor shy, tall nor short, skinny nor fat, old nor young.

"Well well well well," Branstool said, shaking Coffin's hand. "Good to see you again, Detective. Busy times for you these days, eh?"

"Yes."

Branstool sat down and opened a yellow folder on his desk. "You're here for a consult on your mother, isn't that right? Quite a girl, that mother of yours. Keeps us on our toes around here."

"Full of piss and vinegar, my father would have said."

Branstool frowned and pushed his round glasses up a little on his nose. The gesture was fussy; the doctor was a bit of a prude, Coffin thought.

"Hm, well," Branstool said. "Was there a specific concern about your mother's condition, Detective? Something you'd like to discuss about her care here at Valley View?"

A small Jamaican man was mowing the grass outside, pushing the mower back and forth in front of the big window, the sound of its motor building and receding.

"I wonder what your assessment is," Coffin said, raising his voice as the Jamaican yardman passed the window. "Of her mental state. She seems pretty loopy most of the time, but I wonder if I don't set that off in a way. Is she ever lucid? Does she know what's going on around her?"

Branstool leaned back in his chair and laced his fingers together. His glasses glinted in the greenish fluorescent light, and Coffin wondered for a moment if the lenses might be plain glass. Had Branstool chosen to wear spectacles purely out of vanity? Did he think they made him look smarter?

"An interesting question," Branstool said, consulting the folder. "It's difficult to say, really. Your mother's very *secretive,* as you're no doubt aware. Certainly paranoid; sometimes delusional—she's accused her caretakers of all sorts of things, as you know—very common in patients with midstage Alzheimer's. But there are other factors at work, as you suggest. Some Alzheimer's patients develop strong, irrational antipathies to certain people, which may cause them to act spitefully or deceitfully, even to become violent. Your mother has, at times, exhibited all of these behaviors. She threw a baked potato at Mr. Conwell last week, for instance."

"What if she said she'd had a recent conversation with someone that she most likely couldn't have had. That he was in her room."

"To put it bluntly, Detective, Alzheimer's eats holes in people's brains, but the brain is a remarkably resilient organ, with a capacity for creating new pathways, little detours around damaged areas. In Alzheimer's patients, it's not uncommon to have hours or days or weeks of unexpected lucidity, a kind of temporary remission, as a new pathway opens up. Then, eventually, that pathway also becomes damaged. It's one of the saddest things about the disease, really. Now you see them, now you don't."

Outside, the Jamaican man paused by the window and wiped his face with a large red handkerchief. Coffin caught his eye for a moment. The man grinned, showing gold teeth, and twirled his index finger at his temple: *crazy*. Then he turned away and began to push the roaring mower again.

"So you're saying it's possible. She could have been telling the truth."

"Or a version of it. She might have confused one person with another. It's not out of the realm of possibility, certainly. It's also possible your mother is playing some sort of game with you. She can be manipulative. The psychology of confinement."

"What do you mean?"

"It's fairly common for institutionalized persons—those who've lost a degree of personal autonomy—to wage an ongoing power struggle with those whose job it is to oversee them. Your mother's quite clever in this regard. She seems to take pleasure in tweaking us a bit from time to time."

Piss and vinegar, Coffin thought. *Good for her.*

Before he left the nursing home, Coffin stopped in to see his mother. She lay sleeping in her bed with the television on, the remote clutched in her hand. Fox News was running a story about brave American soldiers stationed in a desert somewhere. Coffin stood in the doorway for a moment, looking at her. Asleep, she looked a hundred years old, her cheeks sunken, her forehead deeply lined. An incongruous stuffed duck in a yellow oilskin rain hat sat next to her on the bed. Coffin felt an ache start in the back of his throat.

His mother's eyes flew open. "Take a picture, why don't you," she said.

"Hi, Ma. I didn't want to disturb you."

"Well, you did. Whoever the hell you are."

"It's me, Ma. Frankie."

She glared at him, black eyes glittering in the greenish fluorescent light. "You're not Frankie," she said. "Frankie's dead."

Coffin pointed at the duck. "Is that new?"

"It sings," his mother said. She pressed its foot, and the duck squawked through two choruses of "Singin' in the Rain," flapping its wings and bobbing its beaked head to the rhythm.

"Good God," Coffin said, reaching for the duck. "Where'd you get that thing?"

His mother snatched the toy from the coverlet and hugged it to her scrawny chest. "Keep your greasy mitts off my duck," she said.

"Okay, okay." Coffin held up his hands. "Whatever. I just wondered who gave it to you, that's all."

His mother grinned, sharp-toothed and feral. "That's for me to know," she said, "and you to find out."

Chapter 7

Rodney's was a pretty good piano bar, if you liked that sort of thing. Evening light slanted through the big front windows, golden, autumnal. There were ferns, but only a few. A bartender in a shirt and tie rattled ice and vodka in a stainless steel shaker. It was Happy Hour, and a cluster of tourists drank at the copper and walnut bar, into which a battered but in-tune Steinway baby grand was socketed. A handsome woman sat at the Steinway, big hands tickling out a Cole Porter tune. She wore a black sequined dress and a red wig. Her voice was smoky and low; she did a passable Marlene Dietrich:

> It's not 'cause I shouldn't,
> It's not 'cause I wouldn't, honey,
> And, you know, it's not 'cause I couldn't,
> It's simply because I'm the laziest gal in town.

"This isn't quite what I pictured when you said we were going to a drag show," Lola said.

Coffin leaned in the doorway. "No strobe lights?" he said. "No lip-synching 'I Will Survive'?"

"No Abba," Lola said.

Coffin pointed at the woman in the red wig. "That's Dawn Vermilion," he said. "She's a Provincetown institution."

"In more ways than one, I'll bet," Lola said.

"She's a one-person grapevine," Coffin said. "She hears everything." He looked at his watch. "Show's almost over. Let's wait in the dressing room."

The dressing room was a converted utility closet, cramped and windowless. A pink vanity had been shoved into one corner, its top cluttered with lipsticks, mascaras, and half-used cakes of foundation. Three mismatched chairs sat at odd angles to each other. Racks of dresses lined the walls. Sequined and bright from a distance, the dresses were rumpled and dirty up close.

Dawn Vermilion sat at the vanity, smoking a cigarette and peering dismally into the lighted mirror. "Middle age is such a bitch," she said, lifting her chin and pursing her lips. "What have I done to deserve *jowls*, for God's sake?" Two of the mirror's eight lightbulbs were burned out. The vanity's top was scarred with cigarette burns.

"At least you don't have a bald spot," Coffin said, fingering the top of his head.

Dawn's red wig sat on the vanity. Her real hair was gray, cropped short. Her makeup seemed thick and garish in the harsh light. "No doubt I have that to look forward to," she said. "My father had less hair than a mackerel, the old monster. But I don't imagine you-all came down here just to cheer me up."

"Of course not," Coffin said.

"We came to gossip," Lola said.

Dawn smiled suddenly, a big, lipsticky grin. She made a looping gesture with her cigarette. "Gossip? Honey, you've come to the right place. I take it we're talking about the late, great Reverend Ron?"

Lola nodded.

"I'll dish if you will, darlin'," Dawn said, putting on a New Orleans drawl.

Coffin thought for a minute. "According to the ME, he only had one testicle," he said.

Lola shot Coffin a look, but he ignored it.

"A one-ball wonder?" Dawn rubbed her hands together. "Predictable, but yummy. You cops get all the good dirt. Not sure I can top that."

"Oh, go on," Lola said. "Any little thing."

Dawn leaned toward her. "*Well,*" she said, in a hoarse whisper, "Gordita's boyfriend Edward waited on someone he's *certain* was Reverend Ron and the missus, a few nights ago. They ate like pigs—ran up a huge tab. Very par*ti*cular; nothing suited them. The wine was corked, the fish wasn't fresh—caught that day, but what-*ev*er. Ordered *three* desserts—sat there for *hours*. Then they practically stiffed him. Left a *ten percent* tip. Ten percent! And I thought *dykes* were lousy tippers." She turned to Lola. "No offense, honey."

"Who's Gordita?" Coffin asked.

"Gordita Derriere," Dawn said. "One of my coworkers. Complete slut—but absolutely gorgeous, if you're into chubs."

Lola wrote something in her notebook. "And Edward—where does he work?"

"The Fish Palace, God help him. He's a tiny little gnome. I think he's a feeder."

"A feeder?"

"It's a codependency thing. Very complicated. The bigger Gordita gets, the more Edward loves her, and the more she needs him. I saw it on *Jerry Springer* once."

"Any idea what night this was?" Coffin asked.

"Last week sometime," Dawn said, taking a last drag from her cigarette and stubbing it out in a chipped ashtray. "Gordita isn't good with details."

Lola frowned. "Why do they do it?" she said. "The tall ships, I mean. I don't get it. They never look like they're having any fun."

"They miss their mothers, poor things," Dawn said, brushing away an imaginary tear.

"If you were a tall ship," Coffin said, "where would you hang out in this town? Who would you hang out with?"

Dawn picked up a pair of tweezers and plucked at an errant eyebrow. "Good Lord, I don't know," she said. "I don't think there's any specific gathering place, if that's what you mean—no great hall of tackiness they all seem to gravitate to. They're not really pack animals like we are. They just seem to go galumphing around, looking forlorn—don't they? With their embarrassed wives padding behind, hoping to God they don't run into anyone from back home in Altoona or wherever."

"Loved the show," said Lola. "Sorry we only caught the last part."

Dawn Vermilion winced. "Not my best effort, I'm afraid. Lately, my voice seems to have a mind of its own." She took a bottle of vodka from the vanity's drawer, screwed off the cap, and poured three ounces into a lipstick-smeared water glass. "Show biz'll wear you down, honey. But at least I do my own vocals. So many of us girls just lip-synch it nowadays. It's ruining what used to be a legitimate art form, if you ask *moi*."

"I like your name," Coffin said. "Red sky at night, sailor's delight."

"Red sky at morning," Dawn said, putting on her wig and blowing Coffin a kiss, "sailor take *warning*."

At six o'clock, the line of tourists waiting for tables at the Fish Palace ran out the door and around the corner, almost to the foot of MacMillan Wharf. Mostly they were retirees, bused in for the day, hoping to take advantage of the Palace's early bird special: a one-and-a-quarter-pound boiled lobster, baked potato, salad, roll, corn on the cob, and a half-dozen steamer clams for $14.95, beverage extra. The late-afternoon, late-summer light was slanted and golden; the harbor glittered; a small red boat fluoresced on the beach. The Fish Palace had blinking neon lobsters in the windows. Now and then, a voice rattled out of a plastic speaker, unintelligibly paging customers who were waiting outside.

"My God," Coffin said, as he and Lola squeezed through a clump of thick-legged tourists. "Is it my imagination, or is town even more crowded than usual?"

A doughy woman in shorts and sandals glared after them. "The line forms at the rear!" she said.

"Seems like it," Lola said. "Residual gawk factor from the Merkin killing, maybe."

Inside, the line of hungry tourists extended down a hallway, past the Palace's open kitchen, where a dozen bustling Jamaicans in white jackets and chef's hats sautéed fillets of sole, seared tuna steaks, and deep-fried baskets of oysters. Green-brown lobsters stared accusingly from a gurgling glass tank. Other lobsters, cooked and bright red, crouched on plates next to foil-wrapped potatoes and watery half-ears of corn. The plates, lined up on a high counter, were whisked into the dining room by grim-faced waiters.

The line stopped at the entrance to the dining room, which was cordoned by velvet museum ropes. The hostess—a small, olive-skinned woman—stood guard at a podium while an angry tourist jabbed his finger at her notebook.

"See, there we are," he said. "Hanson, party of four. You've seated all these people ahead of us." He jabbed the notebook again. "We've been waiting over an hour."

"What d'you want me to do, sir?" the hostess said, indicating the packed dining room with a wave of her pen. Every table was full, every seat occupied by retirees or couples with small children. The green carpet was strewn with oyster crackers, bits of lobster shell, dropped napkins. Everyone seemed to be either talking or chewing. "It's high season and we're very busy."

Coffin caught her eye, and she smiled at him over the angry man's shoulder. "Hi, Frankie."

"Hi, Roz," Coffin said.

The tourist pointed at Coffin. "If you seat these people before us, that's it—we're out of here."

"Suit yourself, ace," Roz said. She turned to Coffin and shrugged. "It's like feeding time at the zoo," she said. "Not a pretty sight."

"You got a waiter named Edward?" Coffin said. "Little guy?"

Roz looked around the dining room. "There he is," she said, pointing to a very small man who was plunking salads in front of a table full of retirees. "He's not in trouble, is he?"

Coffin shook his head. "Not at all. We just want to ask him a few questions about someone he waited on."

Roz frowned. "The Merkin guy. I didn't see him, but Edward swears he was in here." She waved to Edward and he trotted over, carrying a big stainless steel tray.

"Are you the police?" he said. "This is so exciting. Just like *Law and Order.*" He was no bigger than a twelve-year-old boy, five-two or five-three at the most. His voice was tinny and high. Like all the waiters at the Fish Palace, he wore a white polo shirt with a tiny red lobster stitched above the right breast.

Coffin held up Merkin's picture. "You waited on this man last week?"

Roz wore reading glasses on a chain around her neck. She perched them on her nose and peered at the picture. "Good grief, what an outfit." She clucked her tongue. "Talk about people who live in glass houses."

"That's him," Edward said. "Him and his wife were in here. It was late—nine thirty or so. They sat upstairs because he insisted on a water view."

His voice made Coffin want to grit his teeth. It sounded like an old reel-to-reel tape deck, playing back a little too fast.

"*What* a pain in the ass they were," Edward said. "A real Preparation H table. Bitch, bitch, bitch. And cheap, too. Practically stiffed me."

"How did they behave toward each other?" Coffin said.

"You mean, were they fighting or anything?" Edward paused for a moment, then raised a hand, palm up. "They seemed—*triumphant*," he said. "Like they'd just won the lottery or something."

"Did you happen to overhear any of their conversation?"

"No, they were very careful about that. When they saw me coming, they'd clam up. Then, as soon as I walked away, they'd get all animated again."

Lola stopped writing in her notebook. "No offense," she said, "but if you'd just won the lottery, why would you come here? Why not someplace a little more . . . upscale?"

"Two things," Edward said. "First, the place is always packed—so it's more anonymous. You're one more tourist in the herd, know what I mean? Moo!"

"What's the second thing?" Coffin said.

"Oysters. I couldn't believe it. They ordered *four dozen* on the half shell. There's only two or three other places in town that serve them. It's like he was an oyster junkie or something. He just kept sucking them down. I've never seen anything like it."

———

The big man left his blue Chevy pickup running, got out, and un-locked the gate that blocked the dirt road into the beech forest. It was almost dark, and the light under the beech forest canopy was watery and green, like the inside of a big terrarium. He drove slowly on the rut-veined road, his pick and shovel clattering in the truck bed. When the road dwindled to nothing in the underbrush, he stopped the truck and climbed out. He stood still for a few sec-onds, listening. Then, satisfied that no one was around, he gath-ered his tools and scrambled down a bank, into a low basin shaded by beeches. The ground was covered everywhere with last year's rotting leaves.

At the basin's lowest point, two small stone grave markers sprouted from the earth, about four inches square and three feet high; a number of others were broken off near the ground. A few yards away, a large circular indentation was still visible in the earth. It was all that was left of the old smallpox pesthouse, to which the good people of nineteenth-century Provincetown had removed the sick, to live or die as God willed, thus sparing the town from epidemic.

"Rest in peace, you antique sons of bitches," the big man said. He dropped the shovel on the ground and took a small compass from his pocket. Starting from the second intact marker, he took fifteen steps heel-to-toe and started to dig.

The digging took a long time; the ground was webbed with roots. He hadn't brought gloves, and by the time he'd dug down a foot he had the beginnings of a blister on his right hand. He paused to rest for a minute, took a silver flask of whiskey from his hip pocket and drank from it, then went back to work.

He dug until it was almost dark. Then, finally, the shovel struck something metallic about three feet down. He'd left his flashlight in the truck, but he didn't really need it. He lay on his belly and reached into the hole—he could feel the hard, square edge of the suitcase that was buried there. Working fast, he widened the hole with the mattock, then shoveled out the loose dirt. Most of the aluminum suitcase was visible. He reached into the hole and pulled it out.

"Atta baby," he said. "Come to Papa." He flipped the two stainless steel latches and opened the lid. There was a brown plastic garbage bag inside. His hands shook and his chest felt tight as he tore it open. The money was still there, still intact. A little over two million, in neat bundles of hundred-dollar bills.

Coffin and Lola sat in the Dodge outside her apartment. He wanted a cigarette but knew she'd disapprove.

"I wonder why they'd be triumphant," he said. "Triumphant about what?"

Lola shrugged. "Maybe they figured out something new to blame gay people for," she said. "Anything to keep the donations rolling in."

"Maybe he'd found a great little boutique, with plenty of stuff in his size," Coffin said.

"I could call the missus and ask," Lola said.

"Worth a shot," Coffin nodded. "She might be more willing to talk to you—she was pretty guarded with me. I want to know everywhere she and the reverend went while they were here—everyone they talked to, and what about. Details."

"Will do," Lola said. She poked a finger into the Dodge's disintegrating upholstery. "Frank?" she said. "No offense, but can we take my car from now on?"

Coffin patted the dashboard. "What's the matter?" he said. "You don't like my Dodge? This is vintage, you know. They don't make 'em like this anymore."

"Huh," Lola said. "Go figure."

"Let's pass among the multitudes outside E Pluribus Pizza to-night," Coffin said. "We'll need copies of the picture of Merkin in his dress, and plenty of business cards."

The passenger door squealed when Lola shoved it open. "I'll pick you up at one o'clock," she said, climbing out. "Unless that's past your bedtime."

"Bedtime?" Coffin said. "Since when do insomniacs have bed-times?"

When Coffin got home, he found a message on his answering machine from Jamie. She wanted a drink, which seemed like a good idea to Coffin. She was on a martini kick, so he got out the shaker and took the bottle of Absolut from the freezer. By the time she arrived, he'd chilled a pair of martini glasses and dropped a few ice cubes into the shaker.

Jamie wore a short sundress and sandals. Her legs were brown; she smelled like suntan lotion.

"Been to the beach?" Coffin said, swirling a little vermouth in the glasses, then dumping it out in the sink.

"Very good, Detective," Jamie said. "What gave me away?"

"You've got sand between your toes." Coffin gave the vodka a final shake and poured. Slight skins of ice formed across the surfaces of the two martinis.

"And elsewhere," Jamie said, squirming a bit. "We went skinny-dipping out at lesbian land."

"I'm jealous," Coffin said. "Who's we?"

"Corinne and me. I. Did you know she has fake boobs? She caused a bit of a stir."

"How many olives?" Coffin said, spoon poised over the bottle.

"Three. And make it a little dirty, *por favor*."

"I hadn't noticed Corinne's boobs, to tell you the truth," Coffin said. He dropped three olives into Jamie's glass, then added a spoonful of brine.

"Liar," Jamie said. "They're huge. How could you not notice?" She sipped her drink carefully; it was very full.

"Never really been a boob man, I guess," Coffin said.

"I don't understand it," Jamie said, shuffling out into the living room, martini delicately poised.

"I'm told I was sufficiently breast-fed." Coffin tasted his drink. The icy vodka had a pleasant, medicinal bite.

"No, I mean why women get boob jobs. It's so barbaric. No different from foot binding, or that African thing with the plates in the lips." Jamie collapsed onto a brocaded sofa. "What is it about the beach? All that sunshine and naked flesh."

"Tired?" Coffin said, sitting next to her.

"Horny," Jamie said, looking at him over the brim of her glass. "It never fails."

"That's good to know," said Coffin.

Jamie set her glass down on a marble-topped end table. "Know what else is good to know?" she said, gently biting Coffin's cheek.

"Uh—"

"I'm not wearing any underwear," Jamie whispered, grabbing Coffin by the ears and slowly pulling him down on top of her.

Later, in the dark bedroom, Jamie lay on her belly, Coffin's head resting comfortably in the curve of her lower back.

"I think I want a boy," she said. "Boys are so elemental. They don't get manipulative until they're thirty."

"Ha," Coffin said.

"Corinne says, if you want to conceive a boy, you're supposed to do it from behind." She waggled her hips a little. "Maybe we should practice."

"In the morning?"

"Poor man. Tired?"

"Yes."

Jamie lay quiet a while. Then she said, "Have you thought about it, Frank? Having a baby?"

"A little."

"And?"

"I don't know. I'm old and weird and solitary."

"Do you *like* being old and weird and solitary?"

"Kids avoid me. I don't know how to talk to them."

"*Your* kid won't avoid you."

"What if something happened?" Coffin said. "Something bad."

Jamie reached for a cigarette, lit it, and blew out a slow plume of smoke. "Like what?"

"I don't know—something. To the child. What if it got terribly sick or hurt in an accident? I don't think I could handle that."

Jamie rolled onto her side and ruffled Coffin's hair. "The boogey-man's not going to get us, Frank."

"You're so *rational*," Coffin said.

"Look," Jamie said. She sat up, pulling the sheet over her breasts. "I'm going to have a baby. I'm not going to be one of these women who waits around for permission till she's forty and then finds out it's too late."

She had once told Coffin that in high school no one thought she was pretty. She was too tall, too lanky, too flat chested to attract much attention; she'd had a bad complexion, worn nothing but black—*queen of the geeks*, she called herself. Now, candlelight sparking her dark, wide-set eyes, Coffin found her wrenchingly beautiful.

He said nothing. The stuffed seagull on the wardrobe stared at him blankly. Jamie got up and went out into the living room to find her dress. "You've got a pretty good deal here, you know—boinking the yoga instructor," she said. "And I'm not the only one who thinks so."

"Oh?"

She padded back into the bedroom, tugging the dress down over her hips. "You heard me, sport. Duffy Plotz has been asking me out. He's cute, in a moderately creepy way. He's got that socially awkward ostrich thing going on."

"Duffy? Jesus. You know the only reason he takes yoga is to meet women, right? Where's he taking you? A romantic evening shooting rats in the dump?"

Jamie laughed, then pointed a long finger at Coffin's nose. "I'm at my sexual peak, boyo—and I'm *extremely* flexible. Don't screw it up."

The man in the blue pickup truck waited a long time while Jamie did whatever she was doing with the cop; fucking him, no doubt. He did not smoke, though he wanted to; he knew the glow of his cigarette would be visible from across the street, if anyone happened to look out the window.

It was getting very late and he was about to give up, but just as he had made up his mind to leave she stepped out onto the screen porch. "Got to get a shot of this," he muttered, picking up the big Minolta on the passenger seat. It had a long telephoto lens and was loaded with very slow black-and-white film. He braced the camera on the truck's window frame. "C'mon, baby," he said. "Put on a show for Duffy."

Jamie paused on the front steps and lit a cigarette. Plotz's stomach fluttered at the sight of her—tall and slim, long hair hanging loose the way he liked it. Backlit for a moment by the yellow porch light, her short white dress turned translucent, revealing the outline of her body. She appeared to be wearing small white panties underneath, but Plotz couldn't be sure—the pale triangle floating under the sundress might have been the tan line from a bikini bottom. Plotz's penis stiffened at the thought.

The Minolta's shutter clunked. The film advanced automatically, with a slight whir. *Clunk, whir. Clunk, whir.*

She got into her old Volvo wagon, backed out of the cop's driveway, and putted away, heading home. When she got to the corner, he started his pickup truck and followed her, staying a safe distance behind.

Chapter 8

Coffin tried to nap after Jamie left but couldn't—every time he started to doze the old, recurring dreams began. He got up, dressed, and went out to the screen porch to wait for Lola. It was late; the neighborhood was quiet except for the crickets, sharpening their little knives. Then, a block or two away, a dog started barking. It sounded like a small dog at first, *yip yip yip*. Other dogs joined in, yipping and yapping their various notes, five or six dogs, and then one of them, maybe a big one, let out a long, ghostly howl, and all the other dogs joined in. *Not dogs,* Coffin realized. *Coyotes. In the graveyard.*

For years, Provincetown had been home to a good-sized pack of coyotes—wolfish and brushy-tailed, low-slung in the hips—they lived in the dunes across the highway and came into town at night, hunting for possums or cats, congregating now and then in the unlit quiet of the cemetery to sing their feral harmony. It was strange hearing them in the summertime, though; usually it was cold weather that drove them into town, the scarcity of rabbits and whatever other wild game they could find in the scrub pines or the beech forest. Sometimes, driving at night, Coffin would spot one or two of them crossing Bradford Street in the distance ahead of his car, eyes glowing yellow in the headlights. They were shy of humans, but leave your cat out at night and likely as not it would end up coyote chow.

The coyotes made Coffin feel better, the weird anachronism of them, the notion of something wild and skittish and a little dangerous roaming the night streets of Provincetown, with its gingerbread trim and pink shutters. Then he thought of the crab that had climbed out of Ron Merkin's open mouth, and he didn't feel better anymore.

On summer nights around one o'clock, a small migration flowed up Commercial Street from the just-closed bars to E Pluribus Pizza; it seemed ritual and prehistoric to Coffin, a kind of pilgrimage, like sea turtles returning to the same lost beach year after year to lay their eggs. They gathered outside, hundreds of men, on the sidewalks and in the street—most with no interest in pizza—a nightly cotillion for those who hadn't yet gotten lucky and those who liked to watch them try. There were men of all descriptions: muscular men, slender men, and fat men; shirtless, smooth-chested men; big-bellied, hairy men; beautiful men and men who were not so beautiful. They wore runner's shorts and muscle shirts, or biker gear, or sailor suits, or cowboy hats, or nondescript jeans and polo shirts, or, in one case, a purple G-string and Rollerblades. Two outrageously muscled men with shaved heads and identical goatees wore nothing but engineer boots, leather chaps, and nipple rings the size of door knockers. A clutch of drag queens tottered on platform heels. There were a few women, too, and a great many dogs, frolicking with one another and barking.

"Last chance to hook up before admitting defeat and going home alone," Lola said. She was carrying a green backpack. They had parked her black Camaro several blocks away.

"Or heading off to the dick dock," Coffin said.

"Ah, the romance," Lola said.

"I don't know how anyone does it," Coffin said. "I'd be too uncomfortable. Everybody looking at me. I'd feel like . . . merchandise."

A car was inching through the crowd while a summer cop tried in vain to clear the street long enough to let it pass.

"Look," Lola said. "It's Pinsky."

"He's got lipstick on his cheek," Coffin said.

"Hey, Pinsky," Lola said to the summer cop. "You going native or what?" She pointed to her cheek.

Pinsky blushed and wiped at the lipstick with his palm. "Aw," he said. "Naw. One of the girls there was just messin' around."

A tall black drag queen turned and blew Pinsky a kiss. She wore a very short chartreuse vinyl miniskirt, a tube top, and a blond beehive wig. "You come home with me, honey," she said. "I'll show you a *good* time."

Pinsky blushed again.

"Maybe you should take her up on it," Coffin said.

"If there wasn't a wiener in those panties, you bet your ass I would," he said.

Lola grinned. "How many times have I said that?"

Coffin lit a cigarette. Two men dressed in hoopskirts and very large straw hats decorated with plastic fruit and Barbie dolls had arrived, to cheers and whistles. "I used to think there were just two genders. Then I thought there were five. Now I have no idea," Coffin said.

"Five?" Pinsky said. "Shit. Who are you trying to kid?"

"Lesbian, gay male, straight male, straight female, bisexual," Coffin said, ticking them off on his fingers.

"Bisexual isn't a gender, honey," the tall drag queen said. Her voice was as slow and rich as molasses. "It's just not knowing your damn mind."

A man with a shaved head and red-rimmed glasses said, "That's not even half. What about butches and femmes, bottoms and tops, and the, like, seventy-eight different shades of transgendered people?"

Lola nodded. "I went to college with a short, fat, hairy guy who had a sex change because he wanted to be a lesbian. Talk about complicated."

"What about you, Detective?" Pinsky said. "You've been here a long time—ever think about seeing how the other half lives?"

"I never get any offers," Coffin said. "It's like I've got a big tattoo on my forehead that says STRAIGHT GUY."

"Oh, come on," Lola said. "No man has ever hit on you?"

"Not never. But not very often, either. And lately not at all." Coffin patted his gut. "I'm not the most buff guy in town, it turns out."

"But when they did?" Lola said.

"Men aren't my type. What can I say?" He shrugged. "I seem to be a hardwired hetero."

"That's right," Pinsky said. "We're all hardwired. Boys and girls." He lowered his voice. "These people here are going against nature."

The tall drag queen made a clucking noise with her tongue and draped a long, elegant arm around Pinsky's shoulders. "You need to relax yourself, baby. Let Lawonda show you how."

Lola laughed, and Pinsky smiled sheepishly.

"So, are you-all a couple?" one of the other drag queens said. She was very slender, sheathed in a sequined minidress. "I mean, are you shopping for a boy-toy or just being, like, *tourists* or something?"

"Actually, we're police officers," Coffin said. He took Merkin's photo from his jacket pocket. "We're wondering if anybody remembers seeing this man."

The drag queens gathered around. "It's Reverend Rhonda," Lawonda said, tapping the photo with a long, sparkly fingernail.

"Oh my *God*," the drag queen in the sequined dress said. "Look at that *sad* little outfit. It's just heartbreaking."

Lola took a fistful of business cards and a sheaf of photos from her backpack. "We need to know if Ron Merkin was with anyone the night of his death, which was last Friday, or anytime late at night that week," she said, passing them around. "Any information you can give us would be very helpful."

There was a low swell of conversation as the photos were passed from hand to hand. Coffin and Lola waited several minutes, but none of the men stepped forward.

"No one?" Lola said. "Are you sure?"

"Our phone numbers are on the cards," Coffin said. "If anyone remembers seeing Ron Merkin late at night, please call us—anytime. We'll protect your anonymity."

After Lola's Camaro disappeared around the corner, Coffin stood in the street for a minute or two, thinking. His house was completely dark. He always left the floor-lamp in the living room on, plugged into a timer. Maybe the bulb had burned out. Or maybe someone had turned the lamp off. The hair on his forearms rose. A blue Chevy pickup truck was parked across the street.

Crouching a little, Coffin peered through the living room window. It was velvety black inside except for the glow of a lit cigarette—someone was sitting in his father's red easy chair, smoking with all the lights out. For a moment, Coffin imagined he was seeing his father's ghost; all that was missing was a glass of scotch and the Red Sox losing a crucial game on the snowy TV. Then the cigarette glow arced up and brightened, partially illuminating a man's face. Coffin stood up and rapped on the window. The man started and dropped his cigarette. Coffin could see his bulky silhouette moving quickly toward the door.

"Relax, Rudy," Coffin said, stepping onto the screen porch. "It's just me."

"Jesus Christ," Rudy said, standing just inside the door. He was a big man with thick gray hair and broad features. He held a large pistol. "You scared the shit out of me." He stuffed the pistol into his jacket pocket. "Got any bourbon? I looked around but couldn't find any."

"Time to start locking my doors," Coffin said, reaching for the light switch.

Rudy grabbed his wrist. "Leave it out," he said. "I'm not supposed to be here."

"That your pickup outside?"

"Tony's. He let me borrow it. He's not the sharpest tool in the shed, but he's a good boy."

Coffin felt his way to the kitchen and fumbled through the liquor cabinet in the dark. "No bourbon," he said. "Scotch or vodka."

"When'd you get so goddamn fancy?"

"Things have changed since you've been gone. The whole town is going upscale."

"The whole town can bite my ass," Rudy said.

"It already did," Coffin said, pouring scotch over ice in the dark, trying not to slop any liquor onto the counter.

Rudy eased his bulk into the red armchair. "You've got a point there," he said, sipping his drink. "But who's to say I won't get the last laugh?"

"Ever the optimist," Coffin said, sitting on the couch.

The room was silent for a while, except for the rusty scraping of crickets outside.

"I suppose you're wondering," Rudy said, when he'd drained his scotch and chewed up the ice cubes, "why I was sitting here in the dark, waiting for you to drag your ass home."

"I am," Coffin said.

Rudy cleared his throat. "There's something I want to give you."

"No thanks," Coffin said.

"For your ma."

"Nope."

"Now how can you stand there and say 'nope' when you don't even know what it is?"

"Is it stolen?"

"Okay, here we go," Rudy said, throwing up his hands. "Just *assume* that anything I'd give you is stolen. Real nice."

"Well, is it?"

"Kind of."

"Then no thanks."

"It's money, Frankie. Lots of it. Untraceable. You could put your poor old mother in a nicer place, down in Chatham or somewhere. You could get the fuck out of here, if that's what you wanted."

Coffin frowned. "And where would I say I got the money, Rudy? When the IRS came to call?"

Rudy snorted. "The IRS. Jesus. Make sure you don't ride your bike on the sidewalk."

Coffin didn't say anything. Outside, crickets sawed in the grass.

"Three hundred thousand, Frankie."

"What?"

"Three hundred large. I got it right here." A briefcase stood on the floor beside his chair—dark object in a dark room. He picked it up and held it in his lap.

"You're riding around in Tony's truck with three hundred thousand dollars?"

"Try twice that," Rudy said. He patted his jacket pocket. "That's why I've got the firearm. This town's gotten dangerous all of a sudden."

"You're fucking kidding me."

"It's a shitload of money, Frankie. Bundles and bundles of it. A present from your old uncle Rudy." He patted the briefcase.

"Look, I know I'm going to be sorry I asked—"

"But you want to know where I got it."

Coffin nodded.

"Your dad and me. We started up a little business venture, back when you were still in high school. You knew about that, right?"

"I figured, maybe. I didn't know for sure."

"Well, now you do. There was a lot of money to be made in those days, if you had some balls."

"You were smuggling."

"I had the connections, your old man had the boat. We had a great thing going—it was bulletproof. We scored big a bunch of times. We never got caught, and we never would've got caught."

"Then Dad was lost at sea."

"Lost at sea can mean a lot of things."

"Like?"

"Like he fell in. Like he was thrown in. Nobody knows."

"You think he was killed?"

"He sure as fuck didn't commit suicide."

Coffin took a deep breath. He felt a curious buzzing in the back of his head; the dark room seemed to swim for a moment, then lie flat again.

"We were dealing with some pretty rough people. The Colombians all went crazy when the coke thing took off."

"So they killed him? Colombians?"

"Maybe. Probably. Hijacked his cargo and chucked him in the drink. They did a lot worse than that sometimes. There'd been a storm, but nothing your old man couldn't handle."

"Jesus," Coffin said.

"This can't be coming as a complete surprise."

Coffin met Rudy's eyes. "No. I guess not."

"Look—your dad was a good man. A little rough on you, maybe, but a good man. He never would have gotten involved, but he had no choice. The fishing was bad. He owed a lot of money."

"More scotch?" Coffin said.

Rudy held out his glass, and Coffin went to the kitchen and re-filled it.

"So you retired from smuggling and stashed the money. Why wait so long to come get it?"

"The DEA was on me like a cheap suit for a while. I mean to tell you, they are persistent sons of bitches. And I figured it was safe enough buried out in the Beech Forest."

"Why come get it now, then?"

"Jesus Christ," Rudy said. "I wasn't expecting the fucking Spanish Inquisition."

Coffin looked at him in the dark.

"Okay—okay. Jesus," Rudy said. "I was broke. I needed the cash, all right?"

"I can't take the money, Rudy."

"Well, you're a damn fool. It's yours—your inheritance, you could say. A reward for playing it straight all these years. It's yours and it's free and no one will ever know unless you're stupid enough to tell them."

"I can't live the rest of my life with a sack full of illegal cash under my bed. I wouldn't be able to sleep at night."

"I admire your scruples," Rudy said. "Where you got them from, I don't know—must have been your mother's side."

"Must have been," Coffin said.

Rudy pondered for a moment. "Look, you don't have to decide right now. It's yours. It was your old man's and he's gone so it's yours. I'll keep it for you. I'll put it in a safe deposit box and send you the key—that way I won't spend it all. It'll be there if you change your mind."

"I wouldn't know what to do with it, Rudy. I mean, sure I could use it—who couldn't? But I don't think I could bring myself to actually spend any of it. Considering."

Rudy squirmed a little in the red chair. He looked at Coffin, looked away. "What if I told you it was more like *five* hundred grand."

"What?"

"Your cut. It's more like half a million. Five hundred and thirty thousand, give or take. I lied, okay? Jesus."

"Half a million," Coffin said. His mouth felt dry. "Holy shit."

"Maybe now your old man will leave me alone."

"What do you mean, leave you alone?"

"I keep dreaming about him," Rudy said, standing up, clutching the briefcase. "His hair's all full of seaweed and shells, and man, is he pissed. It's awful."

"Good seeing you, Rudy," Coffin said.

"Keep it real, Frankie," Rudy said. He turned and walked out onto the porch. The screen door opened and closed softly. Coffin watched Rudy climb into the blue pickup and drive away, taillights dwindling then disappearing as he turned the corner onto Alden Street.

Chapter 9

Right on time," Coffin said, opening the screen door. It was eight thirty on the dot. The morning was cool and clear.

"But of course." Lola smiled. She wore a gray skirt, knee length, with black heels and a white sleeveless top made of silk.

Coffin had never seen her in a skirt before. The heels made her calves bunch a little. He tried not to stare at them.

"There's coffee. Mop water, just the way you like it."

"Ick," Lola said, wrinkling her nose. "Just water's fine." She opened cupboards until she found a glass and filled it from the Brita pitcher on the counter. She leaned a hip against the door frame.

"How's Mrs. Merkin?" Coffin said.

"She sounded pretty frantic on the phone. The state police consider her a suspect, the press is camped out on her front lawn, and the lawsuits have already started to roll in. Tough times back on the farm."

"She's not exactly your favorite vegetable, I gather."

"I'm sorry she lost her husband," Lola said. "Nobody deserves that. But I don't feel bad about the rest of it—the lawsuits and re-porters. They had it coming."

"The Merkins cast a lot of first stones," Coffin said.

Lola shook her head. "It's not even the hypocrisy. They were just so—" She searched for the right word. "So *hateful*. Hateful bigots who got rich playing on people's fears. Some way to make a living."

"Mean, dumb, and energetic is a dangerous combination."

Lola sat down, opened her briefcase, took out three loose sheets of paper, and slid them across the table to Coffin. "I asked her to write out a log of their activities while they were here and e-mail it over to me. Everything they did, everyone they talked to. She said the state police asked for pretty much the same thing, except they weren't so nice about it."

Coffin picked up the papers. "Arrived Wednesday night around six thirty, went straight to their rental condo on the east end. Let's have a look at that today."

Lola nodded and made a note. "They rented a deluxe two-bedroom on the top floor of the Ice House. Booked it through a Re-altor here in town."

"We'll give them a call." Coffin looked down at the paper. "Din-ner out at the Fish Palace. She had the grilled sea bass with mango salsa; he had a steamed lobster and two dozen oysters on the half-shell."

"More like four dozen, according to Edward."

"Afterward, she goes back to the condo, and he stays out by him-self for several hours." Coffin turned the page. "Next day, breakfast in, walk on the beach, home to read and watch TV. Lunch at Bixby's. Home for a nap. Out for dinner at the Cellars."

"She had poached salmon with dill sauce and asparagus," Lola said. "He had oyster stew and grilled swordfish."

"The man liked oysters. After dinner, she goes home, he stays out." He looked at the last page. "Day three, same routine."

"Except when he stays out, he really stays out."

"No mention of any conversations with anybody, except maître d's, shop clerks, and a few business calls back home."

"Nope. Nothing to be triumphant about."

"And she has no idea who he saw or what he did when he was out at night?"

"She said he told her he walked around. He liked being seen in his outfits and not being recognized. That's part of the deal with some cross-dressers, apparently."

"Think she's telling the truth?"

Lola thought for a few seconds. "You mean is she lying about what they did together? Or what he did when he was out on the town?"

"Both. Either."

"Maybe. I kind of get this feeling when I know people are hiding something—it's like a dog when somebody blows one of those whistles. Your ears kind of perk up, know what I mean?"

Coffin nodded. "*What* is she hiding, though? That's the question."

"She's either protecting him or protecting herself," Lola said.

"It's a little late for him."

Lola finished her water and refilled her glass. "True," she said.

"Hang on," Coffin said, padding into his study. "I've been working, too." He came back with a green folder.

"You got the autopsy report?" Lola said. "That was quick."

"Ask and you shall receive," Coffin said. He opened the folder and spread the report and photos on the table.

"The woman at the ME's office—what's her name? She must like you."

"Shelley Block. We go back a few years. We went out for a while, but every time I thought about what she did all day, I got the heebie-jeebies. Still friends, though."

"Yack," Lola said, sorting through the photos. "I see what you mean."

"Here's the summary," Coffin said, scanning the report. "Time of death uncertain; but probably between late the night of the eleventh and early the morning of the twelfth, given the degree of rigor and the extent to which insects and crabs and whatnot had been working on the body when it was found. Definite strangulation; deep ligature wounds, burst capillaries, blah blah blah. Marks on the legs and left foot indicate dragging, probably postmortem. Lots of sand on the body—big surprise. Alcohol zero, *but* the blood work shows significant amounts of ketamine."

"Special K," Lola said. "That's weird."

"There's nothing about this guy that *isn't* weird," Coffin said.

Lola drummed her fingers on the table. "Special K used to be a big club drug."

"In Baltimore the frat boys used it as a date rape drug—wipes out your inhibitions and short-term memory."

"Explains how a guy that big could go out for a walk and end up getting himself strangled," Lola said.

Coffin nodded, unbending a paper clip. "Someone spiked his Diet Coke."

"Any sexual assault?"

Coffin scanned the report, flipped through the pages, flipped back. "No. Want to know what he had for dinner?"

"More than anything."

"Lobster—confirms the wife's account of the meals, anyway—baked potato, salad with blue cheese, chocolate cake. Reverend Ron wasn't exactly counting calories, and here we go again—raw oysters. 'Approximately a dozen.' "

"Did the wife say anything about him eating oysters Saturday night in her highly detailed gastronomic log?"

"Nope. And your friend at the ME's office says they were higher up in the gut than the lobster. Meaning he ate them last."

"Not bad, as last meals go. How many places in town serve oysters on the half-shell, do you think?" Coffin said.

"There's the Fish Palace," Lola said, counting on her fingers, "Al Dante's, and the Harbor Café out in Wellfleet. You wouldn't go to Wellfleet dressed like Aunt Edna, though, right?"

"Don't forget Billy's," Coffin said.

Lola stretched out her legs, pointed her toes, then crossed her ankles. "Only an idiot would walk into Billy's in a wig and a muumuu," she said.

Coffin shrugged. "Merkin was no Stephen Hawking," he said. "Let's call the missus back and find out if he had his dozen raw with her or after she went home to watch *Law and Order*."

"Special K," Lola said. "Does that mean we're back to thinking of this as a hookup that got ugly?"

Coffin fingered his mustache. It had begun to turn gray; the new silver hairs were coarse and prickly. "Secret lives," Coffin said. "You never know what you'll turn up when you're dealing with secret lives."

The Ice House, as its name implied, had originally been built to manufacture ice for the fishing industry. It had been converted to condos in the early eighties, just as the AIDS pandemic was gathering steam. At five stories, the Ice House was the tallest building in Provincetown, except for the Pilgrim Monument.

The Merkins' rented condo occupied the entire top floor. The furniture was a mix of chrome-and-white-leather minimalist and art deco antique. A long balcony stretched across the harbor side, with an excellent view of town beach, the harbor with its scatter of small boats, North Truro, the long, hazed curve of the Cape, and even the ochre strip of smog over Boston.

"Yikes," Lola said from the master bedroom. "Check this out." A polar bear skin—complete with grimacing head—lay sprawled on the floor in front of the gas fireplace. Several paintings of sunsets over sand dunes hung on the walls, and a cabinet opened to reveal a large plasma TV. The bed was enormous. The entire ceiling was mirrored.

"Liberace has entered the building," Coffin said.

"This is one of our premier properties," said the young man from the real estate office. His name was Wendell. "We have quite a distinguished list of renters for this unit."

"Like who?" Coffin said from the bathroom. It had a full-sized marble hot tub and, curiously, a bidet. All of the fixtures were gold plated. "Siegfried and Roy?"

Wendell lowered his voice to a stage whisper. "Miss Barbra Streisand, for one," he said.

"How much does it rent for?" Lola asked.

"In high season?" Wendell said. "Ten thousand a week. More for Carnival."

Coffin opened a closet door. A light came on inside. The closet was almost as big as his kitchen and lined entirely in cedar. "That's a lot, isn't it?" he said. "Even for Provincetown."

"This is a very special property," said Wendell, checking his tie in the big, gilt-framed mirror over the fireplace. It was a pink tie, worn with a shirt made of some shimmering blue-green material. "You can't get this combination of amenities and view anyplace else in town."

"Can't argue with that," Coffin said. He picked up an art deco statuette—a nude girl, standing with one knee raised, holding a bronze tray aloft. Wendell flinched a little, so Coffin put the statuette down.

"How did the Merkins pay?" he asked.

Wendell consulted his BlackBerry. "Bank transfer," he said. "From Tulsa, Oklahoma, under the name Johnson. Same as before."

"Before?" Lola said.

"Yes—they rented this unit last summer, too. As a Mr. and Mrs. Hank Johnson. They liked it so much they tried to buy it, but it's not for sale."

Coffin said nothing. He opened the French door onto the balcony and looked out. It was low tide and the harbor looked drained, exposed sand flats undulating off to North Truro. Here and there a small boat was beached at the end of its anchor line, waiting silently for the bay to percolate back in. "Did they look at any other properties while they were here?"

Wendell leaned toward him conspiratorially. "They looked at several investment properties last year," he said, "but they didn't buy anything. Not from me, at least."

Lola frowned. "But they might have bought from someone else?"

"It's possible, I suppose," Wendell said. He shrugged. "They were interested in new development—but there's not much of that going on. Just those new condos out on the west end, and they're not even officially on the market yet."

"The Moors?" Coffin said.

Wendell nodded. "They're going to be very, *very* exclusive," he said. "Super high-end."

"Who's the developer?" Coffin asked.

"It's all *totally* hush-hush," Wendell said. He lowered his voice to a whisper. "I don't know who's running it—but word is they're mega high rollers. Real Estate Investment Consultants, or something like that."

Lola ran her fingers over the satin duvet cover. "Did it bother you when you found out you'd been renting to Reverend Ron?" she said.

Wendell tilted his head "Money's money," he said. "Baby needs a new pair of shoes."

They ate a quick lunch at Mondo's, an old Provincetown landmark at the foot of MacMillan Wharf. They both ordered baskets of fish and chips and iced tea, which they devoured at a picnic table in the sun, looking out at the water. The cod was perfect, lightly battered, not too much grease. The French fries were hopeless, a limp afterthought. Coffin threw a fry to a one-legged gull standing expectantly a few feet from their table. The gull gobbled it whole, then flew off, screaming.

"Why would the Merkins, of all people, be looking at investment property in Provincetown?" Coffin said, chewing meditatively.

"Where would Jesus buy?" Lola said, licking a bit of tartar sauce from her fingertip. Her black sunglasses glinted in the sunlight reflecting off the harbor. "I guess a good investment is a good investment, even if it's in Babylon."

"I guess," Coffin said. "I wonder if that's what they were celebrating at the Fish Palace—a purchase."

Lola wiped her hands on a napkin. "Could be," she said. "But if that's true, why would Mrs. Merkin want to conceal it?"

"Good question," Coffin said. "Maybe she doesn't want to jeopardize the deal. Bad publicity, and all that."

Lola shook her head and took a bite of fish. "No sense throwing good money after a dead husband, I guess," she said.

Coffin leaned an elbow on the picnic table, sipped his iced tea. "Sort of makes you feel all warm and fuzzy inside, doesn't it?"

It was a warm evening, rich with the scent of lavender and low tide. The harbor glittered; small boats lay stranded on the flats.

Jamie climbed the stairs to her apartment, carrying two plastic bags of groceries from the A&P. She fumbled in her purse for her keys, setting one of the grocery bags down on the wooden balcony. Someone had left an envelope on the mat. She unlocked the door, put the bags of groceries in the kitchen, came back, and retrieved the envelope. It was plain and white, with only her name written on the outside. The flap was loose. She looked inside and slid a piece of folded notepaper from the envelope. When she unfolded it, something shiny fell out and landed on the deck. She knelt down. Razor blades. Three of them—the old-fashioned kind, rectangular with two sharp edges. The first thing she thought was *I didn't know you could still buy them.* She looked at the note, written in black Magic Marker. She felt breathless, suddenly. TWAYI SNIHYAAMI, it said in thick capital letters.

Coffin parked the shuddering Dodge in front of Kotowski's house. The moon was rising nacreous and fat above the harbor; a bright path of reflected moonlight wrinkled from the beach to the bay's black horizon. Coffin could hear the tide sucking through the stone breakwater as it straggled off to Long Point, a jagged barrier separating the tidal salt marsh from the harbor. It sounded like bathwater running down a huge drain.

The last property on Commercial Street's west end, Kotowski's house was a hulking, dilapidated thing, perched precariously above the beach, the harbor waves gumming its cracked seawall. Three large, hand-painted signs stood among the scraggly tomato plants in Kotowski's front yard: one that said $ELECTMEN FOR $ALE, another that said NO JET SKIS, and a third, even more direct, that said THROW THE BASTARDS OUT.

When Coffin knocked on the door, it creaked open a few inches and the pine-smell of turpentine drifted out. The latch had been broken for at least twenty years; as far as Coffin knew, the door had never had a lock.

Inside, the house was cavernous and dusty, cluttered with broken furniture Kotowski had picked up at the town dump: a three-legged coffee table supported by a cinder block; caned chairs, bottoms blown out, mended with squares of plywood. Stacks of books and newspapers teetered on every surface. Every foot of wall space was covered with art—mostly Kotowski's own paintings; the recent ones were images of people under attack by improbable animals: a Jet-Skier mauled by fanged dolphins, a colossal squid engulfing a whale-watch boat.

Coffin had gone to visit Kotowski almost every Tuesday night for the past ten years—ostensibly for a game of chess, which neither of them played very well or liked very much, but more and more to drink beer and argue. The chessboard was already set up on a bent TV tray. One of the black pawns was missing; a bottle cap sat in its place. Coffin opened the wheezing, round-cornered fridge and helped himself to a beer.

Kotowski stood in the kitchen, barefoot, dressed in worn jeans cut off below the knee and a paint-smeared T-shirt. "What do you think?" he said, waving at the big canvas that leaned against the table.

"Nice," Coffin said. "It's new, right?"

"Nice? That's the best you can do? Nice?"

It was a portrait of Spaz, Kotowski's orange tomcat. In the painting, Spaz was the size of a tyrannosaurus, striding through what could only be the Moors, the sprawling new condo complex visible from Kotowski's front door. Spaz had a big, greasy-looking rat in his mouth. The rat's face, on close inspection, bore a remarkable resemblance to Louie Silva, the town manager.

"Very lifelike," Coffin said.

"Thank you," said Kotowski. "I think it has a certain *je ne sais quoi*."

"That's it exactly," Coffin said, sitting in a ratty overstuffed chair beside the chessboard.

Kotowski was a crank, perilously close to tipping over the edge into sheer nuttiness—in serious danger of becoming one of those salty resort-town "characters" the tourists took pictures of. He sold a few paintings every year in Boston and made ends meet by teaching figure drawing at Provincetown's various summer art schools, giving private lessons, and teaching an occasional course at the community college in Hyannis. He volunteered now and then at the high school and once a week at Valley View Nursing Home, instructing the elderly in still-life painting.

"Saw your mother yesterday," Kotowski said. "Entertaining as always. We watched *Jerry Springer* together."

"Thanks," Coffin said, advancing a pawn. "Good of you to stop in and see her."

"She's great. She remembers a lot, knows a lot of history. She just thinks it all happened last week, is the problem."

Coffin nodded. The wind hummed down the chimney.

"Busy day at the office?" Kotowski said, pushing the bottle cap out to meet Coffin's pawn.

"Busy week," Coffin said.

"Any clues? Any suspects?"

"Clues? Suspects? Who are you, Miss Marple?"

"Not exactly what you signed on for, I guess," Kotowski said.

"It's not what anybody in this town signed on for," Coffin said, advancing a knight, taking it back, advancing it again. "Not even Boyle, although he's too stupid and gung ho to know any better. Town Hall's hoping the whole thing is all just a bad dream."

Kotowski snorted. "Town Hall," he said. "Lucky you, working cheek by jowl with our fine Board of Corruptmen. Don't be surprised if they turn your office into a condo."

"Uh-oh," said Coffin. "Here we go. Let the axe-grinding begin."

"Scoff all you want," Kotowski said, crossing his long, skinny legs, "but they're after me again."

"Who's after you?"

"The real estate cabal. The developers and their government lackeys."

Coffin took a sip of his beer. The sliding glass doors leading out to Kotowski's deck were open. Outside, a small boat puttered into the harbor, white paint glinting in the moonlight. "Lackeys?"

"Flunkies. Goons. This woman comes to my door on Monday—never seen her before in my life. Skinny dyke in a power suit. Asks me if I'm Mr. Kotowski. I might be, I said. Who the hell are *you?* She hands me a business card. Says she's with some real estate investment outfit. Says she'd like to come in and talk to me." Kotowski paused and took a sip of his beer. "So I say, what about? And she says she's prepared to make me an offer on my place, right here and now. A *very generous* offer."

"Pretty aggressive," Coffin said.

"No shit," Kotowski said. "I tell her to get lost—not for sale. She takes out another business card, writes a number on the back of it, and hands it to me. 'That's the figure we had in mind,' she says." He rummaged through a stack of papers on the floor and pulled out the card.

Coffin looked at it and whistled a soft, astonished note. "Wow," he said.

"Exactly," Kotowski said. "But I tell her I live here, and I'm not selling. She asks if she can come in and discuss it with me, and I say no. By now I'm getting pissed. I tell her to take her very generous offer and stick it up her ass. She says, 'I want this property. You're going to sell it to me.' Then she hops into her little black convertible and drives off, slick as butter."

Coffin flipped the card over. SERENA HENCH, it said, in embossed script. REIC. Two phone numbers were printed across the bottom.

"What's REIC?" Coffin said.

"Real Estate Investment Company. Consortium. Something like that."

"Must be new. First I've heard of them."

"Know how much I paid for this place, back in '73?" Kotowski said.

Coffin took Kotowski's pawn with a bishop. "Check," he said.

"Forty thousand. Everyone thought I was nuts. I winterized it myself, fixed the plumbing, put in the woodstove. I had to sell my car to scrape up six grand for the down payment. I lived mostly on beans and rice the first few years. I traded sketches for fish, down at the wharf. Know what my tax assessment is now?"

"Everybody's assessment's through the roof," Coffin said. "The tax on my mother's place is killing me."

"Small beans," Kotowski said, dismissing Coffin with a regal wave. "You happen to be sitting in one of the most valuable homes in P'town." He spread his arms. "A fucking palace."

"A regular Taj Mahal," Coffin said, smacking the arm of his overstuffed chair, watching the clouds of dust rise in the lamplight.

"It's the *land*. I'm on three lots here, prime waterfront. Tear the house down and put up deluxe condos, you could multiply this"— he picked up Serena Hench's business card—"by twenty."

They gazed at the chess pieces in silence: white's diffident attack, black's clumsy retreat.

"Ever been to Nantucket?" Kotowski said.

"Once," Coffin said. "When I was a kid. Took the ferry from Hyannis. It was horrible."

"Nantucket?"

"No, Nantucket was fine. The ferry was horrible."

"You and your boat phobia," Kotowski said. "I had some paintings in a gallery there a few years ago. A truly hideous experience.

It was a group show—me, two dune and sunset painters, and a freaking driftwood sculptor, I kid you not. I got drunk and insulted people."

"The trauma," Coffin said, throwing his forearm over his eyes.

"No, no, no—that was the *good* part," Kotowski said impatiently. "*Nantucket* was abominable. Stepford meets the Disney version of *Moby-Dick*. The whole island is perfect and clean and *cute.*" Kotowski curled his upper lip into a canine snarl. "Nobody lives there but rich, glossy white people—self-congratulating lawyers and their lubricious trophy wives, completely zombified on antidepressants. Nothing but suntanned morons wearing Rolex watches, as far as the eye can see. Even the dogs look smug."

"Nobody likes a smug dog."

"There you go again—scoffer. There is no Nantucket anymore. It's all been torn down and replaced with gigantic McMansions. You can't buy a sandwich there for less than twelve bucks. That's Provincetown in a year or two. Except the lawyers and the trophy wives will all be queer."

Coffin yawned. "All the good places get loved to death," he said.

"All the good places get sold to the highest bidder. It's not love that fucks things up—it's money."

"It's both," Coffin said, pondering the board. He considered castling, decided against it, and advanced a pawn instead.

"Ha," Kotowski said, countering with a knight. "Sounds like somebody's got girl trouble."

"Jamie wants to have a baby."

"Well, there it is. Time to jump ship."

"That seems a little extreme."

"It's the trap, man. The female conspiracy. I'll bet she said her biological clock was ticking."

Coffin saw an opening and moved his queen. "Gay man stereotypes straight woman," he said. "Check again."

"I am not *gay*," Kotowski said. "I'm homosexual. To be gay is to be frivolously happy, which I am most definitely not."

"Your turn," Coffin said.

"It's scientific fact. Women only need men around for two things. They need our sperm, and they need us to drag home the occasional mastodon and drive off predators until the pups get old enough to fend for themselves. Everything else is window dressing."

"That's three things. And the window dressing's improved in the last million years or so. Not that you'd be interested." Something was burning, Coffin realized. The smell of smoke drifted in through the open glass doors.

Kotowski shook his head, eyes moist with pity. "A guy your age, getting led around by his dick like a teenage kid. It's pathetic."

"Something's burning," Coffin said. "Smell that?"

Kotowski shuddered, made a retching sound. "I suppose she wants to get married, too."

A deep red glow was visible above the northern horizon. Coffin could hear sirens in the distance. He stood and walked out onto Kotowski's deck. "Actually, no," he said. "You're in check."

Kotowski looked at the board, moved his king a single space to the right. "Don't do it, Coffin. Don't let her turn you into a walking sperm bank. You'll never have a minute to yourself again. Kids are noisy, messy, and expensive, and when they grow up they blame you for all their problems."

"What the hell is on fire?" Coffin said. "Looks like it's up at the Heights."

"Fuck," said Kotowski, staring at the chessboard. "You sly bastard. Time for the Kotowski defense." He shook the board until all of the pieces fell over.

Chapter 10

Trooper Leonard Treadway of the Massachusetts State Police, Cape and Islands Detective Division, flipped open his compact and checked his makeup in the little mirror. He looked good, if he did say so himself. His cheekbones were tastefully accented with a hint of blush, and a careful application of frosted pink lipstick made his mouth look full, almost pouty. *If I was really a girl*, he thought, *I might even ask me out on a date*. His brows lowered. It was a confusing notion—not one he wanted to pursue.

His wig was straight, his makeup tasteful, his clothing attractive but not too far over the top. He wore a short black skirt and a white rayon blouse with a shawl collar. His feet were wedged into size eleven pumps with two-inch heels. They'd taken some getting used to, and he still didn't feel confident walking in them; his ankles turned on every little irregularity in the pavement. The underwear was a revelation, too: Pantyhose were nothing but clinging nylon bags of sweat. Whoever invented them should be shot. And the bra! Bras had seemed insanely complex to Treadway as a teenager, like a test you had to pass to get to second base—all those hooks and catches and straps—but that was nothing compared to wearing one. The underwires dug into his ribs, and he felt weirdly confined, as if he had a big Ace bandage wrapped around his chest.

So far, he and his partner Pilchard had found out exactly zilch about the murder of the cross-dressing minister. None of Provincetown's parade of gender-confused freaks would talk to them: not the homos, not the lesbos, not the drag queens. Trooper Treadway blamed it on Pilchard. His partner was a large, glowering man who favored brown suits and tended to clench up and go into confrontation mode whenever he had to talk to anyone who wasn't straight, white, and at least middle-class. Trooper Treadway had no problem with homos, as long as they obeyed the law and kept out of his face. Besides, it wasn't just the homos that were less than helpful. Even the regular people seemed skittish, reluctant—some kind of weird Yankee reserve, a small town's open distrust of outsiders. Whatever the reason, the result was that no one knew anything, no one had seen anything, no one had anything to say. The cross-dressing weirdo minister had somehow gone invisible on the last night of his life.

So when Treadway's boss, Lieutenant Markham, called on the cell phone to check in with the two detectives, they had little of import to tell him. Yes, they had made contact with a number of gays and/or transvestites. No, no one remembered seeing the Reverend Ron Merkin. Which, in a way, made sense to Trooper Treadway. Cross-dressing was a kind of disguise, he thought, an escape from one's day-to-day identity. If you went to a costume party, you didn't see the people; you saw the costumes. Provincetown was like a huge costume party, everyone trying on one identity after another. He mentioned this observation to Lieutenant Markham, who told him to shut up.

"You two better find something, and you'd better find it fast," Lieutenant Markham had said. "I've got Captain Faucett *and*

Mancini's office climbing up my ass. If they won't talk to you, you're going to have to try to blend in a little."

"Do you mean," Trooper Treadway had said, a little frisson of excitement tingling at the base of his spine, "go undercover?"

"I don't care if you go under*water*," Markham said. "Just get results."

Trooper Treadway's eyes were bright as he hung up the phone. He had never gone undercover before, and the idea had always intrigued him. There it was again, that trying on of new identities.

Then he let Pilchard talk him into going in drag. "How else are you going to check out the freaks?" Pilchard had said. "We've got to try to fit in, like the boss said. I'd do it, too, but where would we find stuff to fit me? Besides, I'm so ugly they'd know I was a cop right away." Pilchard. Fucking Pilchard, who was probably in a bar somewhere drinking beer and watching a Sox game, having a good laugh at his expense.

The town was crowded. A continuous, slow-moving stream of cars rolled down the narrow street, which was all but clogged with pedestrians—families, busloads of camcorder-wielding retirees in khaki shorts, and everywhere men holding hands with men and women with their arms around women, men in leather vests and pants, men dressed up like Cher and Dorothy from *The Wizard of Oz*. People on bicycles rode both ways down the one-way street, weaving in and out of traffic, narrowly avoiding clusters of ambling tourists who strayed from the sidewalks. It all made Trooper Treadway count his blessings and thank God that he, Leonard Treadway, had never felt any confusion about his sexual identity—he was a man, he liked girls, and that was that.

Treadway found the A-House after some searching, following the sound of thumping disco music up a dim, narrow street. He guessed he was in the right place because a lot of young men were milling around outside a rambling old New England house that had two doors facing onto the street. The young men were all smoking cigarettes. Some of them were muscular, and some were small and slender; some were in regular clothes, and some wore sailor suits or cowboy hats or biker gear. A few—and this made Trooper Treadway happy—were even in drag, although their outfits tended more toward sequins or spandex than tweed.

"Hi, sweetie pie," one of the sailor-suited men called from the porch. "Nice *out*fit. Buy you a drink?"

"No, thank you," said Trooper Treadway. "I don't drink. But perhaps you could help me."

The man rubbed the crotch of his white bell-bottoms. "I'll help you if you'll help *me*," he said.

Several of the men on the porch hooted with delight. Trooper Treadway could feel himself blushing. Was this what had happened to the cross-dressing preacher? This sort of harassment?

He brushed past the man in the sailor suit and opened the door on the left, which had a small sign above it that said *THE VAULT* in Gothic letters. It was a heavy, leather-trimmed door. Trooper Treadway stepped inside. The room was very dark, lit only with black light and a flickering strobe. Techno dance music pounded at migraine-inducing volume, and gay pornographic videos played on a dozen big screens around the room. There were no transvestites, only burly men dressed in black leather: black leather chaps, vests, harnesses, shorts, thongs—a great deal of variation on a single theme. Twos and threes of them ground at each other on the dance floor while small clusters heaved and writhed together around the room's shadowed periphery.

An enormous black man in chaps and a peaked leather cap was perched on a stool just inside the door. He waggled a no-no finger at Trooper Treadway, who stopped in his tracks.

"You're in the wrong place, honey," the black man shouted, barely audible above the music's thumping din. "This is a *leather*

bar." He said the words "leather bar" very slowly, as though Treadway might be brain damaged, or from another country.

Treadway smiled. His outfit was almost *too* good: The black man
apparently thought he was a woman. "It's all right!" he shouted.
"I'm a man!"

The black man rolled his eyes and extended a plate-sized hand in
the direction of the dance floor. "Leather," he shouted, leaving a lot
of space between the two syllables. He indicated Trooper Treadway's outfit with his other hand. "*Not* leather." Then he repeated
the process, in case Treadway still hadn't gotten the distinction.

"You mean I can't come in?" Treadway said, nonplussed. It hadn't
occurred to him that there might be places in the gay universe where
cross-dressers weren't welcome. Who knew the rules were so complicated?

The black doorman spun Trooper Treadway around and pro-
pelled him out onto the deck with one big hand between his shoulder
blades. "You want the Dance Bar, honey. First door on your left."

In the Dance Bar, the music was even louder than it had been in
the Vault, but it was different—happier, somehow. A punchy,
disco version of "I Will Survive" thundered from enormous speakers; a DJ stood at the top of a narrow spiral staircase, surrounded
by amps and mixers and other complicated-looking gear.

The room was crowded with men and mostly dark. A mirrored
disco ball hung from the ceiling, and hundreds of bright dots
whirled over the throng of dancers and flickered across the crowds
of men waiting for drinks at the bar.

For the first time in his life, Trooper Treadway felt intimidated.
The dance floor was packed with gyrating men. They ground
against each other in pairs or small pods. Many were shirtless;
Trooper Treadway could smell their sweat, the sheer sexual funk

of it hanging in the air like smoke. The music was deafening. A strobe light fired in the dark room, its bright pulse turning the dancers ghostly and mechanical.

He couldn't imagine entering this world, doing what these men did to each other, what some of them appeared to be about to do to each other in the very near future—it was all so *abnormal*. He shook his head; the images flickering inside it were too disturbing.

It was useless, he decided. There was no talking in a place like this, no chance to ask questions. He wasn't blending in all that successfully, either. He felt a dozen pairs of eyes on him, standing primly at the edge of the dance floor, clutching his handbag. He felt trapped there suddenly—the place was getting more crowded by the moment—felt himself about to drown in a writhing, alien sea. A cold sweat rose on his forehead; he hoped his makeup wouldn't run.

He turned to leave, but a colossally muscled man wearing nothing but a cowboy hat, boots, and white Calvin Klein underwear grabbed his arm and spun him around, practically dragging him out to the dance floor. Treadway was alarmed—it was as if he'd walked into an elaborate practical joke, or one of those dreams in which you've forgotten your pants.

"What's your name, honey?" the man yelled into Trooper Treadway's ear. He was grinding his muscular loins against Treadway's thigh; his long-fingered hands squeezed Treadway's buttocks as if they were ripe cantaloupes. The bulge in the man's white briefs was enormous. The man, Trooper Treadway realized, was getting excited.

"I am Trooper Leonard Treadway of the Massachusetts State Police!" Treadway hollered, trying simultaneously to squirm from the man's grasp and make himself heard over the pounding music. "Take your hands off me, or I'll be forced to place you under arrest!"

"What?" the man said, pulling Treadway closer. "I can't hear you!" The strobe light jittered. The music thumped and wailed.

A number of shirtless men who had been dancing together were now pointing at Trooper Treadway and laughing. Treadway reached into his purse for his ID—his service weapon was in there, too, and his handcuffs—but before he could find it, a second man approached and snatched the purse away, tossing it onto a small round table at the edge of the dance floor. Treadway's handcuffs slid from the open purse and fell to the floor.

"Kinky!" the second man shouted into Trooper Treadway's ear, rubbing his private region against Treadway's buttocks. "I like that!" A hand shot up Treadway's skirt—he struggled to push it away, but its owner was incredibly strong. Another hand went down the back of his pantyhose as the first hand squeezed his testicles through the taut nylon, forcing him onto his tiptoes.

"Awk!" said Trooper Treadway, squirming in the tentacled embrace of the two men. Panicked, he heaved with all his might, and the three of them staggered a few steps backward. The man who was grinding his pelvis into Trooper Treadway's buttocks bumped into the table on which his bag lay crumpled, and Treadway's service weapon—a chunky Glock nine millimeter—slid out of the bag and fell to the floor, where it discharged with a flat *crack,* barely audible above the music. The bullet pinged off the frozen margarita machine and blew a large hole in one of the DJ's black metal boxes, halting the music abruptly.

Everyone froze. The smell of cordite hung in the air, sharp and dangerous. For a moment, the silence in the big room was absolute, crystalline. The two men who had been happily groping Trooper Treadway took several steps back. Treadway dove for his gun, retrieved it, scrambled to his feet in the preposterous heels, then dug into his purse, intending to produce his badge and brandish it before him like a crucifix in a den of vampires. He gripped the badge, but before he removed it from the bag a little red flag popped up in his head—there was a chance he could still escape without further embarrassment, the collegial jeering, the damage to his career that would certainly result if he revealed his identity. He collected his handcuffs, held the gun down at his side, and bolted for the door as the bartender frantically dialed the phone, no doubt calling the local police.

Trooper Treadway kicked off the wobbly pumps when he reached Commercial Street and ran as fast as he could down a dim alley, out onto the town beach, past the backs of restaurants and souvenir shops, then up a quiet side street near his hotel. "Mother-*fucker!*" Trooper Treadway gasped, though he was not a man much given to vulgarity. His wig was cockeyed, his pantyhose torn. He had a raging erection.

Months later, Trooper Leonard Treadway would wake up after a darkly erotic dream filled with flashing lights and the shadowy, muscular forms of men. Sweating and aroused, he would lie awake until the clock radio went off at six, unable to sleep for the cloying dough-smell of his wife's body and the occasional sound of her teeth grinding, like a car driving slowly over china plates and cups.

On his way home, Coffin drove toward the red glow and column of smoke through the tall wrought-iron gate that separated the Heights from the rest of Provincetown. One of the enormous new trophy houses on top of the hill was spectacularly engulfed in flames. Fire spouted from its doors and windows, and the roof was beginning to burn; big, flaming cinders drifted through the air like demonic kites, threatening to torch the houses next door. The volunteer fire department was there, its two small pumper trucks throbbing, red lights whirling, pathetic streams of water pissing from their hoses. The EMS boys leaned against their ambulance;

the house was an inferno—if anyone was inside, there was nothing they could do.

It had been a gorgeous house, three full stories with banks of floor-to-ceiling windows facing Herring Cove. It had a broad upper deck, which would have been perfect for watching the sun set over the water while sipping a cold drink.

Coffin shut off the rumbling Dodge; it shuddered and clanked for several seconds before it died. He shouldered open the squealing door and climbed out. Two police cars sat at the bottom of the drive, lights flashing. A nervous cluster of neighbors stood in the street. Tony was smoking a cigarette, discussing the Sox and their annual late-season swoon with one of the summer cops. Lola was talking to two middle-aged men: one small, the other large and barrel-chested and wearing a cowboy hat. The fire crackled and popped like a Civil War skirmish.

"Anybody inside?" Coffin said.

"Don't know for sure," Lola said. "There was a dog barking and whining in there for a while, but it stopped."

"Crispy critter," Tony said. He rolled his eyes back in his head, held his curled hands up like begging paws.

Coffin looked at Tony, then at Lola, who was pointedly scribbling in her notebook. He wanted to smack Tony in the head. Instead he said, "Got a cigarette?"

Tony pointed his flashlight at Coffin. "Thought you quit."

"Just give me a cigarette."

Tony dug in his shirt pocket and pulled out a pack of Marlboros and a plastic lighter. He handed Coffin a cigarette and lit it for him.

Coffin took a deep drag. It tasted terrible. He took another.

"Gentlemen say they heard an explosion," Lola said, pointing her pen at the two men. "Around ten fifteen."

"Not an *explosion*, exactly," said the big man. "Sort of a *foomp*."

"*Foomp?*" said Coffin.

"Yeah," the man said. He draped a thick arm around the small man's shoulders. "Like when your furnace comes on in the winter? But louder."

"Did you see anything?" Coffin asked. "Flames? A flash of light?"

"Not till later," said the small man. "We were out for an after-dinner stroll. On our way back, we saw flames through the down-stairs windows. We ran right home and called 911."

Coffin watched the big house burn for a few minutes. The fire-fighters were having trouble; they kept slipping and falling on the wet lawn, and one of the trucks was only producing a weak, inter-mittent spritz. The fire was beautiful, like a great, hungry animal, feasting on joists and windowsills. "Whose house is this?"

Lola looked at her notebook. "Belongs to a Mr. Jason Duarte. Belonged."

"Any relation to Rocky Duarte? As in Duarte Construction?" Coffin said.

Tony nodded. "He's Rocky's grandkid. Took over the business a couple years ago."

"Rocky was a nice old guy," Coffin said. "He used to come around when I was a kid and watch the Celts games with Pop—they didn't have TV."

"Some house," Lola said. "The Duartes have done all right for themselves since then."

"My brother-in-law's a builder," one of the summer cops said. "Once you get a good line of credit, you can build these big tro-phy houses, live in them a few years, then sell them for a fortune and build another one."

"What if the market goes down?" Coffin asked.

"Sicilian foreclosure," Tony said, nodding at the fire. He shrugged. "But since when does the market go down?"

Coffin flipped his cigarette butt onto the pavement and ground it out with his toe. "I wonder what went *foomp*."

The house groaned, and a large section of the roof collapsed; a cloud of sparks burst upward into the night sky.

"Anybody call the fire marshal?" Coffin asked.

"I did," Lola said. "He's on his way up from Barnstable."

"I'm going home, then," Coffin said. "Call me if you need me."

Chapter II

It's quiet, except for the hiss and clank of the old-fashioned radiators. There's a short hallway with a closet, then a living room. Coffin makes a mental catalog: recliners, green carpet, old console TV. The colors are weirdly intense, as if the whole room is suffused with the green light before a storm.

The first bedroom is empty. The bed unmade. Clothes strewn on the floor—jeans, a flannel shirt, women's cowboy boots, shoddy and worn at the heel. There's a wall hanging, a big image of a wolf howling at a bright moon, printed on black plush. There's a boom box on the nightstand, a mostly empty bottle of Jim Beam, a glass pipe and a lighter.

"Hillbillies on crack," Rashid said. "The black man's revenge."

The second bedroom is bad. There's blood everywhere—smeared on the floor, soaking the bedclothes, spattered on the walls and ceiling. Coffin has seen hundreds of homicide victims, hundreds of rooms and apartments and houses where murders have been committed; his first year as a Baltimore cop, he vomited from one end of his precinct to the other. But this is one of the worst—the two battered children in their beds, the covers twisted around them. Their faces are horribly damaged, *their skulls caved in. Coffin realizes he's making a sound, a kind of whimper in the back of his throat. Rashid is doing his job, taking Polaroids, but Coffin can't stay in the hot little bedroom anymore. He wants to flee, but where? There's a small crowd of people outside the door. He considers opening the window and climbing down the fire escape, but then Rashid comes out of the bedroom, shaking his big head. Coffin expects him to make a joke, some wisecrack that will make him feel better, less out of control.*

"This is bad, Coffin," Rashid says. "This is really incredibly fucking bad."

Later in the dream, the phone began to ring, and Coffin searched for it in a lightless room, worried he might fall down the stairs in the dark. Something fell on the floor and broke. The phone stopped ringing, and Boyle's voice came out of the answering machine.

"For fuck's sake, Coffin," he said. "I blame this entirely on you."

Coffin turned on the light and, squinting, picked up the phone. The digital clock said 5:17. "What's that, Chief?" he said, rubbing his eyes.

"We've got *another one*," Boyle said, as if he'd discovered a rat in the laundry hamper.

Coffin knew but asked anyway. "Another one what?"

"Dead guy, is what—Jesus Christ, Coffin. Up at the Heights—the fire department found a dead guy in that house that burned down."

Coffin grimaced, swung his legs out from under the bedclothes. "Is it Jason Duarte?"

"Beats me, Coffin," Boyle said. "What does Jason Duarte look like? 'Cause this guy's crunchy, black, and smoldering."

Coffin sat on the edge of the bed for a minute or two. He felt disoriented and dizzy; his hand shook slightly as he brushed his teeth. He put on old clothes—poking around in burned-out buildings was a dirty job—and a pair of ancient L.L.Bean duck boots. It took him a long time to hunt down his keys. It was still dark outside. The air was damp and cold, and the whole town smelled like smoke.

The smell was worse at the Heights; stronger and more complex. There was the stink of charred wood, of course, but also melted plastic and a burnt-wool smell that Coffin guessed was expensive carpet. Beneath it all, something horrible, something animal and a little sweet that made the back of his throat close a bit.

A few volunteer firefighters were still there, leaning against a pumper truck and smoking cigarettes, keeping an eye on the blackened skeleton of Jason Duarte's house. Lola and Jeff Skillings had cordoned the lot with yellow police tape. A gaggle of neighbors hovered in the street; Coffin wondered if they'd been there all night. Pete Wells, the fire marshal, was sitting in the open rear door of his van, drinking coffee from a Styrofoam cup. "Mornin,' Frank," he said.

"What've we got here, Pete?" Coffin said.

Wells was about thirty-five, with a mop of curly brown hair. He wore jeans, yellow rubber boots, and a plaid cowboy shirt with pearl snaps instead of buttons. "Two bodies," he said. "One human, one canine. In the basement. That's where they ended up, anyway, when the floors caved in."

"Coroner not here yet?" Coffin said.

"Nope. Nor the state police. There's a wreck out on Route Six, apparently. Big pileup in the middle of suicide alley. Guess I just missed it."

"You got a minute? Can you give me the tour?"

"Have I got a minute," Wells said, dumping the last of his coffee into the street. "Time is *all* I got, my friend."

The house had burned to the sills; only the poured concrete foundation remained, the basement a blackened hole in the ground. Dead cinders and wet wads of pink insulation were scattered across the lawn. Charred timbers lay everywhere, broken, at odd angles.

"Jesus," Coffin said, climbing down an aluminum ladder into the basement. "The place looks like a bomb hit it."

"Nothing as exotic as that," Wells said, climbing down after him. "Simple arson fire."

"How do you know?"

Wells pointed. "See here? Scorch marks on the concrete slab, from the stairs to what was the laundry room. Looks like somebody doused a pile of dirty clothes with gas or kerosene, poured a trail out to the stairway, lit it, and walked away. Arson 101. They didn't try to conceal it, either. I wouldn't be surprised if there was an empty gas can lying around."

"Look at the washer and dryer," Coffin said. They lay crumpled on the basement floor, as if they'd been thrown from the cargo hold of an airplane as it flew overhead.

"Yeah—the fridge melted, too. Pretty hot fire. Ready to look at the bodies?"

Coffin's vision began to warp and swim. He stuck a hand out, leaned against the foundation wall and took a few deep breaths.

"You okay?" Wells said. "You don't look so good, Frank."

"I'm fine," Coffin said. His palms tingled. His heart thunked in his chest. "It's nothing that'll kill me, anyway."

They picked their way through half-devoured floor joists, blackened doors, and stumps of stud wall, all of which had collapsed into the basement as the floors gave way.

"Here's the dog," Wells said. The charred body lay near the

furnace. It could have been any small four-legged thing—a cat, a raccoon. The reek of its burned flesh was almost overwhelming.

"And the man?"

"I didn't say it was a man." Wells stepped around a bent and blackened clawfoot bathtub. "I said it was a human. Your guess as to the gender's as good as mine."

The body was black and stiff. Most of its clothes had burned away. Coffin was glad it was facedown. The smell was horrible. He coughed, gagging a little. His boots were smeared with ash.

When Coffin got home it was almost noon. He checked his answering machine. There were nine messages from reporters requesting interviews and one message from his cousin Tony, inviting him over to watch a ball game—the Sox versus the Yankees. Coffin pictured Tony's chaotic house, the explosion of plastic toys all but obscuring the floor, Tony's three young children screaming back and forth in front of the TV screen, his wife, Doris, hollering at them, somebody always crying.

Coffin thought about Tony—wondered how he could stand it, all that mess and commotion at home. Tony seemed to take the whole business in stride, like a big, good-natured Buddha. Coffin liked the peace that living alone brought, liked eating when he wanted, going to bed when he wanted, not having to pick up anyone's mess but his own. He'd been married for five years, in Baltimore, but things had gone sour—the divorce a cold slap in the face. His wife had gotten pregnant toward the end, but then she'd had a miscarriage.

He tried to sleep for a while, but whenever he began to drift off he felt dizzy; the darkness behind his closed eyes was a bottomless pit into which he fell and fell. He got up and made coffee and toast. He put half-and-half and sugar in the coffee and buttered the toast and then threw the toast away. As he sat and sipped his coffee he saw that Jamie had left most of a cigarette in the ashtray—she'd apparently lit it, then put it out almost immediately. He eyed it, deciding to let it be. He showered and shaved and dressed in his least-rumpled khakis and flannel shirt. On his way out the door, he picked up the cigarette and put it in his pocket.

Chapter 12

A half hour later, Lola sat in Coffin's desk chair, flipping through her notebook. Coffin was on the phone with Shelley Block.

"Thanks for the Merkin report, Shel," he said.

"Hope it helps," she said. "Just don't tell anyone you got it from me. You're not authorized, you know."

"Any ID yet on the body from the Duarte house?"

Someone flushed a toilet upstairs, and water rushed through the sewer pipe above Coffin's desk.

"It's wall-to-wall gorks here," Shelley said cheerfully. "Haven't had a minute. But hang on—I've got his stuff here somewhere." There was a rustling of papers. "Here we go. Personal effects. Wallet, watch, two rings, earring. Let's just look in the bag, shall we?"

She paused a moment; Coffin heard plastic rattling.

"All righty," Shelley said. "One wallet, smoky and wet, containing bank card, credit cards, insurance card, nude photo of girlfriend—nice dye job—and Mass driver's license, issued to one Jason Duarte."

"So it's him, then."

"Unless somebody went to the trouble of putting Jason Duarte's wallet in someone else's pocket before they killed him, yes. Once we get dental records, we'll know for sure."

"Great," Coffin said. "When can you do the autopsy?"

"*Now* he's interested in my work," Shelley sighed. "*C'est l'amour.* Your guy's at the top of the list. I'll shoot for this afternoon."

"I owe you lunch," Coffin said.

Shelley laughed. "Yeah, yeah. Anything but barbecue."

Coffin's phone buzzed as soon as he hung up. It was Boyle.

"Coffin? Mancini's here. He's holding a briefing in ten minutes. You and Winters are required to attend." He hung up before Coffin could say anything.

"Mancini's here," Coffin said. "He's going to brief us on the murders."

"That should be interesting," Lola said.

At one o'clock precisely, Vincent Mancini strode into the cramped squad room, with Boyle two steps behind him. The Cape and Islands district attorney was tall and tight-lipped. He wore round-rimmed glasses, a blue suit, and a red power tie. His hair was gelled into a premeditated rumple. Mancini set his briefcase down on the desk, stood behind the small lectern, and looked at his watch. The gabble of conversation died.

"As you know, the CIDA's office and the state police detectives division are now investigating two homicides committed this week in and around Provincetown," he said. "While we are making good progress, we ask that you keep your eyes and ears open and notify us at once if you obtain any information that may prove to be pertinent."

Tony raised his hand. "Like what kind of stuff?" he said.

"Facts. We're interested in Merkin's movements in the hours before his death. The PPD should *not* directly question potential witnesses, but we do ask that you notify us immediately if you *hear* of anyone who might have information pertaining to either of these cases."

"That sucks," Tony said softly.

Mancini frowned and straightened his tie. "While you will not be an active part of the investigation, I thought it wise to come here today and fill you in on where we stand at the moment. You may want to take notes." He held up three fingers. "In a homicide investigation, we look for three things: means, motive, and opportunity. Let's begin with motive. Murder happens for one of two reasons. Who can tell me what they are?"

Mancini waited, eyebrows raised expectantly. No one moved.

"All right," Mancini said. "I see we're starting from square one. The two basic motives for homicide are sex and money. Everything else is just a variation on those themes."

"Mr. Mancini?" Tony said.

"What is it, Officer?"

"What about revenge?"

"What do you mean, what about revenge?"

"You said there were only two motives for murder, but you didn't say revenge."

Mancini rolled his eyes. "All right, Officer. If you insist. Sex, money, and revenge."

Jeff Skillings raised his hand. "What about self-defense?"

Mancini glared at him. "All right, all right—sex, money, revenge, and self-defense. Is that it? Is everybody happy now?"

Two more hands went up. Coffin looked down at the floor, hoping Mancini wouldn't see him grinning.

"Jesus fucking Christ," Boyle said, standing near the door. "Can we get on with this? Would that be all right with you people?" No one spoke for a moment.

"As you all know," Mancini went on, "the majority of homicides are committed by the victim's family members or acquaintances, so that's where homicide investigators tend to look first. At the moment, our best suspect in the Merkin killing is Merkin's wife, who stands to inherit his entire estate, valued in the range of one hundred million dollars. She had motive and opportunity and no alibi for the time period in which Merkin most likely was killed. That is where our investigation will focus."

Tony raised his hand again. "What is it, Officer?" Mancini sighed.

"What about means?" Tony said, looking down at the scrap of paper on which he'd been taking notes.

"What's that, Officer?"

"Before, you said you had to have motive, opportunity, *and* means. Then just now you said the wife had motive and opportunity, but you *didn't* say means. Does that mean it's okay not to have means?"

Coffin cringed. Several officers were visibly struggling to suppress the giggles.

Boyle's face was very red. Coffin imagined his head popping like a balloon.

"Are you just about through, Santos?" Boyle demanded.

"But—"

"Santos!"

A quick bark of laughter popped out of Jeff Skillings's mouth. It seemed to hang in the air for a moment, like a small but lethal cloud of poison gas. Then there was another sound, out in the hallway, muffled a bit by the squad room's closed door. Someone was shouting, and another someone was shouting back. The first voice sounded a lot like Kotowski's. The voices got louder. The

Kotowski-sounding someone said, "Hold still, you fucking weasel!" Then the second someone yelled, "Get him off me!"

The officers in the squad room leapt to their feet in almost perfect unison. They charged into the hallway, skidding on the polished terrazzo. En masse, they rounded the corner, charged up two flights of stairs, and barreled toward Louie Silva's office, where the sound of shouting was now punctuated by a heavy, wet thwacking noise.

Coffin pushed through the knot of cops who'd gotten stuck in Louie's doorway. Kotowski was there, standing over Louie, who lay in front of his desk curled in the fetal position, arms protecting his head. Kotowski brandished a large dead fish. "You had my house condemned, you crooked little cocksucker!" he yelled, thwacking Louie over the head with the fish.

"Lunatic!" Louie said. "I had nothing to do with it!" His left eye was puffy, and his upper lip was split. His face and hair were slimed with scales.

Pinsky drew his service weapon and assumed the textbook firing position: feet at shoulder width, right arm extended, heel of his left hand bracing the gun butt. "Drop it!" he said.

Kotowski waved the fish. It was shiny and appeared to be very fresh—its eyes were black and unclouded. "Back off, stooges," Kotowski said. "This is between me and Mr. Greasy Palms here."

"For Christ's sake," Coffin said. "Put your gun away."

"But he's assaulting Mr. Silva with a codfish, Detective," Pinsky said.

"It's a striped bass, you ignoramus," Kotowski said, giving Louie a backhanded smack.

"I think you've made your point, Kotowski," Coffin said. "Whatever it was." He held out his hand, and Kotowski handed him the fish.

"This little douchebag let them condemn my house," Kotowski

said. He let go of Louie's tie. "Monday that blond dyke showed up and tried to buy me out, and today the building inspector comes by and tells me he's condemning the place. Bad wiring, he said! Rotten sills! Unfit for human habitation!"

"I had nothing to do with it!" Louie said, wiping his reddened, fish-slimed face with a handkerchief. "That's the building inspector's *job*."

"He said *you* ordered the inspection," Kotowski said.

"We had a complaint!"

"From who?" Coffin said.

"That's confidential," Louie said, pointing a pudgy finger at Kotowski. "Confidentiality's written into the statute—protects people from *lunatics* like him."

"All right, boys," Coffin said to the gaggle of police offers crowding Louie's office. "Fun's over. Everybody back to work."

"Um, Frank?" Tony said as the other officers filed out. "Shouldn't we arrest him?"

"Arrest who?"

"Kotowski."

"For what?"

"I don't know—assault with a big-ass fish, I guess."

"Louie? You want to press charges against Mr. Kotowski for assault with a big-ass fish?"

"Go ahead," Kotowski said. "Then we can tell the judge and the newspapers about how you're in league with these real estate sharks."

"Just get him out of here," Louie said, struggling to his feet, "and keep him the fuck away from me."

"I'll keep him away from you if you uncondemn his house," Coffin said.

"I can't do that. Once the citation's been handed out, you can't just take it back. But there's an appeals process."

"Nice little striper," Coffin said, handing the silvery fish back to Kotowski. "What is he, about ten pounds?"

"Okay! Okay!" Louie said, holding out his hands in a gesture of surrender. "Jesus Christ. I'll take care of it. But I don't ever want to see this nut-job in my office again."

Chapter 13

Anywhere else in the world," Coffin said, "a two-hundred-forty-pound man in a floral muumuu would have been about as anonymous as a circus clown at a Mafia funeral."

They were walking the block and a half to Al Dante's. Commercial Street was mobbed; the sidewalks overflowed with lesbian couples pushing strollers and knots of retirees and lean, muscled young men, some with their shirts off, displaying their carefully depilated chests. Adolescents, pierced and tattooed, rattled past on skateboards. Children gawked while their parents window-shopped. The line of traffic was blocked by the fake trolley that ran tours of Historic P'town all day long; bicycles whisked by in both directions, missing cars, pedestrians and telephone poles by millimeters. Three TV news remote vans were parked in front of Town Hall, beside the horse and carriage you could rent for a scenic jaunt around the Commercial Street–Bradford Street loop, at fifty dollars an hour. A group of women beat drums arrhythmically in front of the Unitarian church, which appeared to annoy the carriage horse; it tossed its head and snorted as a family of tourists climbed into the ornate buggy, helped by the driver, a tall woman in a top hat with a red plastic rose tucked into the band. The horse had a small sign on its forehead that said DON'T TOUCH! I BITE!

"A man in drag wouldn't necessarily stand out here," Lola said, "but a man in really *bad* drag might."

Al Dante's was on the inland side of Commercial Street, in the basement of an upscale boutique called Num Num. The walls were brick, the low ceiling supported by stout timbers. Most of the dining room's heavy oak tables were occupied, and the long, boat-shaped bar was packed. The customers were mostly well-dressed gay couples, tanned from long days at Herring Cove, nibbling appetizers and sipping green or red or blue cocktails from martini glasses.

"I've always wanted to eat here," Lola said.

"After you win the lottery?" Coffin said.

Lola took a menu from the rack by the hostess station, glanced at it, put it back. "Yowch," she said.

A woman emerged from the kitchen and drifted toward them. She was young and very thin, with jet black hair cut in a twenties bob and two gold rings in her left eyebrow. She wore low-riding black leather bell-bottoms and a short black top; six inches of flat, tanned belly showed between them. A third gold ring glinted in her navel.

"Dinner for two?" she asked, turning the reservation book on its little podium. "Name?"

Coffin showed his ID. "Detective Coffin, Officer Winters," he said.

The hostess put a slender hand over her heart. "Oh my," she said, smiling at Lola. "Am I under arrest?"

Lola shot Coffin a glance—*see what I mean?*

Coffin arched his eyebrows.

"Ah, no," Lola said. "We're looking into the movements of Ron Merkin on the night of his death."

The hostess's lip curled a bit. "Why bother?" she said. "The world's better off."

"Hate the sin," Coffin said, shrugging. "Love the sinner. Were you working Friday night?"

"Yes, of course."

Coffin held up Merkin's picture. "This is him. If he came in, he might've headed for the bar, ordered a couple of dozen on the half-shell."

The hostess took the picture and sniffed. "I don't know," she said. "We get a lot of tall ships in here. After a while they just merge into one big, tacky blob. Seen one, you've seen 'em all."

"Mind if we ask Cal?" Coffin said, pointing his chin at the bar.

"Help yourselves," the hostess said. She wrote a phone number on a card and slipped it into Lola's hand. "Here," she said. "In case you'd like to interrogate me further."

"Cute girl," Coffin said, as they climbed onto a couple of just-vacated bar stools. "She likes you."

"Too young," Lola said. "Too skinny. Too—I don't know—*fancy*. I like tomboys."

"Aren't you even curious?" Coffin said.

"About what?"

"Where else she was pierced."

Lola punched him in the arm. It hurt.

"Lecher," she said. "Stop projecting."

Coffin waved at the bartender, who was pouring two purple martini drinks from a chrome shaker. The bartender waved back and flashed a smile. He was tall, broad-shouldered, and remarkably handsome.

"That's Cal, I presume," Lola said.

Coffin looked at her. "Handsome, isn't he?"

"Gorgeous," she said. "He must be a popular guy."

"He's been with the same partner for ten years. They own a place out in Truro. They're getting married in September, I think."

"That crashing sound? Hearts breaking all over P'town," Lola said.

"Well, if it isn't my favorite peace officer," Cal said, leaning across the bar to give Coffin a hug and kiss on the cheek. "You two look like you're out on a date."

Coffin introduced them.

"I'm honored, ma'am," Cal said. He kissed Lola's hand. "Drinks?"

"Absolutely," Coffin said. "Scotch for me. And a dozen raw, if they're fresh."

"Came in at lunchtime," Cal said. "They don't get much fresher than that."

"What are those purple things you just made?" Lola said.

"Black orchids," Cal said. "Black vodka, Chambord, and cranberry."

Lola wrinkled her nose. "Stoli martini, dry as dust," she said.

Cal smiled. " 'Atta girl," he said.

"I can't believe you actually eat those things," Lola said when Cal had gone to make their drinks.

"Oysters? You don't like them?"

"I don't even like to think about them."

Coffin looked at her. "You've never tried one, have you?"

"Well, no," Lola admitted. "They look nasty. Just the thought kind of makes me queasy."

A waitress brought the oysters on a stainless steel platter. They glistened in the muted light. Their shells were wonderfully complicated—rough and ugly on the outside, smooth and pearlescent on the inside.

"What they look like," Coffin said, squeezing a lemon wedge

over three of the oysters, "are big old blobs of sea snot." He pierced one with a small fork and chewed it slowly. "Mmmm," he said. "*Delicious* sea snot."

"They're full of germs, you know. Hepatitis and God knows what. Not to mention mercury."

Coffin ate another. "The mercury," he said, "is what makes them so good."

Lola laughed.

Cal arrived with the drinks. "Plain old boring scotch for you," he said. "Kick-ass martini for the lady. How are the bivalves?"

"Fantastic," Coffin said. He picked up one of the oysters and slurped it from its shell. "People who won't even try them are big wussies."

"I'd never date a man who wouldn't eat oysters," Cal said, leaning a hip against one of the chrome beer coolers. "It's a very bad sign."

"Wussies?" Lola said. "*Wussies?* What is this, seventh grade?" She lifted an oyster from its shell with the little fork, dunked it in cocktail sauce, and put it in her mouth.

"Well?" Coffin said, watching her face.

"Not bad," Lola said through the mouthful of oyster. She swallowed, then washed the oyster down with two large slurps of martini. "Reminds me of someone I used to date."

"You're very brave," Cal said, making a face.

"Thanks," Lola said. She drank more of the martini, then pulled the picture of Merkin out of her briefcase. "We actually came here for a reason. Was this guy here on Friday night? Doing what my esteemed colleague is doing?"

Cal held the snapshot at arm's length, then took a pair of reading glasses out of his pocket and held the picture under his nose, shooting an *I dare you* look at Lola.

"Ha!" Cal said. "Reverend Rhonda. I almost called you guys on Sunday, when I heard he was dead."

"He was here?" Coffin said. "Are you sure?"

"Sure I'm sure. We get some big uglies in here, but not many as big and ugly as him. Besides, I'd recognize that wig anywhere—the man's wearing a spaniel on his head."

"Was he with anyone?" Lola said. "Or by himself?"

Cal leaned toward them. "Funny you should ask," he said. "With someone. A woman."

Lola looked at Coffin. "The wife?"

"Short brunette?" Coffin asked. "Big head, eighties mall hair, diamond the size of a horse suppository?"

"Not even close," Cal said. "Skinny blond in a black Armani suit. No makeup. No idea what to do with her hair."

"Who paid?"

"She did," Cal said. "It was funny, so it stuck in my head. The power dyke and the tall ship, out on the town."

"Credit card?" Coffin asked.

Cal nodded. "Super duper titanium. And very particular about the receipt."

"Remember the name?"

Cal thought for a second, then tapped the side of his head with his index finger. "Early Alzheimer's. Weird name—it's on the tip of my brain."

"Could you go through Friday's receipts and see if anything rings a bell?"

"Sure. As soon as we close, I'll get the boss to dig them up."

Coffin climbed the two steep flights of wooden stairs to Jamie's apartment slowly. He was tired and half drunk; he felt old.

Jamie's lights were on, and sitar music was playing softly inside. Coffin thought he could hear the shower running. He knocked and nothing happened. He tried the door; it was locked, which was unusual. Coffin leaned against the rail of the long wooden balcony and lit a cigarette. The deep indigo sky and the moon and the silhouette of the Pilgrim Monument looked like a painted backdrop. Coffin's cigarette tasted bad, so he flipped it over the rail into the bushes, its orange coal streaking downward like a little meteor.

When he heard the shower stop, he knocked again, and in a minute Jamie came to the door wearing the big terrycloth bathrobe he'd given her. She'd wrapped a towel around her head like a turban. A trail of wet footprints led down the hall to the bathroom.

"Been here long?" she said, leaning against the door frame.

"Just a minute or two."

"I was in the shower," she said.

"I can see that."

The robe had slipped open an inch or two; Jamie pulled it together with one hand. "Well, don't just stand there, Detective. Come on in." She turned and padded into the living room.

"Your door was locked," Coffin said. He followed her down the short hallway, liking the way her hips moved under the bulky robe, her slow, fluid walk. "That's good."

"I guess I'm a little spooked," Jamie said. The apartment smelled like hot water and Jamie's grapefruit shower gel.

Coffin perched on the big, lumpy sofa while Jamie opened the fridge, then came back with two bottles of beer. She sat in a green vinyl armchair, left foot tucked under her right thigh. Coffin twisted off the bottle caps and handed one of the beers to Jamie.

"The killings," Coffin said, "have spooked a lot of people."

"There's definitely that," Jamie said, "and something weird happened yesterday. Like really kind of creepy. I wasn't going to bother you with it, but it's sort of freaking me out." The white envelope was on the end table. She handed it to Coffin. "I found this on my doorstep yesterday morning."

Coffin looked inside. "Jesus," he said. "That's pretty fucking creepy, all right." He unfolded the sheet of paper. "Twayi sni-hyaami?" he said, haltingly.

"It's Sanskrit. I learned some when I was studying in India. It means 'I love you.'"

Coffin dumped the razor blades out on the coffee table and looked at Jamie. "Hell of a way of showing it," he said. "Any idea who the creep in question might be?"

"Remember the other day, when I said Duffy Plotz had been asking me out?"

Coffin nodded. "Maybe he's not so good at taking no for an answer," he said. "I'll have a talk with our friend Plotz, first thing tomorrow. He needs to know this is totally over the line."

Jamie clasped her hands together and grinned. "What a man!" she said in her best South Carolina drawl.

Coffin grunted, caveman style. Then he leaned back and sipped his beer. "I've been thinking about the baby thing," he said.

"Me, too."

Coffin set his beer on the coffee table, next to a greenish bronze statuette of an Indian god. The god had a human body and an elephant's head—a long, elegant trunk snaked over its belly. "I don't think I'm ready," he said.

Jamie smiled and leaned back in the big chair. "Well, you better *get* ready," she said. "Today was my last birth control pill."

Coffin picked up the bronze figurine; it was heavier than it looked. It wore a crown, like Babar. He set it back down. "Jamie," he said. "I can't. Not now."

"You most certainly can," Jamie said. "Unless there's a vasectomy you haven't told me about."

"No vasectomy."

"Car wreck? Football injury? Tight shorts? Bicycle balls?"

"No. It's nothing physical. That's all fine, as far as I know."

Jamie pursed her lips. "Well, what, then, Frank? What *is* it?"

"I tried to tell you, night before last."

Jamie frowned, thought for a minute. "You're afraid something will happen? To the baby?"

Coffin nodded. "I know it sounds crazy."

"A little, yeah."

Coffin took a sip of beer, then pressed the cool, moist bottle against his forehead. "I saw a lot of stuff, working homicide. Things people had done to each other, to women and children." He shook his head. "Horrible things."

"That would be hard to walk around with," Jamie said. She touched his hand.

Coffin shook his head. "I'm just saying—if anything really bad like that happened to my kid, I couldn't handle it."

"It won't, Frank."

"Probably not. But it could. It *does.*"

Jamie shifted in the green chair, tucking her legs up under the bathrobe. "I had a friend in college whose parents were both doctors," she said. "They were always making her get all these tests. Every time she got an ache or pain, they had her tested for cancer or MS or whatever. Now she's the biggest hypochondriac who ever lived."

"Too much information," Coffin said. "Fucks with your head."

"You did counseling, right?"

"A year and a half. It helped. I'm working. I'm more or less functional—although these two murders have been kind of a nasty déjà vu."

Jamie moved to the couch, leaned close. "I don't know how you do it," she said. "I think you're incredibly brave. I'd be a whimpering pool of jelly if I were you."

Coffin's eyes hurt. He closed them and rubbed the lids lightly with his fingertips. "I'd like to say that when things calm down a little, I won't be such a freak, but I'm not sure that's true."

"How do we find out?" Jamie said.

"I don't know. Wait a little, maybe."

Jamie leaned back and pulled the hem of the robe down over her feet. "Okay. How long's a little, do you think?"

"Assuming no more dead people show up," Coffin said, "a week or two. Boyle and Louie will lose interest; the town will return to business as usual. The state police will arrest the most likely suspect or give up and go home. I'll go back to investigating bad checks and break-ins."

"Look, Frank," she said, draping her arm around his shoulders. "We're all spooked. These murders have got the whole town looking over its shoulder, but it won't always be like this. At some point you have to choose your life story, you know what I mean?"

"I think so."

Jamie looked into Coffin's eyes. "I know what I'm proposing is radical," she said with a half-smile, "but it's basically a simple choice. You can have a rich and rewarding life with me, or you can end up like your friend Kotowski—cranky, smelly, and peculiar."

"I'm already cranky, smelly, and peculiar."

Jamie kicked him in the shin with her bare foot. "Smellier," she said.

"Ow," Coffin said, rubbing his leg.

"You're tired," Jamie said. "Look at you."

He nodded.

"I know you'll say no, but do you want to stay over?"

"Yes," Coffin said. "But I have an early morning tomorrow. I should go home." He plucked a cigarette from Jamie's pack and lit it with her plastic lighter. His vision tilted and warped a little as he stood up.

Jamie stood, too, and put her hands on his shoulders. The

bathrobe slipped open. She pressed her body tight against him, her skin still sheened with moisturizer. "You're a complicated package, Coffin," she said. She tilted his head a bit with her hands and lightly bit his neck. "Sure you won't stay?"

"That's not fair," Coffin said. "My whole body is one big goose bump now."

"What's fair got to do with it?"

They kissed good night on the balcony, in the yellow glow of the porch light. It was a long kiss. Jamie's bathrobe fell open again and Coffin cupped her breast, gently pinching the nipple between his thumb and forefinger. She groaned a little, took Coffin's hand, and placed it between her legs. She was very wet; he pushed a finger inside her.

"Now who's not being fair?" she said into his ear.

"Sorry," Coffin said.

"I'm not," Jamie said. She grabbed his sleeve and pulled him inside.

Chapter 14

Windless dawn, the sun coming up red behind the Pilgrim Monument. Kotowski sat on his sagging deck, staring out at the harbor through a pair of army surplus binoculars. The Jet-Skier made a big, looping circle on the still water, throwing up a curtain of spray, then zoomed off in the direction of the sunrise, thwomping hard across his wake. Zooming and thwomping seemed to be the whole point of a Jet Ski—that and the noise. The noise! It was unbearable, like a herd of chain saws all running at once, shattering the morning silence, rendering sleep or thought or stillness of any kind impossible.

As usual, the Board of Corruptmen was responsible. The town had resisted the overtures of a number of Jet Ski rental franchises over the years, had even at one point banned the damned things from the harbor. Three months ago Louie Silva had changed all that, claiming that the town's lawyer believed the ban to be unconstitutional. Silva had pushed through new rules in a closed door meeting of the board, with no input from the community. Kotowski and a few others had raised a stink, and Silva and the board had promised to review the new policy at the end of the summer. The corruptmen had won, Kotowski knew, without a fight. Most of the harborside properties were owned by absentees who rented them out for astronomical sums; they couldn't care less. What mattered was the money. That's what New Improved Provincetown was all about.

The Jet-Skier looped again, throttle wide open. He was heading straight for Kotowski's house and would have to turn soon to avoid the breakwater. Kotowski put the binoculars down and picked up his rifle, an old .30-06 he'd bought years ago at a yard sale. The gun had a pretty good scope, and Kotowski fixed the crosshairs on the Jet-Skier's head.

"Bang," Kotowski said under his breath. "Gotcha, you son of a bitch."

Coffin woke up early in his own bed, showered and dressed, and drove three blocks to the Yankee Mart for a cup of coffee. He was tired and a little hungover. Town was busier than ever: Bradford Street was a slow bumper-to-bumper. The inside of the Dodge smelled like something aquatic and dead. He left it idling in the parking lot, afraid if he shut the engine off it might not start again.

Inside, Cassie Ramos was just starting her shift. Coffin had gone to high school with her father; Cassie, he knew, was short for Cassiopeia. She was a slim, olive-skinned girl the age his own kids might be, if he'd had them, if things had worked out differently. She had a slight, heartbreaking mustache; every time Coffin saw her, he fell hopelessly in love with the faint strip of down on her upper lip. Sooner or later, he knew, Cassie would move to Boston or New York—all the smart, pretty girls did; why would they stay here?—and the mustache would be history. She'd wax it at home in her bathroom or pay a lot of money for electrolysis, but either way it was a goner, like everything human that was real and unself-conscious. He squirted coffee from the chrome air pot into a tall paperboard cup.

"Everyone goes to Milton's for lattes now," Cassie said from behind the cash register. "Four dollars for coffee and steamed milk. There's even a name for the person who makes them. Know what it is?"

"Milton?" Coffin asked.

Cassie laughed, which made Coffin happy. "A barista. I think it's Italian."

"You can't just drink coffee anymore," Coffin said. "Coffee's for rubes. You have to drink chai while doing Pilates and listening to your iPod."

Cassie laughed again. "Dude," she said, "you're so, like, 2003."

Coffin felt good until he walked out to the parking lot: The Dodge had stalled. A ribbon of white smoke drifted from under the hood.

Duffy Plotz ran the dump that served Provincetown and Truro. It was off Route 6 at the end of a short, unpaved service road. The landfill itself had been closed years before, but there was still a large corrugated-steel shed where residents could drop off trash in Dumpsters and recycling in neatly labeled barrels. There was also a low, rambling thrift store stocked with donated and discarded items—everything from secondhand baby clothes to used mattresses, old books, and vinyl LPs—which was open only on Saturdays. Plotz's office was a small Airstream trailer beside the recycling shed; a used air conditioner wheezed in its front window. A TV antenna and a galvanized stovepipe sprouted from its roof.

Coffin climbed out of the Dodge and knocked on the door.

The curtains moved beside the window; then the door swung open.

"Well, well—Officer Coffin," Plotz said, his tall frame stooped in the doorway. "Kind of unusual, seeing you out here."

"Is this a good place to talk?" Coffin said. "Or should we go somewhere a little more private?"

Plotz looked at his watch. "I'm kind of working," he said. "What are we talking about, exactly?"

Coffin pulled the envelope out of his shirt pocket. "You left this on Jamie's doorstep, Duffy. That was a highly inappropriate thing to do."

"I don't know what you're talking about," Plotz said. "I didn't leave any envelope on anybody's doorstep."

"I'm going to give you one warning, Duffy." Coffin waved the envelope under Plotz's nose. "No more of this creepy shit. You're messing with the wrong people, and if you do it again you're going to be very fucking sorry. Do you understand me?"

Plotz was two or three inches taller than Coffin and a decade younger. He was lean and sinewy from years of advanced yoga classes. "Are you threatening me as a private citizen," he said, stepping out of the trailer and down its two wooden stairs, "or as a public official?"

He does *look like an ostrich,* Coffin thought. *A big, pissed-off one.* He hadn't been in a physical fight in twenty years, but he still remembered his training. He stamped hard on Plotz's instep with the heel of his boot. Plotz yelped, half-doubled in pain, and Coffin clipped him on the point of the chin with his elbow. Plotz sat down abruptly, banging his head on the side of the trailer.

"Both," Coffin said. He climbed into the sagging Dodge and turned the key. Mercifully, for once, it started on the first try.

———

At his office, Coffin sipped cold coffee from his paper cup. "That the Duarte autopsy report?"

"Hot off the fax machine," Lola said.

"Any surprises?"

"Well, it's definitely him—extensive bridgework perfectly matches Duarte's dental records. But the autopsy still raises a couple of questions. He had enough heroin in his blood to kill a mule."

"So he OD'd?"

Lola pushed the report across the desk toward Coffin. "No. But he would've, if the smoke hadn't killed him first. Which it did— lots of particulate in the lungs."

"So," Coffin said, flipping through the pages. "Somebody injected him with an overdose of smack and then set the house on fire?"

"Maybe he did the injecting himself. No shortage of junkies in P'town."

"Could he have set the house on fire, too?"

Lola's brow furrowed. "Maybe before he shot up. But wouldn't that be like drinking poison and then shooting yourself? Kind of overkill?"

"Since when are suicides rational?"

They sat in silence for a long moment. "You think he committed suicide?" Lola said.

"No. Wishful thinking."

Lola reached up with both hands and fiddled with her ponytail. Coffin couldn't help observing the round swell of her breasts through her silk blouse.

"I wonder what Duarte was doing for money," Lola said. "Big house, drug habit—he must've needed a lot of cash."

"Shouldn't be too hard to find out. We can check his bank records. Wouldn't hurt to talk to his dad, either."

"Who's his dad?"

"Sonny Duarte—son of Rocky. He lives in my neighborhood. I think you should go talk to him."

"Me? He knows you."

"That's the problem. He and my father hated each other." Coffin paused. "But he'll like you just fine."

Lola raised a finger. "Almost forgot," she said. "Cal from Al Dante's called. They found the receipt, they're pretty sure."

"And the name?"

"Serena Hench."

Coffin scribbled the name on a legal pad and underlined it twice. "*That's* interesting," he said. "She's the woman who was trying to buy Kotowski's house."

Lola stood. "And she was with Merkin shortly before he died. When do we go see her?"

Coffin shook his head. "You drop in on Mr. Duarte. I'll call Fishermen's Bank. Then I'll have a talk with Ms. Hench."

It was just after 10:00 A.M. and already hot. Three enormous sunflowers leaned beside Sonny Duarte's house like bright prehistoric showerheads. A scruffy militia of starlings picked their way across the lawn. Lola was sweating in her slacks and silk blouse. She knocked on the screen door a second time. Inside, a television blared and a dog started a deep, phlegmy barking. A man's voice said, "Go away, dammit."

"Mr. Duarte?" Lola called. The screen door opened directly into the kitchen. The linoleum was worn, a green and yellow checkerboard. The walls were painted robin's egg blue. There was a stained Formica table and chrome and vinyl dinette chairs. The barking stopped. A bulldog waddled up to the screen door, toenails clicking on the linoleum, and stood looking up at her, breathing in labored snorts through its mashed-in snout.

"Go away!" the man's voice said. "Goddamn Jehovah's Witnesses—I told you I don't want no Jesus bullshit."

"Mr. Duarte? I'm Officer Winters of the Provincetown Police Department. Can I talk to you for a second?" Lola could hear sweaty bare feet approaching on the linoleum floor—*squish squish squish*.

The voice said, "Police? I'll be goddamned. Who called the police?" Then a small, wiry man appeared in boxer shorts and a stained white T-shirt. "You ain't no police," the little man said, looking Lola up and down. "But you don't look like no goddamn Jehovah's Witnesses, either."

"Police, honest injun," Lola held up her shield. "What do Jehovah's Witnesses look like?"

Duarte grinned. He was missing one of his front teeth. "They was just here, this morning. Big fat people. I thought you was them, but you ain't."

"Can I ask you a few questions about your son?"

"You can ask me anything, hot stuff," Duarte said. He opened the screen door. "Take a load off while I put some goddamn pants on." He padded off into the dim recesses of his little house.

The bulldog sniffed Lola's calf, then sat down on its haunches. Its left eye was clouded and white. The refrigerator hummed loudly. It was ancient and rusted in spots. Dishes were piled in a sinkful of greasy water. A dirty saucepan sat on the stove. In the next room, the TV was tuned to *The Price Is Right*.

Sonny Duarte emerged from the bedroom, zipping a worn pair of chinos. "Jason was a good boy. He worked hard. He got some problems, but who ain't got problems?" Duarte opened the fridge and took out a beer. "You want a beer? I got Busch Light."

"No, thanks, Mr. Duarte. You said Jason worked hard. What was he working on when he died?"

"What-you-call-it. Goddamn big condos down on the west end.

Building foreman. Real big shot, but does he give me any work? No, he don't." Duarte's face crumpled then, and fat tears rolled down his cheeks.

"Mr. Duarte—are you okay? Do you want me to come back later?"

"No, it's all right." He wiped the tears away with the back of his wrist, then took a long swallow of beer. "Go on. Ask your goddamn questions."

"You said Jason had problems. What kind of problems?"

"Okay," Duarte said, leaning close to Lola. "What can it hurt if I tell you?" He lowered his voice. "He likes the needle. Too much. So he got problems."

Lola tilted her head. "The needle?"

"He shoots that smack shit. Heroin. First a little bit, no big deal. Then more, more, more. He's working hard; he can afford it, he says. Goddamn it, I say," Duarte shook his skinny, gnarled fist. "But he don't listen."

"Who was financing the Moors project, Mr. Duarte—do you know?"

"Some company. Something-or-other Real Estate—I don't know."

Lola flipped through her notebook. "Real Estate Investment Consortium?"

Duarte took a long gulp of beer. "Yeah, maybe. Something-or-other."

"Who was his boss there?"

"Beats me. Look, we don't talk much, me and Jason. He got his big house in the Heights and he got his smack and his girls and I got this ugly dog and Bob Barker and Busch Light and a bad back. Different lives. We don't talk so much."

"Did Jason go out with a lot of girls? Or was there one in particular?"

"Ho!" Duarte waved a bony arm. "That goddamn kid, he always got lots of girls. Like you wouldn't believe. Blond, brunette, whatever you got. Last time I seen him, he got some skinny artsy chick. Nice little ass on her." Duarte grinned and held out his hands, squeezing invisible buttocks.

"Mr. Duarte," Lola said, leaning forward in her seat. A fly landed on the table in front of her, rubbed its forelegs together, took off. The bulldog snapped at it as it flew by. "Can you think of anyone who would want to kill Jason?"

Duarte scratched his ear with a ragged fingernail. "Well, maybe he owed somebody some money. Maybe some drug dealer or something. I don't know."

"Do you know for a fact that Jason owed money?"

"No, but he was broke all the time—always got the bank after him. He asked *me* for money. Me—and I'm livin' on disability."

Lola looked at the bulldog, which gazed back at her with pop-eyed, frowning adoration. "What's your dog's name? He's kind of cute."

"His name? Sonny Duarte, just like me."

"You named your dog after yourself?"

"Sure. Why not? I'm a hell of a guy."

Chapter 15

offin hung up the phone and looked at his notes. According to Jeff Skillings's boyfriend, who ran the loan department at Fishermen's Bank, Jason Duarte had bounced checks all over town between December and the end of March. Starting in early April, he'd begun depositing checks from Real Estate Investment Consortium totaling almost fifty thousand dollars.

Coffin thumbed through the phone book, picked up the phone again and dialed.

"Serena Hench Investments," a female voice said.

"This is Detective Coffin, Provincetown Police Department," Coffin said. "I need to speak to Ms. Hench."

"I'm sorry, she's in a conference right now. May I take a message?"

"No. It's very important. Perhaps I'll come by and see her in person. Do you think she'd mind if I brought a few officers along, with lots of sirens and flashing lights?"

"Please hold for one second, Detective. Ms. Hench is just coming out of the conference room."

Hold music played briefly, muted guitar and flute, noodling through "Greensleeves."

"Detective?" A different woman's voice. "This is Serena. How do you feel about drinking on duty?"

"Ms. Hench—"

"Meet me at Pepito's for cocktails. Four thirty. I'll be on the upper deck. Don't be late." She hung up.

Coffin left his office, trotted upstairs, and poked his head into the property tax assessor's office.

"Hey, Marv," he said.

Marvin Jones was a tall, heavy black man who shaved his head and favored sweater vests, even in the summertime. "Frank," Jones said without looking up from his computer.

"Sorry to bother you, Marv, but can you tell me who owns the Moors?"

"It's Marvin, and you can find that information on our Web site. Just download the Excel spreadsheet."

Coffin pursed his lips. "What's an Excel spreadsheet?"

Jones sighed and looked up at Coffin. His eyes were sapphire blue. "Would you like me to look it up *for* you?"

"That would be great. Thanks."

"Address?"

"I don't know. It's the big new condo farm out on the far west end. The Moors."

Jones sighed again. "That's so *extremely* helpful," he said, tapping away on his computer keyboard. "All right—I found it in spite of you. That's how good I am."

"You're the best. I've always said so."

"You are *such* a charmer. Not. It's an et al."

"A what?"

"An et al. Means it's owned by more than one person. Only one name's listed."

"And that name is . . . ?"

"Serena Hench. How'd you like to walk around with *that* for a handle?"

"Let's not go there."

"Sorry."

"No you're not." Coffin turned to leave.

"What," said Marvin, "no thank you?"

By late afternoon it was hot and surprisingly humid; the sky was pale, the western horizon blurred by a blank white haze. Always, on days like these, a storm was in the making—rolling up the eastern seaboard, pushing the mainland smog and funk ahead of it like a railyard switcher muscling a boxcar. By nightfall, the rain would have come and gone.

Coffin walked slowly down the Town Hall steps, a chilly drip of sweat oozing from his left armpit. Unfazed by the heat, the verdigrised soldier on top of the World War I monument brandished his rifle and gazed out to sea. Tourists jammed the street and filled the stone benches in front of Town Hall. A man in a clown suit did tricks with balloons while a woman played a blue guitar. Coffin counted a half-dozen TV news remote vans, throbbing in their illegal parking spaces along Commercial Street.

In the parking lot, little heat waves shimmered off the Dodge's peeling vinyl roof. The starter made a loud grinding sound when he turned the key; the engine cranked and sputtered, then roared to life, a greasy cloud of blue-black smoke billowing from the exhaust.

Coffin's head ached. The car's interior was sweltering; he turned on the air conditioning, but only a rancid blast of hot air came out.

It took a long time for a break to appear in the stream of traffic going both ways on Bradford Street; when it finally did, the Dodge stalled as he began to back out. He turned the key and pumped the gas—the Dodge sputtered and died. The cloying smell of gas hung in the car's interior. He turned the key again, and a single dry click emanated from somewhere among the dark tangle of belts and hoses under the hood, but nothing else happened. *Click . . . Click . . .* It was lucky, Coffin thought, that in eight years on the PPD he had never felt the need to carry a gun; otherwise he might have done something stupid. *Like what? Get out and shoot the car? Why stop there?*

"Fuck it," he said and climbed out. He stalked off, not bothering to shut the door. He hadn't had a day off in two weeks. *Here we go*, he thought. *The cracks are starting to show.*

Coffin walked up Commercial Street from Town Hall. He passed the town library, with its cupola and gingerbread trim, and turned right when he reached Spank Yo Mama, a head shop that was famous in equal measures for the florid nude murals that adorned its exterior, the twin nine-foot albino pythons sleeping companionably inside its glass-fronted counter, and the quantity and variety of dildos for sale in its back room, the largest of which hung from the low ceiling like a forest of lewd stalactites.

He turned down a narrow alley on the harbor side of Commercial Street. Pepito's was a "casual expensive" restaurant of a type peculiar to seaside resorts: The customers wore shorts and sandals; the cheapest dinner entrée cost twenty-three dollars. Appetizers were less expensive, but not much. Coffin checked his wallet, in case Serena decided to change her mind about picking up the tab. Pepito's only accepted cash.

The upper deck was crowded—early cocktail drinkers lined the bar and packed the café tables, shielded from the late afternoon sun by big blue and red umbrellas emblazoned with the Cinzano logo.

A thin blond woman was sitting alone at a table overlooking the harbor. She wore a black tailored suit and Gucci sunglasses. When she saw Coffin, she waved.

"It's very interesting to meet you, Detective," she said, offering Coffin a thin pale hand. Her handshake was limp and dry as tissue paper. "I've never met one before. A detective, I mean."

"No one from the state police has spoken to you?" Coffin said, wedging himself into a metal café chair.

"Whatever for?" Serena said. "Have I done something wrong?" A waiter arrived. He was a very handsome young man with olive skin and shoulder length black hair.

"Care for a drink?" Serena said. "I know it's early, but I'm just dying for a martini."

Coffin ordered a beer for seven dollars and an appetizer plate of fried calamari for nine.

"Grey Goose martini," Serena said. "Very dry, up with a twist. And the tuna sashimi appetizer."

The waiter smiled with very white teeth. "Excellent," he said. "Be right back with your drinks."

Two tables away, a middle-aged lesbian couple were trying to shush a screaming baby. The baby was fat and waxy. It looked like Don Rickles.

Serena slitted her eyes and said, "Send it back. It isn't done."

"No one's suggesting you committed a crime, if that's what you mean," Coffin said when the waiter was gone, "but I'm a little surprised that the Cape and Islands DA's office hasn't contacted you."

"Because I was out with poor Mr. Merkin the night he died—is that it? You found out about that."

"Yes."

"But the state police don't know yet." Serena smiled broadly. "You see? You're very clever after all, Detective."

"What were you and Mr. Merkin discussing that night?" Coffin said. "If you don't mind my asking."

Serena was looking over the railing at someone on the beach. "Good God," she said, pointing. "Look at that horrible fat man wearing that tiny Speedo. How appalling."

Coffin squinted. "I think that's Norman Mailer," he said. "He has a house just down the beach from here."

"Well, whoever he is, he shouldn't be allowed to go around like that," Serena said. "It's the kind of thing that's ruining this town for normal people."

The waiter brought their drinks, smiled brilliantly, and went away again.

"About Mr. Merkin," Coffin began.

"I *do* mind," Serena said, looking at him over the rim of her glass, a faint half-smile on her lips.

"Excuse me?" Coffin said.

"I mind if you ask questions about my private conversations, Detective."

"Why's that, Ms. Hench?"

"Because they're private, that's why. And because I did a bit of checking, and you've got no authority to ask me anything. You're supposed to refer all witnesses to Mr. Mancini. Isn't that right?"

Coffin poured his seven-dollar beer into a Pilsener glass. It was a little flat. "That's technically correct, yes," he said. "Would you rather talk to the State Police detectives? Is that what you're saying?"

"If I do, I'll be sure to mention our little lunch date," Serena said. "But you wouldn't tell them anyway. You'll let them figure it out for themselves. Am I wrong?"

Coffin sipped his beer. "We'll see," he said.

"I didn't kill him, I can tell you that, and I have no idea who did."

"When did you last see him?"

"Around midnight. He said he was going for a walk, then heading back to his condo."

The smiling waiter arrived with their food. The calamari was lightly breaded and fried with a dash of red pepper, the way Coffin liked it. "One more question," Coffin said, slowly chewing a rubbery band of squid. "Once the Moors is built, what's next for REIC, exactly?"

Serena's smile tightened, then disappeared. "That's out of bounds, Detective," she said. The smile returned. "Now be a good boy and let Serena taste one of those lovely calamari."

Coffin walked back to Town Hall and climbed into the Dodge. It started on the third try. He drove to Sal's Auto Repair, just off Shank Painter, across from the A&P.

Sal was standing under one of the garage's two lifts, draining the oil from an aging Volkswagen. A big-bellied man in his sixties, Sal wore Elvis-style sideburns and a tall gray pompadour. The garage smelled like grease and carbon and recapped tires.

"Sure, I'll take a look at it," Sal said, wiping his hands on a greasy rag. "But why don't you junk that piece of shit, Frankie? Buy yourself something nice. I got a real clean Subaru wagon at home, all-wheel drive. Make you a good deal on it."

"Can't afford it, Sal." Coffin held his hands out, palms up. "I'm broke."

"What's the matter? I figured you'd be getting rich on overtime."

"No such luck."

Sal lowered his voice. "I got a theory about these two killings—Jason Duarte and the Merkin guy. Want to hear it?"

"Sure," Coffin said.

"I figure it's a conspiracy. Who gains, that's my question."

"So?"

"The merchants. The guest house owners, the restaurant people, the whale-watch industry. The chamber of freaking commerce. I mean, look around. I've never seen this town so busy. People are coming from all over to see the place where Reverend Ron was found dead in a dress."

"So you're saying the chamber of commerce killed two people to stimulate tourism?"

"Bingo. I called the state police and told them to check it out, but they treated me like I was nuts."

"Assholes," Coffin said, shaking his head.

Sal climbed into the wrecker, cranked its big diesel engine, and then reached for something under the seat. "I figure they're in on it, too, somehow," he shouted, over the diesel's clatter and growl. He held up a long-barreled revolver with a bore the size of a dime. "With all that's going on, I don't trust nobody but my wife, my dog, and Mr. Smith and Wesson here," he shouted, dropping the truck into gear. "And I'm not so sure about my damn wife!"

The Oyster Shack was slower even than usual. The jukebox was quiet. Two discouraged fishermen sat at the end of the bar, long noses in their glasses of beer.

"He ain't here," Billy said when Coffin pushed the screen door open.

"He who?" Coffin said.

"Whoever you're looking for." Billy waved at the two fishermen. "Unless it's one of these dumb-asses."

"Hey!" said the fisherman on the left. He was tall and lean, bald on top with long hair hanging down his back—a skullet. "We don't come here for that kind of abuse, y'know."

"Sure we do," the other fisherman said.

Captain Nickerson climbed the slender bars of his cage: claw, claw, beak. "Show us your tits!" he said.

"What makes you think I'm looking for somebody?" Coffin said.

Billy grinned. "Investigating two murders, you *better* be looking for somebody."

Outside, the sky had turned green. The wind picked up, scattering bits of trash around Billy's parking lot.

"Right now I'm just looking for a drink," Coffin said.

"How about a little shot of the monster?" Billy said. He opened a small cabinet behind the bar and took out a dusty cloth bag, from which he extracted a brown bottle. A sea serpent swam across its peeling and faded label.

Billy winked apishly at Coffin, took two rocks glasses down from the overhead rack, uncorked the bottle, and poured a small shot each for Coffin and himself.

"To the seafaring Coffins," Coffin said, toasting.

"Roger that," Billy said. They clinked glasses and sipped the whiskey. It tasted old and warm and enormously rich, like something that should have been illegal.

"Hey, I'll have a shot of that," said the tall fisherman, waving a ten-dollar bill.

"When monkeys fly out of your ass," Billy said. "Put your damn money away."

"Jesus Christ," the fisherman said. "Excuuuuse *me*."

"Why do you call it the monster?" the other fisherman asked.

Billy grinned. "This here," he said, holding the bottle up to the light, "is one of three remaining bottles of Old Loch Ness, a single malt scotch made by the Loch Ness distillery in 1928—right before it burned to the ground." Billy pointed a thick finger at Coffin. "His granddad was a rumrunner during Prohibition days. This bottle is from his famous last run."

"Why famous?" said the tall fisherman.

"Famous on account of his boat was rammed and sunk by the Coast Guard just twenty yards off of Herring Cove beach, and the old man drowned in eight feet of high tide, 'cause he couldn't swim. A few cases survived, and this bottle, like I said, is almost the last of it."

"A fascinating tale," said the tall fisherman. "Let's shake this peanut stand."

"Okay, okay," his friend said, downing his beer.

"Eat me!" said Captain Nickerson. "Eat me!"

Coffin sipped the monster, closed his eyes, swallowed. The whiskey burned pleasantly on the way down. He opened his eyes and leaned his elbows on the bar. The sky had grown dark. Lightning jittered in the western sky.

"I've got a new theory about this whole murder deal," Billy said.

"Great," Coffin said. "Another theory." He lit a cigarette. It tasted good with the scotch.

"I figure Merkin and Duarte were lovers. The wife found out and had them both whacked. What do you think?"

Coffin reached for the monster, uncorked it, and poured himself another shot. "I think it makes as much sense as anything else that comes out of your mouth on a given day." He pointed out the window. "Here it comes," he said.

The rain had finally started. A few fat drops pelted the parking lot; then the downpour began in earnest.

Billy shrugged. "Okay, fine. Don't take me seriously. But I'll tell you, people are starting to get spooked. They're locking their doors, loading their guns, and looking under the beds at night."

"I don't blame them," Coffin said. "I'm pretty spooked myself."

"Comforting words from your local police department," Billy said.

"Thar she blows!" shrieked Captain Nickerson.

"Shut the fuck up," Billy said.

"Shut the fuck up," said Captain Nickerson, fluffing his neck feathers.

Coffin frowned. "Most of the time, murders are obvious. You show up at the scene and there's a woman lying dead with a bunch of stab wounds, the knife still stuck in her chest. The boyfriend's there, covered with blood. You ask him if he killed her, and he says no, he found her like that. You say, you mean you walked in and she was lying there dead and then she sprayed blood all over you? He says yeah, and you arrest him. Once in a while you get a planned killing, and those are always tougher. A lot of them go unsolved."

Billy's eyebrows went up. "So you're saying this guy might get away with it?"

"Maybe," Coffin said, drumming his fingers on the bar. "With Mancini running the investigation, I'd say his chances are pretty good."

Billy squinted. "You ever get pissed off enough that you wanted to kill somebody?" he asked.

"Sure. Rolled up at a crime scene in Baltimore once, and a guy shot at us through the window. He was a terrible shot—all wiggy on crystal meth—but I was enraged."

"So?"

"We had four uniforms there. We decided not to wait for the SWAT guys. We used garbage can lids as shields and stormed the place. Turned out the guy was out of ammo by then anyway."

"What happened to him?"

"He slipped and fell down a couple of flights of stairs. Broke his pelvis. Cops hate being shot at."

They said nothing for a while. Billy wiped the bar in slow, greasy circles.

"How about you?" Coffin said. "Ever get mad enough to kill somebody?"

"Me? *I've* got nothing to get mad about, Frank." Billy grinned, tossed the sopping bar towel into a bucket on the floor, then spread his arms wide. "Look around—I'm building an empire."

The rain had stopped, and the clouds were slowly opening like enormous curtains. A ragged fog oozed off the bay, slowly wrapping the town in its gray tendrils. Coffin decided to walk home from Billy's the back way, through the cemetery on its nameless gravel road. The night was warm, the moon off-kilter and egg shaped, three-quarters full. Little puffs of fog swirled around the gravestones. They looked like rows of bad nineteenth-century teeth, mossed and tilting. The narrow road curved between ornate mausoleums and monuments to sea captains, including his great-grandfather's—a tall column topped by a carved marble globe. To Coffin's right, down a rutted lane, squatted the granite crypt of three young girls, all dead of diphtheria in the 1860s. Their names were carved into the lintel: Temperance, Chastity, and Silence Bledsoe. They were the ghosts of Provincetown past.

The cemetery was deserted, quiet; the small echoes of Coffin's footsteps between the gravestones, like something scurrying among the markers, made his heart beat faster and the hair on the back of his neck prickle. He almost jumped out of his skin when a pair of dark, brush-tailed shapes emerged from a copse of trees a few yards away and regarded him for several moments, eyes gleaming orange in the fog-dimmed moonlight.

"Hey!" he shouted, clapping his hands. The two coyotes trotted away, glancing at him over their furred shoulders before they disappeared into the mist.

Coffin kept walking. Twin shafts of yellow light swept up slowly from his left; a car had turned into the cemetery from Shank

Painter Road, its headlights throwing Coffin's long-legged shadow on the grass in front of him—ambling along, gangly and monstrous.

He could hear the low throb of the engine and the sound of the gravel under tires, like popcorn popping. The headlights seemed very bright; he turned to look and had to visor his eyes with his hand. It was a pickup truck, a big one. He could just make out the gold Chevy logo on the grille.

"Rudy?" Coffin said.

The truck stopped and the lights went out. A big hand beckoned from the window. "Got a second, Frankie?"

"I don't remember you being so theatrical, back in the old days," Coffin said.

"These are theatrical times," Rudy said. "Shakespearean, almost." The ropy tang of marijuana smoke drifted from the rolled-down window.

"I thought you'd left town," Coffin said.

"I had a business matter to attend to," Rudy said, shoving the lit joint at Coffin. "I'm heading out tomorrow. Gene-spliced, Key West mastuba nativa. Want a hit?"

Coffin waved the joint away.

Rudy shrugged. "Your loss," he said. He took a deep hit and held the smoke in his lungs before blowing it out in a thick blue stream. Then he licked the tips of his thumb and index finger, snuffed the joint, and put the scorched roach in his shirt pocket. "Listen," he said, "I've got to tell you. I think you're losing it."

"How's that?" Coffin said.

"You're chasing your tail on this thing with the Moors," Rudy said. "It's killing me. I can't stand to watch it anymore."

"So don't watch," Coffin said. "It's not your problem, right?"

"Look—what do Merkin and the Duarte kid have in common,

besides the Moors complex?" Rudy took the roach from his pocket, waved it under Coffin's nose. "It's obvious."

"Drugs? That doesn't make sense. There's no evidence that Merkin was a habitual drug user."

"Don't be a dope, Frankie," Rudy said. "He was taking a trip down the K-hole, wasn't he? I mean, the guy liked to dress himself up like the school librarian—who knows what else he was up to?"

Coffin rubbed his chin. "Even if he was, I still don't see the connection. Heroin and club drugs, those are whole different worlds."

"Maybe, maybe not. Things change fast in the recreational pharma biz, Frankie. You know that as well as anyone. There's a business cycle—diversification, then consolidation. We're in a con-solidation phase right now."

"We?"

"The town, I mean. So I hear."

A long, quavering wail started up from the Catholic section of the graveyard, first one coyote, then two and three. Before long, all the dogs in the neighborhood had joined in.

"We used to shoot those son-of-a-bitching coyotes when we saw them," Rudy said. "Now they're a damn protected species. Wait till they drag somebody's kid off their front porch—we'll see how protected they are *then*."

"I guess the drug angle's a possibility," Coffin said, lighting a cigarette. "In the Duarte killing, anyway. His old man said he owed a lot of money."

"There you go," Rudy said. "There's a good chance he was deal-ing. If his accounts payable situation got out of hand, he might have run into trouble with his suppliers. There are some rough Cape Verdean boys operating out of New Bedford, you know. And I hear some of the local Jamaicans are trying to move in."

"Dogfish would know about Duarte," Coffin said.

"Dogfish *would* know, you're right," Rudy said, relighting the joint with the truck's dashboard lighter, the red glow filling the cab for a second or two. "If I was you, I'd saddle up the lesbo-cop and go roust his ass. Catch him first thing in the morning, when he's asleep."

Coffin shivered a little. Dogfish lived on a houseboat that was almost always anchored in the harbor. He was a twenty-year junkie and small-time dealer who knew everything there was to know about Provincetown's heroin trade. The police let him operate in exchange for information, though that was likely to change under Boyle's clean-sweep regime.

"One other thing," Rudy said. "About your ma. I've made some arrangements."

"What kind of arrangements?" Coffin said.

"She's not as loopy as you think, you know," Rudy said. "There are times she's sharp as a tack."

"The doctors say she comes and goes. When you say 'arrangements,' what do you mean, exactly?"

Rudy spat out the window, narrowly missing Coffin's shoe. "Pah!" he said. "Doctors. What the fuck do they know? If you lived your life according to doctors, you'd do nothing but exercise and eat broccoli. I'd rather be dead."

"Rudy—"

"Okay, okay. It's a small investment. I can't give you the details yet, but if it works out, it should be enough to keep her in style the rest of her life."

"Is it illegal?" Coffin said.

Rudy started the truck. "God, she was gorgeous, back in the old days," he said. "I had kind of a thing for her, I don't mind telling you. A real spitfire, gave your old man all the hell he deserved, and then some—but Christ, the awe-inspiring *rack* on that woman." He grinned and dropped the truck into gear. "Don't let your meat loaf, Frankie," he said, reaching a big paw out the window and waving the thumb-pinky "hang loose" sign at Coffin. The truck pulled away.

"Rudy!" Coffin said, walking after it, watching it accelerate rapidly down the gravel road. "Hey—what *kind* of investment?"

Chapter 16

PPD 2 was a twenty-seven-foot Boston Whaler, powered by two big Mercury outboards. It was Provincetown's only police boat—PPD 1 had been swamped and damaged beyond repair in Hurricane Charley, back in 1986.

Coffin felt nauseous and dizzy, even though the harbor was almost dead flat and he was standing on the Coast Guard wharf, where PPD 2 was secured by a stout line. The Mercuries rumbled to life. There was a sickening whiff of gasoline in the air.

Teddy Goulet, the harbor cop, stood in PPD 2's pilot house and pointed at his watch. "You coming, Frank?"

Coffin swallowed hard. "Sure," he said. "No problem."

"Just undo the bow line there and hop aboard," Goulet said. "Chop chop—haven't got all day."

Coffin unlooped the line from the big brass cleat and tossed it onto PPD 2's deck, then scrambled awkwardly aboard. He felt light-headed, out of breath. His forehead was sheened with cold sweat.

"You all right, Frank?" Lola said.

"I'm not that crazy about boats," Coffin said. PPD 2 eased away from the wharf, and he grabbed the rail hard. His mouth tasted sour.

"Really?" Lola said. "I love boats. My folks had a lake house when I was a kid, up in northern Wisconsin. We had a little Sunfish, and we'd go sailing every day. I got pretty good—my dad used to call me Captain Ahab, because I was kind of obsessed."

"That's great," Coffin said. "Ha ha."

"Let's blow the carbon out, what do you say?" Goulet shouted, one hand on the wheel, the other holding a travel mug full of coffee.

"Go for it!" Lola shouted back.

"Do we have to?" Coffin said.

Goulet pushed the throttles up, and the big outboards roared happily.

Coffin almost fell over as the bow lifted and PPD 2 surged forward, cutting a foaming wake across the harbor.

Dogfish lived on a ramshackle pontoon boat, anchored just inside the breakwater. He'd built it himself, out of scrap lumber and fifty-gallon drums. He appeared to be in the process of painting it Di-Gel green but had evidently run out of paint halfway through; the old paint was chipped and peeling, and had faded to nondescript gray.

Coffin stood on the pontoon boat's deck as it rocked sickeningly in PPD 2's wake. He took a deep breath and knocked on the door, which had been discarded or stolen from a home renovation project. Its veneer was warped and peeling.

"Dogfish?" he called. He knocked again, then tried the door. It was unlocked. He motioned to Lola, who took the big flashlight from her equipment belt. Coffin pushed the door open, and Lola aimed the flashlight beam into the cabin.

"Holy crap," Lola said. The cabin was small and dim, lit only by daylight filtering in through two dusty, curtained windows. She swept the flashlight beam slowly around the cabin's interior. Every inch of wall and ceiling space was occupied by some bit of flotsam found on the beach: broken lobster pots, gull feathers, brightly painted wooden buoys, skulls of seals and fish and birds, hairless plastic baby dolls in various sizes and degrees of dismemberment, hundreds of luminous shards of beach glass, the washed-out flags of several nations, pennants of inscrutable nautical significance, chunks of driftwood shaped like animals or human body parts, and an almost infinite variety of faded plastic toys, including an Etch A Sketch, two model airplanes, and a large purple dildo. A table and two chairs—painted highway-cone orange—stood bolted to the floor. A small potbellied stove crouched in the corner. A twin bed, shoved up against the far wall, appeared to be occupied by a pile of dirty laundry. The pile sat up and rubbed its eyes.

"Jesus," it said. "What fucking time is it?"

Coffin looked at his watch. "Quarter to seven," he said. "We wanted to make sure we caught you at home. Rough night?"

"The usual." Dogfish pushed the covers aside. He was naked—skinny and hairy, with dark, bruised-looking veins in his arms and legs. His right hand was wrapped in an ace bandage. The outline of a shark was tattooed on his left forearm, with the word DOGFISH stenciled below it in wavery blue script. "Excuse me," he said, pulling on a pair of shorts, "while I go outside and take a piss."

"Would you look at this place," Lola said, peering at the forest of junk bristling from the walls. "It's incredible."

"He goes out every day just after high tide and combs the beach," Coffin said. "If you wonder why you never find any good stuff when you're out on a walk, it's because Dogfish already got it and tacked it up on his wall."

Dogfish stuck his head in the door. "Admiring my collection, I see," he said.

"It's very impressive," Lola said. "Do you always just pee off the deck?"

"The world is my toilet," said Dogfish.

"What happened to your hand?" Coffin said.

Dogfish looked down. "I slammed it in a door," he said. "While I was stoned."

"How's business?"

"Oh, you know. Slow. The gay guys are all into crystal meth now. It's crap, but it's cheap and it'll keep you going all night—in more ways than one. Nobody cares about a quality high anymore." Dogfish busied himself starting a small fire in the potbellied stove. "I'm gonna make some coffee if you want some," he said. "Just take a few minutes."

"Not for me," Lola said, eyeing Dogfish's rusty coffeepot.

"No, thanks," Coffin said. "What about Jason Duarte? He a customer of yours?"

"Off and on," Dogfish said, striking a kitchen match and lighting the newspaper he'd wadded carefully into the stove. "Usually when he was broke, 'cause he knew I'd sell to him on credit. I had a good supply of A-grade Burmese that wasn't super expensive—good clean stuff." Dogfish looked at his bandaged hand, then looked down at the plywood deck. "But then he got flush all of a sudden and started buying this Afghani flake from some Cape Verdeans out of Fall River. He gave me a hit once. That shit was dangerous."

"Dangerous how?"

Dogfish looked up, met Coffin's eyes. "Very, very pure and extremely potent. You know, the Afghani poppy was almost wiped out under the Taliban. Now the market's flooded with incredibly cheap, incredibly high-grade stuff, thanks to the CIA and the Afghan warlords. George W. Bush, making the world a safer place. To shoot up in."

"Did Jason ever deal?"

Dogfish looked at his hand, looked down. "Some. I don't know. Sure. He'd sell a little bit to friends or something, just to help cover his costs."

"Enough to rile the Cape Verdeans? Or the Jamaicans?"

Dogfish frowned, tilting his head. "Jamaicans? What Jamaicans? There are no Jamaicans moving heroin out here."

"The Cape Verdeans, then."

"Maybe," Dogfish said. "They're some crazy motherfuckers."

"They have any trouble with you?"

"Me? Nah. I'm small beans. Hardly a blip on the radar. The Cape Verdeans are mostly trying to expand along the I-95 corridor. They wouldn't give a fuck about P'town, unless something big was going down."

"But you said Jason was only selling to a few friends."

"Yeah, well," Dogfish said, blowing into the woodstove, then shutting the little door. "That was the old Jason. He changed a lot in the last six months or so. Suddenly he had *money,* man. Wads of it."

"Must be hard, shooting up with just one hand," Coffin said.

"It ain't easy," Dogfish said, looking at the bulky, pink bandage. "If you were an amputee or something, I don't know how you'd do it."

"What kind of door did you say it got slammed in?" Coffin said. "Pickup truck, by any chance?"

"No, man," Dogfish said, putting the coffeepot down with a sharp little *clang*. "That's just wrong." He held up his bandaged hand. "Rudy had nothing to do with this."

Coffin and Lola both stared at him.

"Oh, fuck me," Dogfish said.

"So," Lola said, when they were back on the Coast Guard wharf. "Why would your Uncle Rudy slam Dogfish's hand in a door?"

Coffin's stomach was still churning. "Rudy wants me to think Duarte was killed by Cape Verdeans," he said.

"Why?" Lola said.

Coffin bent over, elbows on knees. "I'm not sure," he said. "To keep me busy for a little while. It's a diversion."

"You all right, Frank?"

Coffin took a deep breath, straightened up. "Well, I'm not going to barf. God, I hate boats."

"Diversion from what?"

Coffin thought for a minute. "I don't know. From whatever we're getting too close to."

Lola laughed. "You're kidding," she said. "Right?"

Chapter 17

She'll run, for now," Sal said, slamming the Dodge's hood, "but I can't make any guarantees as to how long."

"What's the damage?"

"Well, I gave her a tune-up. She needed that real bad, Frank. I replaced the fuel pump, which was just barely working—that's why she was stalling out going uphill. I changed the oil and filters, which was all real nasty. But I gotta tell you, we're just rearranging the deck chairs here."

"Bad?"

"Terrible. Your brakes are shot, your tires are bald, your shocks are a joke, she burns oil like crazy, and your head gasket leaks."

"Anything else?"

"The valves are bent, the rings are worn, your wheel bearings are about to seize, the front end's dangerously out of whack, the frame is bent, and your radiator's full of gunk. And you got a nest of field mice in your trunk. You're basically a danger to yourself and others every time you start this thing."

"So what do I owe you?"

"Well, the fuel pump's a rebuilt—I'll give you the plugs, wires, oil, and filters at cost. No charge for labor. Let's say a hundred and fifty bucks."

"You sure?"

"Sure I'm sure. This way, I call the cops, I figure you'll at least show up."

"What, are you worried?"

"Wouldn't you be?" Sal said, picking his teeth with a blunt thumbnail. "Knowing what I know?"

Jamie's advanced class hadn't gone well. She'd felt flustered and out of sorts; she hoped her students hadn't noticed. Every time she looked at Duffy Plotz, her skin crawled. She couldn't help thinking of the three gleaming razor blades in their white envelope.

The students filed out in chattering twos and threes until only Plotz was left, standing in the doorway. Jamie groaned inwardly. *Now what?* she thought.

Plotz smiled with closed lips, then stuck out his tongue. It was long and purple, almost like a dog's. A double-edged razor blade lay on its meaty flat, glistening wetly. Plotz reeled in his tongue and the blade disappeared. He smiled again, turned, and walked out.

The dump was closed, the sandy parking lot deserted. Coffin knocked on the door of Plotz's trailer, but he knew there was no one inside. The day had turned hazy and a little humid; there was hardly any wind in the scrub pines. Several gulls argued over some delicacy that lay in the dirt outside the corrugated shed.

"Let's try his apartment," Coffin said, lowering himself into Lola's Camaro.

"He might have left town," Lola said, pulling onto Route 6 and accelerating.

"That would be the smart thing to do," Coffin said. "So I'm guessing he's still around."

Lola passed a slow-moving Winnebago. "Poor Jamie. What a creepy thing."

"She's okay. Tougher than she looks."

"If you say so. I'd be freaked," Lola said. "Maybe she should move in with you for a few days, just to be on the safe side?"

"I suggested that, and she said I was being patronizing, thank you very much. She says she can handle Plotz."

Plotz lived on Duck Lane, on the far east end. The narrow road was paved with crushed oyster shells. They crunched under Coffin's feet as he stepped out of the Camaro. A cat watched him from the window of a tiny cottage. Coffin made a kissing sound, and the cat blinked its orange eyes.

Plotz's building was an old rooming house that had been condo-ized: a narrow, rambling structure shingled in weathered cedar shakes. His apartment was at the top of a ramshackle flight of wooden stairs, which appeared to tilt a few degrees to the left. Coffin knocked on the door, but no one answered.

"Duffy," he said, "open up!"

No lights were on inside; except for the wind, everything was quiet. The sun was going down, and the sky over the harbor was streaked in crimson. The whole town seemed to be glowing—pale magenta, suffused and throbbing.

Coffin clambered back down the stairs and lowered himself into

Lola's car. "Maybe you're right," he said. "Maybe Plotz is smarter than I think. Maybe he did leave town."

Serena Hench's cell phone rang while she was having dinner and cocktails at La Bistro with an *extremely* wealthy client who, thank God, was also extremely gay, which meant she wouldn't have to sleep with him. Ordinarily she liked it when her cell phone rang in public—she'd become quite the mover and shaker in Provincetown's soaring real estate market, and she didn't mind who knew it—but now it was annoying. She had spent the better part of a week wooing this man, a potential investor who now, over his third martini, seemed about to say yes, *yes,* he would like very much to put up three or four million to help begin the construction of her next big condo project. For Serena, the first rule of business was never, *ever* take risks with your own money.

She flipped open the tiny silver cell phone and said, "Serena. Talk."

"Miz Hench?" said a gruff male voice, followed by a surge of static. Cell phone reception in Provincetown was always hit-or-miss; the nearest tower was in Truro, almost ten miles away.

"Yes?" she said. "Who is this?"

"This is Dan Roby, over at the Moors," said the voice.

Serena's heart tightened. The Moors was her biggest project to date, a thirty-unit, high-end condo development that would net her millions, if it ever got built. So far the construction had been plagued by one fiasco after another.

She put her hand over the cell phone's miniature mouthpiece. "Excuse me a moment," she said to the blandly smiling investor sitting across from her. "Serena will be back in two shakes of a little lamb's tail." She stood up and walked a few feet away, to a quiet spot next to a large potted hibiscus.

"All right," she hissed into the phone. "This better be important, Roby."

"We've found some broken pots and stuff, digging the hole for number five. Looks like maybe Wampanoag Indian artifacts. I was hoping you could come by the site and talk about what to do next."

"Broken pots? Who gives a fuck—throw them away."

Roby cleared his throat. "I'm afraid I can't do that, ma'am. The building code's real clear on this stuff. We've got to stop construction and report the artifacts to Town Hall."

"Perfect," Serena said, mentally calculating the size and number of the bribes she'd have to hand out to keep the project moving. "*Just* what I need."

Roby had been Jason Duarte's underling and had stepped in as construction foreman when Duarte died. He was clearly an idiot—even dumber than Duarte had been, if that was possible.

"All right, fine," Serena said. "I'll be there in an hour."

"Yes, ma'am," said the voice. "See you then."

The little phone went silent, and Serena flipped it shut and dropped it into her bag.

"Problems?" said the investor, eyebrows raised.

"Nothing major," Serena said, tossing her lank blond hair. "Nothing Serena can't handle." She raised her nearly empty martini glass. "I'm game for one more—how about you?"

If Serena Hench had been less distracted or less impatient, or had consumed less vodka, she might have thought more about the man who had called her, the man who said he was Dan Roby. It might have occurred to her that Roby sounded older than she remembered him, and that thought might have made her hesitate, for a moment, as she drove to the site in her black Porsche convertible.

But she did not hesitate; she drove to the west end as fast as she could, furiously honking at a ponderous Winnebago when it pulled out in front of her on Bradford Street.

When she arrived at the Moors, she parked her car in the sandy, not yet paved lot and got out. The buildings, all in varying stages of completion, rambled up the hillside overlooking the tidal salt marsh. Mosquito Central, the construction workers called it. There was no sign of Dan Roby—only the rattling throb of the crew's big air compressor and, from inside the skeletal frame of Building 1, the *thwack, thwack, thwack* of a pneumatic nail gun.

Chapter 18

*I*n the kitchen, blood is everywhere, pooled on the counter, streaking the fridge, the walls; it's sprayed on every surface in tiny droplets. A woman lies on the floor in a wide red smear. She's wearing a fleece nightgown with a picture of a bunny rabbit on the front, sitting in a field of pink flowers. Her face is destroyed, caved in so completely that it's impossible to tell which of her features are which. An aluminum softball bat lies next to her on the green linoleum floor.

There's a dinette set, yellow Formica and chrome. A man is slumped in one of the chairs, torso flopped forward onto the table. His head is all but gone—Coffin notices his jaw lying on the floor, near the refrigerator. There's a sawed-off shotgun clenched in his big, rawboned hands. Coffin hears himself whimpering again, but he can't make it stop. He's aware of looking out of himself, keeps noticing the rims of his own eyes.

"Hey," Rashid says. His voice is gentle. He grips Coffin around the bicep. "Hey, Frank."

Coffin swallows. His mouth is very dry. "Jesus, Rashid," he said. "Jesus Christ."

"Fuck!" Coffin said, lurching suddenly awake. He felt the chill of an adrenaline surge and shook himself involuntarily, like a dog after a cold swim.

He turned on the light and drank water from the plastic bottle on the nightstand. His heart galloped. He sat still and waited for it to settle down, head cocked, listening. After a minute or two, he looked at his watch. It was twelve thirty—he'd only been asleep for an hour.

He got out of bed, pulled on a pair of jeans and a T-shirt. He thought about calling Jamie, making sure she was okay. The impulse was silly, he knew—calling would just wake her up, make her anxious. He picked up the phone and dialed her number.

"Mmm?" she said.

"It's me," Coffin said.

"Frank? What time is it? You okay?"

"I'm fine. I just wanted to check in."

"Sweet . . ." she said.

Coffin heard her roll over, bedclothes stirring. Her breathing slowed, and she began to snore a little. He looked at the phone and pressed the OFF button.

He was wide-awake. Going back to bed seemed out of the question. So did sitting around the silent house alone.

"What are *you* looking at?" he said to the stuffed goat. It leveled a yellow stare at him as he tied his running shoes, grabbed a sweatshirt, and pulled the front door shut behind him.

As usual, Billy's was almost empty. An old woman sat at the bar drinking Chivas Regal. Her dentures sat on the bar beside her, a lit cigarette clenched between the uppers and lowers.

Ticky sat two stools down, watching the Red Sox lose to Oakland. "Son of a bitch," he said, face twitching as though his gonads were wired to a twelve-volt battery. "Could one of these multimillionaires hit the damn ball, for Chrissakes?"

Captain Nickerson swung in his cage. "Frankie! Frankie! Frankie!" he said.

"Well," Billy said, "if it ain't the constable, out drinking when he ought to be investigating."

"What makes you think I'm not?" Coffin said.

"Why?" Billy said. "Am I a suspect?"

"Sure. Why not. You're crazy enough."

"Everybody I know is crazy," Billy said. "That doesn't mean anything."

"I didn't say crazy. I said crazy *enough*."

"Everybody I know is crazy *enough*. Hell, we started a pool last week. Two bucks a shot, winner take all. Want in?"

"You're a sick man," Coffin said. "Let's see."

Billy fetched a big piece of posterboard from behind the bar. A Magic-Markered list of twenty names ran down the left side. Coffin saw his own name there, along with Kotowski's, Louie's, and Tony's. A second column listed dates by the week, projecting a year into the future. "You pick a suspect and an arrest date. You can share a suspect, you can share a date, but only one customer to a particular date *and* suspect—get it? Right now most of the money's on Kotowski. You're in third."

"You guys seem pretty convinced it's a local," Coffin said. He took a pen from his pocket and made two new entries at the bottom of the posterboard, NONE OF THE ABOVE and NEVER, then signed his name next to each.

"Aren't you?"

"Anything's possible," Coffin said. He fished a cigarette from the almost empty pack in his shirt pocket and lit it.

"Thought you quit," Billy said.

"Quit is a relative thing, my friend," Coffin said, exhaling a stream of blue smoke.

Billy wiped the bar in front of Coffin with a stained towel, leaving long, greasy smears. He stopped, lifted his ball cap and scratched his head with a ragged fingernail. "I've been thinking the same thing. Just when you think you're done with something—really done with it—back it comes, bigger than ever."

"What something are we talking about?"

Billy swallowed half his whiskey and leaned across the bar. "Remember when I had my prostate surgery? Five years ago?"

"Sure. We took up a collection."

"Yeah. Sixty-eight bucks. Thanks."

"Better than a poke in the eye."

"Depends how you look at it," Billy said. He coughed wetly, spit something into a paper towel, and threw it into the trash. Then he grinned. "When you survive a thing like that—a big old tumor up your asshole—you kind of figure there's got to be a trade-off. It's got to cost something. Cosmic balance."

"Cosmic balance," Coffin said, toasting with his glass of whiskey.

"Exactly. It costs a lot of money, for one thing, and afterward it hurts a lot. You expect that with any surgery."

"But that's not enough."

"Right. I assume you know what happens to people who've had prostate surgery."

"Mr. Floppy," Coffin said.

Billy cackled, then coughed.

"You all right?" Coffin asked.

"Bronchitis," Billy said, thumping his chest with a loose fist. "Secondhand smoke."

Coffin looked at his cigarette, then put it out in one of the green glass bar ashtrays. "Sorry," he said.

"After prostate surgery," Billy went on, fixing Coffin with a yellow goat-stare, "Mr. Floppy comes to stay. So you pretty much give up on the sex thing—especially at my age. After a while you make peace with it, and there's a way it comes as a kind of relief. I mean, desire is a lot of work."

"So say the Zen masters. The end of desire brings peace and enlightenment."

"Exactly. It's like a Zen thing. Sixty-two years old, and for the first time in my life I can think two consecutive thoughts without one of them being about pussy. Amazing. But then along comes Bob Dole and fucks everything up."

"Bob Dole?"

"Yes, Bob fucking Dole. You know—he did those ads. There he is, this old fart with his withered arm talking about prostate surgery and Viagra."

"And?"

"And Kathleen's *interested*."

"Yikes."

"Why don't you *try* it, she says. Next thing I know, I'm standing in line at Adams Pharmacy, me and about five other old geezers, getting a prescription filled."

"So, did it work?"

"Does Bill Clinton like a blow job?"

"So much for enlightenment."

"Exactly. Kathleen's decided we're having a goddamn renaissance in our marriage. The woman won't leave me alone; she's leaving little blue pills around the house like a trail of freaking bread crumbs. But that's not the worst part."

"It gets worse?"

"It's opened up a whole new range of possibility, Frank. For the first time in years, I could have sex with any woman who was dumb enough to say yes. It's staggering."

"Well, how many could there be?"

"So far, none. But that's not the point—I'm *thinking* about it, Frank. Wondering if today might not be the day. I'm on the lookout, for Christ's sake." He shook his head, swabbed at the bar with the greasy rag. "It's really not what I want to be doing with my brain, at this point. It's ridiculous. It pisses me off."

"What *do* you want to be doing with your brain?"

"Pondering the great cosmic mysteries," Billy said, grinning with his big yellow teeth. "What else?"

As Coffin passed through the dark cemetery on his way home, he saw a furred shape moving like a wraith among the tombstones. Coffin stopped walking, and the coyote turned and stared at him. Its amber eyes glowed in the moonlight.

"What're you doing out by yourself?" Coffin said. "Don't you know this town's gotten dangerous?"

The coyote stared a moment longer, tongue lolling. It seemed to Coffin as though it were about to speak. Then it turned and loped off into the deep shadows, vanishing into the darkness.

Coffin walked past his great-grandfather's column and the Bledsoe girls' crypt. He passed the faithful alabaster dog that slept at the foot of Captain Jeremiah Slocum's grave and wondered, as he often did, whether the dog and the captain were buried together. He turned when he heard the sound of an engine and tires rolling slowly on the gravel road. A blue Chevy pickup was following behind him, lights out.

The pickup rolled to a stop, and the driver gunned the engine twice, the muffler growling as though it had a hole in it. The lights flicked on, blinding Coffin momentarily.

"Rudy," Coffin said, impatient. "For Christ's sake. What's wrong with a phone call?"

He started to walk toward the headlights, shading his eyes against the glare. He heard a hard *clank* as the driver dropped the truck into gear. The engine roared again, and this time the back wheels sprayed gravel against a row of tombstones and the truck shot forward, coming straight at Coffin.

At first, he didn't react. He had the odd sensation of being outside his body, watching himself, dazzled by headlight glare as the truck bore down on him. He made his body take two awkward steps to the left, onto the grass—still thinking it must be a joke. The truck veered in response, two wheels halfway down the slight embankment, close enough now that Coffin could hear not just the engine's rising howl but the suck of air through the intake. The pickup was almost on him before he could gather himself and jump clumsily out of the way, landing belly-down in a muddy ditch as the pickup sped by, side mirror missing his head by a couple of inches.

The truck fishtailed in the road as the driver steered all four tires back onto the gravel and accelerated hard, sliding through a curve before disappearing into the fog, the red glow of one taillight diminishing into the distance.

Coffin lay in the ditch for a moment, ticking through a mental checklist of major body parts. He wasn't dead. He hadn't cracked his skull or broken his neck. His arms and legs worked.

He sat up. His wrist hurt. His left pants leg was torn and his knee was bleeding. Wet and smeared with mud, he felt woozy when he stood, so he sat on a gravestone and took deep breaths until his head cleared.

"Holy shit," he said, still out of breath. "Holy fucking shit."

Coffin was out of scotch. There was only one ice cube in the tray. He poured a tall glass of vodka, dropped in the ice cube, and called Town Hall. He got Jeff Skillings on the line.

"Somebody tried to run me down just now," Coffin said. "In the cemetery. Blue Chevy pickup, maybe ten years old. Bad muffler. One taillight out."

"Jesus, Frank—you all right?"

"Fine. Covered with mud and scared shitless, but fine."

"You think it was intentional?" Skillings said. "Not just some drunk?"

"It felt pretty fucking intentional. Just get the word out, okay?"

"Sure, Frank. We'll keep an eye out. You get a license plate, by any chance?"

"Not unless it's embedded in my ass. Do me a favor—get on the phone with the BMV and have them run every blue Chevy pickup registered on the outer Cape, from Orleans to Provincetown. Maybe the gods will smile and something'll jump out at us."

"Sure, Frank. Got it."

After he hung up, Coffin went into the bathroom and took a hot shower. He put peroxide on his scraped knee. Then he rummaged through his dresser, looking for his father's gun—a Colt .45 automatic. He finally found it in the hall closet, in a shoe box behind an old set of golf clubs. The clip was empty, but there were five or six bullets, he remembered, rolling around in his desk drawer. He thumbed them into the spring-loaded clip, then slid the clip into the gun butt and slapped it home with his palm. He was too charged with adrenaline to sleep. He refilled his glass and took it and the gun out to the screen porch. He sat on the swing and drank, looking out at the roiling fog. After a while the gun started to make him feel foolish, and he put it back in the closet in its shoe box. The stuffed goat's head stared at him as he crossed the living room. It seemed amused. Coffin gave it the finger and went to bed.

At 3:00 A.M., the parking lot above Race Point beach was deserted except for two vehicles: a blue Chevy pickup truck and a silver Mercedes. It was very dark; the moon had set and thin, high clouds blurred the stars. Beach grass ruffled in the small wind. Below the dunes, surf whomped and slid. The truck stood empty, the driver's side door open. Two men sat in the Mercedes. Provincetown was a pale glow above the southern horizon.

"This is extortion, is what it is," Louie said. "My own cousin. I can't believe you're fucking me like this."

Rudy peered into the fat manila envelope Louie had just given him. "Fucking you? I'm doing you a favor by keeping your little secrets. You should be down on your knees kissing my ass instead of complaining."

"Frankie's not buying the drug angle," Louie said.

"I told you. He ain't Tony, for Christ's sake. If I was you, I'd put him on that wacko Kowalski. Keep him busy for a day or two, at least."

"Kotowski's his buddy. Frankie protects him. You heard what that lunatic did to me—I've still got a lump on my cheekbone. Does Frankie throw him in jail? No. You can't even count on your own blood anymore." Louie touched his bruised cheek. "Jesus. I never should have gotten Frankie started on the Merkin thing."

"I could have told you that," Rudy said. "You were crapping your drawers about Mancini turning over the wrong rock—and finding you underneath."

"I thought it was a hookup. Merkin takes some twink out to Herring Cove for a hummer, weirdness ensues, Merkin ends up dead. I thought Frankie'd be able to wrap it up quick and easy and keep Mancini out of my business. How did I know Duarte was going to get himself barbecued?"

Rudy took a joint from his shirt pocket and lit it with a chunky Zippo. For a moment, the smell of marijuana smoke and lighter fluid mingled inside the big Mercedes. "Frankie doesn't do quick and easy. I used to hate watching him work on a case—he'd drive me nuts. Let me guess: He's expensing the department for lunches and drinks all over town and it looks like he's not doing shit, right? But I'm here to tell you—the wheels are turning." Rudy took a hit from the joint, held it, blew it out. "He's a nonlinear thinker—jumps around from A to R to Z and back to F until he gets the whole picture. It works, but it's like watching a bear peeling a grape."

"That's the problem," Louie said. "He's going to nonlinear my Mediterranean ass out of a goddamn fortune and into the penitentiary." Louie waved his hands in exasperation. "Do you have to smoke that in here? This is an eighty-fucking-thousand-dollar car, you know."

"So pull Frankie off the case. You put him on, you can pull him off."

Louie thought for a minute. "Too risky," he said. "Then he'd *know* something was going on."

Rudy shrugged. "At least this way he has to report back to you."

"He's not telling us shit."

"That doesn't surprise me. He never told me shit, either."

Louie groaned, rubbing his temples with his fingertips. "I'm *so* screwed. I'm a target, you know. Whoever this maniac is that's killing people—you can bet your ass I'm on the naughty-and-nice list."

Rudy took another hit from the joint. "Near the top, probably. It sucks being you, ace."

"Maybe I should let Frankie in on the Project," Louie said, pushing the power-recline button on the driver's seat. The moonroof was open; the clouds were slowly breaking up, sliding away to the east. "Some of it, anyway. Cut him in for fifty grand. He's broke—why not?"

Rudy scratched his ear. "You could try. Trust me when I say he's not all that motivated by money. Five to one he pulls the plug on your whole operation."

Louie groaned again and closed his eyes.

"If you ask me, you're thinking about this all wrong," Rudy said. "You're waiting around for the duly appointed constabulary to protect you, but you can't tell them you're a target—and if they really do their jobs, you go to jail. For a smart guy, that's pretty fucking stupid."

Louie sat up, looked at his cousin. "You think you can make this murdering nutbar go away?"

"It'll cost you," Rudy said.

"Two fifty," Louie said. "That'll buy you a hell of a lot of weed."

Rudy shook his big head. "Two fifty? What am I, some hired stooge? I want points," he said. "Twenty percent of the gross."

Louie's smile disappeared. "You would, you prick. Twenty percent's outrageous. I can tell you right now, the other partners will never go for it."

Rudy snubbed out the joint on the Mercedes's gleaming dashboard and put the roach in his shirt pocket.

"Son of a bitch!" Louie said, pointing at the scorch mark on the dash. "That's burl walnut you just defaced!"

"I guess you'll just have to hope Mancini gets lucky. Him and his two goons. Dumb, dumber, and dumbest." He pulled the big pistol from his jacket pocket. "In the meantime, here. Try not to blow your own dick off."

"Jesus," Louie said, hefting the gun in his soft hands. "What am I supposed to do with this?"

"If somebody's hiding under your bed, shoot the motherfucker," Rudy said. He tapped the barrel. "The bullets come out of this end."

Louie put the gun in his briefcase. "What about you? If you're going to be a partner, shouldn't you be scared, too?"

Rudy grinned, climbed out of the car, stretched, and stood looking out at the dark Atlantic. "I'm like the shadows of the fucking night," he said. "Nutbar'd better be scared of *me*."

Chapter 19

ere's what I can't figure out," shouted Tony over the whoop of the cruiser's siren. "Why would anybody still eat margarine? I mean, they did that study a few years ago that shows how margarine's just as bad for you as butter—worse, maybe—but people still buy it. What the fuck is up with that? I mean, what *is* margarine, anyway? It's just like this yellow *grease,* right?"

Coffin blew cigarette smoke out the window; he was smoking one of Tony's Marlboros. His car had refused to start, so Tony was driving him to the Moors construction site, where a woman's body had been found by the framing crew when they arrived for work. "Tony," he said, "not now, okay?"

"Hey, sure. Whatever."

Tony roared into the compacted sand parking lot, just ahead of the Rescue Squad. Something hung from the skeletal frame of the first, most complete building.

"Holy shit," Tony said.

It was a woman, dressed in black. She hung, arms outstretched, beside the building's main doorway.

Lola and Skillings were already there, wrapping the whole construction site in yellow crime scene tape.

Coffin got out of the squad car. "Jesus," he said. His jaw felt tight, as if his teeth had been wired shut. "She's been crucified."

Blood had streamed down her arms, spurted from her feet, run down the side of her face. It was pooled beneath her and had started to dry. There were a great many flies. Something, Coffin realized, had been stuffed into her mouth.

"Who is she?" Tony said, thumbs hooked into his belt.

"Serena Hench," Lola said. "We found her ID in the car." The black Porsche sat like a gleaming insect in the parking lot.

"Jesus Christ," Coffin said. "I just had drinks with her."

"How do we get her down from there?" Tony said. "With a crowbar?"

The construction crew had all gathered around the two police cruisers in a loose semicircle. One of them spoke up. "I'd break out the Sawzall," he said. "Cut right through them studs." The rest of the crew nodded.

"You guys got a ladder?" Coffin said.

One of them, a skinny blond Coffin thought he recognized, trotted off to his pickup and brought back a short aluminum ladder. Coffin carried it up the rough-framed steps to the building's front deck. Bloody footprints were everywhere—but they stopped next to the stairs, where a pair of rubber Wellington boots stood discarded. A nail gun lay just inside the door, still attached to its long rubber air hose.

Coffin set up the ladder next to the suspended corpse and climbed to the third rung. His stomach lurched and his vision dimmed, and he thought for a moment that he might vomit or faint, or both. Four big sixteen-penny framing nails had been punched through each of Serena Hench's wrists, into the two-by-four studding of the building. Her knees were bent slightly, and two nails pierced each of her feet. The hair on the side of her head was matted with blood. A nailhead glinted in the sun where it protruded from Serena Hench's left temple. A big piece of crumpled paper was crammed into her wide-stretched mouth. *Blueprint,* Coffin thought.

"Jesus Christ," he said. His vision narrowed, then blurred, and something in the back of his head began to buzz. It was familiar yet terrifying, like a recurring nightmare of drowning or being buried alive. His chest felt tight; he was short of breath. He thought he might be having a heart attack. He climbed down the ladder awkwardly—his legs were rubbery, and both of his hands tingled. He stumbled across the deck and down the stairs.

"Frank?" Lola said. "Are you okay?"

Coffin stared at her for a moment. Her face was weirdly distorted—all eyes and nose. "No," he said. Then the ground hinged slowly up and hit him hard in the face.

"Frank? Frank?"

Somebody was shaking him. Coffin opened his eyes and scowled, hoping it would make whoever it was stop. A small crowd of people had gathered. A big hand swam into view and tried to press an oxygen mask over his mouth and nose. The hand belonged to Ed Voorhees, one of the volunteer EMTs. Coffin pushed it away.

"C'mon, Frank," Voorhees said. "Just a little oxygen. Make ya feel better."

"Get away from me, Ed," Coffin said.

Lola was kneeling, peering down at him. She looked worried. "Frank—you all right?"

Coffin sat up. "Well, I'm not dead. I guess that's a good sign."

"You look like crap, Frankie." It was Tony. He bent down and squeezed Coffin's shoulder. "You should let the rescue boys check you out. Make sure you're not having a stroke or something."

Coffin shook his head. "No, thanks," he said. "I'm okay. Just get out of my face."

A sleek black Lexus pulled into the parking lot. Mancini got out, along with Pilchard, the big detective in the brown suit. Mancini's jeans were beautifully pressed. He wore artfully weathered loafers and a crisp green polo shirt with a little horse embroidered above the left breast.

"Detective Coffin," he said. "You *do* look pale. Everything all right?"

"Never better," Coffin said, struggling to his feet. "But I'm a little worried about Ms. Hench." He nodded in Serena's direction.

"Hench?" Pilchard said, opening his notebook. "How d'ya spell that?"

"Never mind," Mancini said. "We'll take it from here, Detective Coffin. You really don't look well. Maybe you should go lie down."

Lola tugged at Coffin's elbow. "C'mon, Frank. Let's get out of here."

"So what happened out there, Frank?" Lola said, swirling a double shot of scotch in her glass, watching the ice cubes whirl slowly around in the amber fluid.

"It's why I quit being a cop in Baltimore."

They were sitting in Coffin's living room. The stuffed goat's head leered at Coffin. As usual, it seemed about to speak.

"What is it," Lola said, "vertigo or something?"

"Panic attacks. I feel like I'm going to have a coronary or a brain embolism or something, and if it's really bad I pass out. It seems to be triggered by dead people."

"Bummer," Lola said. "And there's nothing you can do to fix it? No drugs?"

"I tried Xanax for a while. The problem with Xanax is, you're so freaking calm you don't give a rat's ass about anything. Your house could collapse with you in it, and you wouldn't care. It's kind of creepy after a while. Stepford Frank."

"That it? Just Xanax?"

"I tried Paxil, too. It made me sleepy, itchy, and impotent."

"That's not good."

Coffin finished his scotch and refilled his glass. "No," he said. "Not good at all. The best solution seems to be to avoid the company of dead people. It was working fine till two weeks ago."

"Rough little life you've been having, all of a sudden."

"The truck thing. Yeah, that kind of sucked."

"You okay?"

"A couple of scrapes. Scared the hell out of me. Otherwise fine."

"Any idea who tried to flatten you?"

"Nope. The BMV's working up a list of blue Chevy pickups for me. Maybe we'll get lucky."

"Tony drives a blue pickup."

"So does Kotowski."

Lola's eyebrows went up. "Kotowski does seem kind of— unstable."

"Absolutely. Crazy as a bedbug. Which is to say, no crazier than anybody else that's lived here for thirty years."

"Know what I'd do if I was you?" Lola said, propping her feet on the coffee table.

Her eyes were a bit glassy, Coffin thought. She was getting drunk. Maybe the stress was getting to her a little, too.

"What's that?" Coffin lit a cigarette and offered one to Lola. She waved it away.

"I'd quit my crappy job and make babies with Jamie."

"You would?"

"Yeah. I mean, I don't know her very well, but she seems smart."

"She is. Extremely."

"And she's very attractive."

"Absolutely."

"And she obviously thinks the world of you, Frank. So I don't understand what the problem is."

"I'm not sure there's a *problem*," Coffin said. "I'm just not a hundred percent ready, and it would be dishonest to go forward if I wasn't."

"Because of your history, you mean? Your divorce and everything?"

"It's not that so much. Just the idea of having kids. It's terrifying. What if they hate you? What if you're a lousy parent? What if something happens to them? Wouldn't that scare *you*?"

"No. Not with the right person."

"I'm too old to have kids now. By the time they're in high school, I'll be sixty. Sixty! That's if Jamie gets pregnant *now*."

"So? Older guys make great dads. They're more patient, not so self-absorbed."

"I'm *hideously* self-absorbed. You wouldn't believe it."

"Know what I think?"

"Here we go."

"I think you're a great big chicken. If you don't do this, you'll kick yourself for the rest of your life."

Coffin took a deep drag on the cigarette and blew the smoke out through his nose. "Can we talk about *your* personal life now?"

Lola laughed. "Four."

Coffin frowned. "Four?"

"The hostess at Al Dante's—Morgan? That's how many other places she was pierced."

"*Four?*" Coffin pondered for a moment. "I'm stuck at three."

"Tongue stud."

Coffin let out a low whistle. "How'd I miss that?"

"Sometimes you've got to do a little old-fashioned, down and dirty detective work."

"So?"

Lola shrugged. "I don't know. We had fun, I guess."

"*Fun?* The girl is twenty-one, gorgeous, multiply pierced—and you *guess* you had fun?"

"Twenty-three," Lola said. "We just didn't have that much in common. She's *fancy*. Her parents live on Park Avenue. She writes experimental poetry."

"Good God. I see what you mean. What you need is a *nice* one. Girl-next-door type."

"I think I scare the nice ones," Lola said. "All they see is Super Butch, the lesbo-cop. So I get the not-so-nice ones. The needy neurotics and the *oh my, are you going to arrest me* ones."

"Sounds a little fishy, if you ask me," Coffin said.

"I'm not sure I *did* ask you," Lola said.

"I'm just saying, maybe it's a two-way street. Maybe part of you likes the not-so-nice ones."

"Past tense, maybe. When they're all twisted up and ironic, it just feels like too much work for what you get back."

"Jamie's ironic. But not twisted up."

"The not wanting to marry you thing is kind of inside out."

"I don't know," Coffin said, dropping his cigarette into the quarter inch of scotch in the bottom of his glass. It sizzled and went out. "I'm neurotic and cranky and I drink too much. I've got hair growing out of my ears, for God's sake. I don't think I'd want to marry me, either."

Chapter 20

Serena Hench's house was a newly built, six-bedroom, octago-
nal trophy model that dominated the bluff overlooking the
breakwater and Long Point. Inside, Coffin found himself thinking
like a real estate ad: *The cathedral-like spaces of the living area afford
panoramic water views.* In fact, the banks of floor-to-ceiling windows afforded an almost 360-degree view of the outer Cape: Long
Point, the harbor, North Truro and Corn Hill—where Edward
Hopper's house still stood above the long sweep of beach curving
off toward Wellfleet—Provincetown's tight grid of cedar-shake
saltboxes, the phallic jut of the Pilgrim Monument. The enormous
living room was done in blond leather sofas, track lighting, and a
self-consciously eclectic mix of antiques and art: a few ebony
African masks, a couple of small Motherwell prints, and several
dune-and-sunset paintings of the sort that would have sent Kotowski off on a twenty-minute rant about money not equaling
taste.

Serena Hench's personal assistant was a blonde in her early
twenties named Devon. She looked exhausted—her hair hung

limp, there were dark half circles below her eyes. Still, she was pretty in the slightly equine way of moneyed New England girls.

"Serena was not an easy person," Devon said. "She was very *aggressive*, in a way that women aren't supposed to be, and I think sometimes people resented her for it. But I couldn't imagine anyone wanting to *kill* her—it's just so crazy."

Her accent was subtle, something she'd worked to get rid of, but still there if you knew what it was—that slight swallowing of the vowel-following *r*: South Shore working class, belying the long-limbed tweed-and-field-hockey appearance of patrician breeding. *New Bedford*, Coffin thought. *Fall River, maybe.*

"Why did Serena go to the Moors last night?"

"I don't know. Sometimes she visited her construction sites, just to make sure things were moving along."

"At night?"

"No."

"Was she here last night?"

"No. She was out with a client."

Coffin took out his notebook. "Got a name?"

"Henderson, I think. Brian Henderson."

"I'd like to see her appointment books, e-mail, phone logs—" Coffin said.

"I'll have to speak with her attorney first."

"Why?"

"Serena was . . . secretive." Devon shook her head. "That's not quite the right word. Protective."

"Protective of what?"

"Her clients. Her partners. Her projects. Her money."

"Who were her partners in the Moors project?"

"I don't know."

"Don't know, or won't tell me?"

Devon smiled for the first time. "Both."

Coffin shifted on the leather couch, which made a soft farting sound as he moved. "Who's in charge of Real Estate Investment Consortium?"

Devon furrowed her blond, professionally shaped brows. "I don't know. Never heard of it."

"Really? Serena had business cards with her name at the top and REIC at the bottom."

"Serena had a lot going on. She didn't tell me everything."

"If you say so."

Devon's face softened. "Really. I don't think she trusted me to keep my mouth shut."

"What about Serena's personal life?" Coffin asked. "Did she have a partner? Boyfriend? Girlfriend?"

Devon frowned. "Not in the way you mean," she said. "Serena was completely . . . unsentimental. For her, all relationships were business relationships. She didn't have time for anything else."

"So she never had sex? Is that what you're saying?"

"No—I mean that when she did have sex, it was usually motivated by business considerations, not romantic attachment."

One way of closing the deal, Coffin thought. "And her relationship with you? What was that like?"

"I worked for her—kept track of her appointments, answered her calls and her e-mail, that kind of thing."

"You live here, is that right?"

"Yes. There's a small apartment downstairs—it came with the job."

Coffin sat quietly and watched her cross and uncross her arms, then push a lank strand of hair behind her ear. Amazing how uncomfortable people got when you didn't talk.

Devon leaned forward, looked at the floor. "Sometimes we slept in the same bed. It wasn't really sexual, though—not after the first couple of months. I think I was mostly . . . *decorative*." She gestured at one of the big dune paintings. "I went with the sofa."

"So what was in it for you?" Coffin said. "I mean, you're young—didn't you feel like you were missing something?"

"Look, Detective," Devon said, her pale blue eyes meeting Coffin's, "sex is just sex—I could have that with just about anybody. What I had with Serena was security. Sorry if that's not enough for you."

Coffin put his hands up halfway, palms out. *Don't shoot.* "Sorry," he said. "I'm just trying to get a sense of who Serena was. No offense, okay?"

"Whatever," Devon said, suddenly teary. She honked her nose into a cocktail napkin, folded it twice, and dabbed at her eyes.

"One more question," Coffin said. "Don't take it the wrong way."

Devon raised her eyebrows.

"Who inherits? Serena had a ton of money, right?"

Devon pressed her lips together into a grim little smile. "I don't know," she said. "I never asked."

Coffin let himself out, climbed into the Dodge—which bucked and coughed before thundering to life—and backed down the long, steep driveway. Serena's house was less than a mile from Coffin's neighborhood, but she might as well have lived in a different universe. There was no panoramic view from Coffin's house, no Motherwell prints artfully arranged. His windows all looked out at other people's houses, shingled in gray cedar, packed in tight.

When Coffin arrived at his office, Lola was sitting at his desk, leafing through a pile of curling fax paper. A list, he could see. He picked up the cover note: It was from Hank Walters at the BMV, apologizing for the delay—their computers had been down for most of the morning.

"You're looking over my shoulder, Frank," Lola said.

She'd changed out of her uniform. Coffin thought she looked like a young attorney in her pale silk blouse and dark slacks.

"Sorry," Coffin said. He pulled up the orange plastic guest chair and sat down next to Lola. The list contained the year of manufacture, registration number, and name and address of the current owner for all the blue Chevy pickups registered on the outer Cape—a grand total of forty-one. Coffin slid his desk drawer open a couple of inches and picked out a green highlighter.

"Looks like there are nine blue Chevy pickups registered in Provincetown," he said. "Five in Truro, and another twenty-seven in Wellfleet, Eastham, and Orleans."

He found Tony's name right away and drew a bright transparent streak over it. "No surprises yet," he said. He drew another streak over Kotowski's name.

Coffin ran his finger down the rest of the list, stopped, went back. Plotz—there it was. Dunbar Plotz, of Provincetown. *Duffy* Plotz.

Coffin drew a bright green circle around Plotz's name and leaned back in his chair.

"Plotz," Lola said. "What an idiot."

Coffin shook his head. "The man's a vegetarian, for God's sake. He does yoga. Shouldn't he be free of aggression?"

"Vegetarians are always in a bad mood," Lola said. "It's an amino acid thing."

Coffin shrugged. "I guess I pissed him off, out at the dump."

"Maybe he's the killer," Lola said. "Maybe he thinks you're getting too close." She guffawed and put a hand over her mouth.

Coffin shot her a look. "Very funny."

"Sorry."

"It's too impetuous, anyway, trying to flatten a police detective. It's out of character for our guy."

"What's out of character is you still being alive."

"On the other hand, you can't eliminate Plotz altogether. He's not exactly the sanest guy in the world if he's going around trying to run over people."

"What about Kotowski? Shouldn't we take a look at him? He's kind of a loon, right?"

Coffin stood up and turned out his desk lamp. "He's a total loon, but I'm pretty much the only person in town he's *not* mad at. No reason he'd come after me."

Lola cleared her throat. "For the murders, I mean."

Coffin frowned. "Why? Because he smacked Louie around with a fish?"

"Well, duh. I mean, if anyone in this town's got an axe to grind, it's Kotowski."

Coffin steered Lola out of the office and pulled the door shut behind them. "Kotowski's all show," he said. His voice echoed in the stairwell. "You know the joke about how many old Provincetownians it takes to change a lightbulb?"

"No," Lola said. "Tell me."

"Twenty. One to put in the new lightbulb, three to do an environmental impact study, five to hold a protest vigil in support of the old lightbulb, three to do a nude performance art piece called 'Changing the Lightbulb,' and eight to throw a lightbulb-changing theme party."

"Did you just make that up?" Lola said, following Coffin up the narrow metal stairs.

"The point is, there are lots of wackos in Provincetown. Lots of *vocal* wackos. Kotowski's just the most visible."

Lola paused at the landing. "He's a friend of yours, right?"

"I've known him for thirty years, almost," Coffin said.

"I guess what I'm saying is—"

"That he seems like kind of an obvious suspect."

"Well, yeah."

"And you think he might be crazy enough to start killing people."

"Well, yeah."

"I don't think so."

"So you think he's rational."

"I didn't say rational. I just don't think he's irrational *enough*. Besides, he's got a stone-cold alibi for one of the killings."

"He does? I thought he was a hermit, almost. Which one?"

"Jason Duarte."

"Okay. What's this great alibi?"

"He was with me. We were at his house, playing chess. I saw the fire from his deck."

"Oh. Sorry, Frank."

"Forget it. How busy are you right now?"

"I was just about to clock out."

"Put your uniform back on, and I'll grab us a squad car. Let's go pay Mr. Plotz a visit."

Chapter 21

Coffin knocked on the door of Plotz's apartment, but no one answered. He did a palms-up shrug at Lola, who was waiting in a borrowed squad car. A gray armada of clouds steamed across the sky. The harbor was green and choppy.

"Mind hanging around a little?" Coffin said, climbing back into the car.

"Sure, why not," Lola said. "We can pretend we're cops on a stakeout."

Lola pulled around the corner onto Bradford. She parked at the Pilgrim Market, nose out, within view of Plotz's back windows.

Coffin smoked a cigarette. Lola waved at the smoke, gave him a look, rolled down the windows. After a while, a beige Toyota sedan puttered down the hill on Bradford, swung into Duck Lane, and parked. Lola waited until Plotz had climbed most of the way up the stairs before she stuck the patrol car into drive and pulled into Duck Lane, stopping at the foot of Plotz's stairs. Both Coffin and Lola climbed out.

"Hey, Duffy," Coffin said. "We need to talk."

Plotz stared at Coffin for a long second. "Are you going to assault me again?" he said.

"Assault is one of the things I'd like to talk to you about. Mind if we come in? You know how people gossip in this town."

"Out here's fine," Plotz said. "Safer that way. People can gossip all they want."

"Where's your truck, Duffy? The blue Chevy."

"I don't know what you're talking about."

"According to the BMV, you own a blue 1993 Chevy pickup. I'd like to take a look at it."

"I changed my mind," Plotz said, pushing his front door open. "I don't want to talk to you after all."

"Arrest him," Coffin said. Lola started up the stairs, moving fast. She took them in three loose-limbed bounds and got a boot inside the crooked door before Plotz could slam it.

"You can't come in here," Plotz said, backing toward his kitchen. The apartment was long and narrow, like the cabin of a sailboat. "You don't have a warrant." He lunged for the coatrack and picked up an umbrella, which he brandished like a sword.

"Oh, for God's sake," Lola said, grabbing the umbrella and twisting it out of Plotz's hand. She hooked the umbrella's handle behind Plotz's neck and yanked it down and sideways, forcing the recycling engineer off balance. He stumbled, and Lola kicked his feet out from under him. Plotz fell heavily, grunting as his shoulder hit the floor. Lola rolled Plotz onto his belly and, with a knee in his back, snapped handcuffs onto his wrists.

Tears welled up in Plotz's eyes. "*Fuck,*" he said. "That *hurt.*"

"All you had to do was show us the truck," Coffin said. "Now you're going to jail."

"Hey, Frank," Lola said, wiping her hands on her uniform pants. She tipped her head toward Plotz's bookshelf. "Check it out."

There were at least a dozen photographs on top of the small

bookshelf, crowded together, some in frames, some leaning or lying flat on their backs. They were all pictures of Jamie—Jamie loading grocery bags into her car, Jamie on her front porch, Jamie at yoga class—grainy black-and-whites, mostly taken with a telephoto lens. A scatter of razor blades lay among them. One of the photos—Jamie in silhouette, shot through the window of Coffin's house—had been cut into jagged strips.

"I'm not answering any questions," Plotz said as Lola stuffed him into the back of the squad car.

"Fine," Coffin said.

"Not without my lawyer," Plotz said.

"Okay."

Lola started the engine.

"So what am I being charged with?"

"Right now? Assaulting Officer Winters with an umbrella."

Lola steered the car onto Commercial Street. The clouds had moved on, and the harbor glinted in the afternoon sun. A big whale-watch boat was rounding the breakwater, nosing toward MacMillan Wharf, engines rumbling. After dark, the same boat would head back out to the Atlantic, taking several hundred men, a DJ, and a great deal of liquor on an all-night dance cruise.

"Look, I'm sorry about the umbrella thing," Plotz said. "I felt threatened. It was just instinct."

"Bad instinct," Coffin said. "What about last night, in the cemetery? Did you feel threatened then, too?"

"I don't know what you're talking about."

Coffin turned around and looked at Plotz through the wire mesh separating the front and rear seats. "You really suck at lying, Duffy. I'd be embarrassed, if I was you."

"Whatever," Plotz said. "I'm not answering any questions."

"We're fucked," said Louie Silva. Louie was pale; the rims of his eyes were pink, as though he hadn't slept. His hair, which had always been jet black, was suddenly flecked with gray. "We are officially one hundred percent fucked up the ass."

Brandon Phipps raised a finger. "What Mr. Silva means is that the business climate shows signs of deteriorating."

They were in Louie's office, on the third floor of Town Hall. Louie sat in an antique office chair behind a big oak desk. Phipps and Boyle sat on the leather sofa. Coffin stood near the windows, watching a green sailboat as it tacked slowly across the harbor.

"Is that what you mean, Louie?" Coffin said.

"Yeah," Louie said. "We're fucked."

"Who is we, exactly?"

"Mr. Silva is referring to the business community in general," Phipps said.

Coffin leaned toward Louie. "Can you talk while he drinks water? I mean, I'd be impressed if you could do that."

"Very fucking funny, Frankie," Louie said.

"More to the point," said Phipps, raising a neatly groomed eyebrow at Boyle.

"More to the point," Boyle said, "what have you got? Who are your suspects?"

Coffin shrugged. "Beats me," he said.

Louie groaned audibly. Phipps threw up his hands.

"What do you mean, *beats me?*" Louie said. He was fiddling with a black and silver fountain pen—taking the cap off, putting it back on. "How can you not have suspects when corpses are piling up all over town?"

"We've got no witnesses to any of the killings. We've got very little in the way of physical evidence, and limited access to forensic lab reports on what evidence there is. What we *do* know is that the killings all appear to be connected to the Moors condo development. I'd like to know more about the consortium that owns it—it's very secretive."

"Quite the investigation you're running, Detective," Phipps said.

Coffin met his eyes. They were a foggy blue, the color of bread mold. "Last I heard, this was an unofficial, off-the-books investigation. We can't just start busting heads and serving warrants."

"But you arrested the Plotz guy," Boyle said. "What's that about?"

"Unrelated, probably. He tried to run me down last night."

"Jesus. What'd you do to piss him off?"

"He's been stalking my girlfriend. He followed me into the cemetery and tried to flatten me. Or maybe just scare me. Anyway, he's in jail."

"So," said Phipps, pursing his lips. "You've basically got nothing."

"We're *so* fucked up the ass," Louie said, furiously capping and uncapping the fountain pen.

Coffin shrugged. The green boat was turning at the breakwater, heading for Race Point and the Atlantic. "We can narrow things a little," he said. "Our guy is probably male, pretty big and strong. He's probably local; he knew Duarte and Serena were involved with the Moors. He had Serena's cell phone number."

"You checked her incoming calls?" Boyle asked.

Coffin nodded. "Her cell phone and PDA were in her car. Lola got a look at them before Mancini showed up. Serena had dinner with a client at eight o'clock. Got a call on her cell at nine seventeen. We talked to the client—guy named Henderson. He says the call seemed to upset her. She wrapped things up with him and took off."

"So . . . ?"

"Dead end. The call came from the pay phone outside Adams Pharmacy."

Louie groaned softly. Phipps folded his arms across his muscular chest.

"How sure are you that the killings are related?" Boyle asked. "That's not what the state police think."

"You talked to Mancini today?"

"Yup. He's working on Merkin's wife and Serena's girlfriend. Duarte he figures is drug related."

"Maybe—but then you've got three unrelated murders in less than two weeks, in a town that hasn't had three murders in ten *years*. Pretty freaky coincidence."

"Okay," Boyle said. "What's your game plan?"

"Keep poking at Real Estate Investment Consortium," Coffin said. "See what crawls out. Find out who's involved, how they're making money. Look for anyone connected who had a reason to start killing people."

"The *Moors*?" Louie said. "You think someone involved in the *Moors* did this? These are wealthy, prominent businesspeople, for God's sake. They don't go around nailing people to freaking *buildings*." He uncapped the fountain pen. It made a faint blurping sound, and ink splattered all over his hands. "Fuck," he said.

Coffin shrugged again. "If these are motiveless killings, we *are* screwed."

Silva glanced at Boyle, who nodded. "We need results, Coffin," Boyle said. "This thing cannot drag on till fucking Judgment Day. We like your pal Kotowski for Serena's murder, and if he did that one, he probably did the others, too."

"He's completely fucking deranged," Louie said, wiping his hands on a white handkerchief. "Capable of anything."

Coffin watched the green boat as it passed Long Point. The water was pale turquoise near the shore, deep blue farther out. It sparked and glittered in the sunlight. "Kotowski hasn't killed anyone," he said. "I was with him when Duarte's house caught fire."

Boyle waved a hand. "Doesn't matter. Duarte may not be related. Maybe Mancini's right about him. The point is, we want you to take a good, hard look at Kotowski."

"Trust me, Frankie," Louie said, dropping the ink-smeared handkerchief into the wastebasket beside his desk. "The Moors angle's a loser. It's going nowhere."

"Obviously," said Phipps.

"Fire me," Coffin said.

"Now, Frankie—" Louie said.

"You force me to open an off-the-record, probably illegal investigation, and now I've got a committee telling me how to run it. Fuck you. Fire me."

"Think about your mother, for God's sake," Louie said. "What happens to her if you lose your job?"

"Look, Coffin," Boyle said, "maybe you're right, but maybe you're a little too close to this Kotowski guy to see the situation clearly. All we're asking is that you take a look. Talk to him. See if he's got alibis for Merkin and Hench. If it doesn't pan out, you can poke at whatever you want."

Chapter 22

Coffin knocked on Kotowski's door. It was locked, which surprised him—Kotowski had never even had a working latch, to Coffin's knowledge, much less an actual lock. The house was quiet. Kotowski's truck sat in its usual spot in the scraggly front yard.

Kotowski had probably pedaled his rattletrap bike to the Yankee Mart for coffee or a pack of cigarettes, or over to Billy's for unhappy hour. Coffin decided to wait on the front porch, but after a few minutes he got restless and walked around to the back of the house, figuring the sliding glass door that opened onto the deck was almost certainly unlocked.

Late afternoon slantlight, the sky luminous and clear, only a few wisps of cloud at high altitude, mingled with the contrails of passenger jets heading into Boston. Coffin hopped from Kotowski's low seawall onto the beach. A pair of gulls shrieked at each other at the water's edge, fighting over some dead thing they'd found in the sand. The tide was going out, sucking through the breakwater, speaking a thousand watery tongues.

Kotowski might have gone to the Little Store, to peruse a fresh shipment of porn magazines. He could have been paddling his kayak around Long Point, nude except for his conical Vietnamese straw hat. Or maybe he was inside, asleep or sitting in one of the moldering armchairs with headphones on, smoking hashish and listening to Rostropovich play the Bach cello suites.

A flight of rotting wooden stairs ran from the beach to Kotowski's deck, with a little gate at the bottom to discourage tourists from trespassing. Spaz, Kotowski's scruffy orange tomcat, sat on the warped railing, licking his paw. Coffin swung the gate open and climbed the stairs, which sagged a bit under his weight. He crossed the weathered deck and peered in through the glass door, cupping his hands around his eyes to block the glare. Kotowski's rusted three-speed leaned against the shingled wall. There were no lights on inside, no Kotowski. Coffin tried the door, but it was locked. He thumped on the glass with the flat of his hand.

"Kotowski!" he called, but there was no movement inside. He thumped on the glass again. Nothing. Kotowski wasn't home.

Coffin clambered awkwardly over the seawall, crossed Kotowski's yard, and got into the Dodge. He turned the key, and the engine roared to life instantly, a black plume of smoke belching from the tailpipe. The Dodge backfired loudly twice, then stalled.

"Fuck me," Coffin said. "Motherfucking fuckball." He climbed out of the Dodge and stood staring at it, pondering revenge. Something smelled like melted plastic. He opened the hood. Green flames flickered up from the carburetor.

Kotowski's garden hose was snarled in the front yard, near the scraggly tomato plants. Coffin turned the water on at the house, grabbed the hose, and trotted toward the car. The flames were bigger, rising two or three feet above the engine compartment. Coffin trained the garden hose on the fire, a miserable spritz aimed at its heart. The flames grew. It occurred to Coffin that if the fire spread to the gas tank, he might be killed by the explosion—or at least maimed by flying shrapnel. He tossed the hose aside and backed off.

"Burn, then, motherfucker," Coffin said. "Go on and burn." The fire hissed and steamed and went out. The smell of burnt radiator hose hung in the air.

Coffin crossed the yard, jumped over the seawall, then came back a minute later with Kotowski's decrepit three-speed over his shoulder. He set it down, climbed aboard, and rode off, wobbling. He'd call Sal when he got home.

Chapter 23

Jamie napped fitfully on Coffin's sofa. The day was warm; the couch was lumpy and narrow, upholstered in something itchy. She dreamed a woodpecker was drilling a hole in the house. It knocked, paused, knocked again.

It knocked.

Jamie's eyes snapped open. Someone was *there*—outside the screen porch. A dark figure stood on the doorstep, peering in, silhouetted against the late afternoon light. Jamie's heart was pounding. *Plotz?* she thought.

"Frank? You in there?"

"Oh my God," Jamie said. "Lola, is that you?" She climbed off the sofa, walked out to the screen porch, and unlatched the door.

"Hi," Lola said. "You okay? Did I catch you at a bad time?"

Jamie pushed the screen door open. "Come on in. I was napping. I had back-to-back classes this morning, and with everything that's been going on I haven't been sleeping very well."

"Oh, no," Lola said. "Sorry to wake you. I just wanted to drop something off for Frank."

"He's not here." Jamie padded into the kitchen and poured herself a glass of water from the Brita. "I thought he'd be with you."

"I can come back," Lola said.

"You're welcome to wait. He's probably over at Billy's, having a drink. Water? Glass of wine?"

"Sure—water. Thanks."

Lola was dressed in jeans, a black T-shirt, and engineer boots. Her hair was pulled back in a short ponytail. *A tomboy,* Jamie thought. *A cute one. No wonder Frank likes her.*

"So Frank tells me you're thinking about having a baby," Lola said, sipping her water. "That's a pretty big step."

"The end of self-indulgence, or something. At least until they start day care."

"I'm not sure I could handle the responsibility. I don't even do very well with houseplants."

Jamie blew a strand of hair out of her eyes. "Apparently people don't usually forget their babies at the grocery store. Or eat them. It's nature's way."

"Can I ask another personal question?"

Jamie smiled. "My life's an open book."

"It's none of my business," Lola said, leaning against the kitchen counter, "but I've been wondering about the not-getting-married thing. It's kind of unusual."

Jamie waved a hand. "Marriage," she said. "You get a piece of paper that says you're stuck with each other until you die. It seems like the quickest possible way to suck the life out of a relationship, doesn't it?"

"Besides," Lola said, "now that gay people can get married in this state . . ."

"It just *ruins* it," Jamie said. "Up in Canada, straight people have stopped getting married altogether."

Lola grinned. "You know, suddenly wine sounds like just the ticket."

"When doesn't it?" Jamie said. She opened the fridge, found a cold bottle of pinot grigio, and went to work with a corkscrew.

Coffin wobbled into his driveway on Kotowski's bike, nearly crashing into Jamie's old blue Volvo. The bike had no brakes at all. He climbed off and wiped a sleeve over his brow. He was soaked with sweat. Lola's black Camaro was parked at the curb.

The house was alive. Music and women's voices drifted through the open windows out into the summer evening. He opened the screen door and stepped onto the porch and said, "Hello?"

"You're in trouble, mister," said a voice from inside the house. It was Jamie. Another woman laughed. Coffin stuck his head into the living room. Jamie and Lola were in the kitchen, drinking wine and making a salad. A jazz record was playing—Chet Baker singing "The Best Thing for You."

"I am?" Coffin said.

"No fair not telling me when someone tries to kill you," Jamie said, wagging a finger at Coffin. "That's very, very bad. Bad!"

"Nobody tried to kill me," Coffin said. The goat's head goggled at him incredulously. "Duffy just wanted to scare me, I think." He put his hands on Jamie's shoulders and tried to kiss her, but she ducked away.

"Don't *ever* do that again," she said, pointed index finger an inch from his nose. "I hate that stupid stoic shit."

"Sorry," Coffin said.

"Hi, Frank," Lola said. "Want me to hit him for you, Jamie?"

"Hey!" Coffin said.

"Yes," Jamie said, "but let's give him a drink first."

Coffin scowled at Lola. "You told on me," he said.

"Sorry, Frank," Lola said. "I had no idea you were playing tough guy."

Coffin sighed. The pinot grigio was so cold that the bottle was beaded with condensation. "What's for dinner?" he said, pouring himself a glass.

Something squirmed in a bag on the counter. Jamie reached in and pulled out a brown, struggling lobster. "Sea bugs," she said, holding the lobster by its thorax. "I got you a big one. Two pounds." The lobster waved its claws at Coffin.

"You're getting very sleepy . . . ," Coffin said, stroking the lobster's spiny head with his fingertip. The lobster's antennae drooped. Its black bug-eyes grew dreamy.

"Plenty for the three of us," Jamie said.

Coffin looked at Lola. "You staying?"

"That okay?" Lola said.

Coffin shrugged. "Of course."

Jamie took the other lobster out of the bag. "Let's race them," she said.

"Two bucks on the smaller one," Lola said. "The big one seems kind of sluggish."

"Frank hypnotized him," Jamie said.

Coffin refilled his wineglass. "Don't tell the lobster racing commission."

Jamie set the two lobsters down on the linoleum floor. "And they're off!" she said. The big lobster waved its antennae dreamily. The smaller one ambled slowly toward the living room.

"I came by to give you something," Lola said. "Jamie forced me to drink wine."

"See? I told you she was bossy."

"Hey!" Jamie said.

Lola fished a single sheet of paper from her briefcase and handed it to Coffin. "It's the cross-reference with your list of blue pickups. The one you asked Jeff to do."

"Well," Coffin said, reading. "You think you know people."

Six of the forty-one pickup owners had criminal records. Three of them had Orleans addresses, one lived in Wellfleet, and two were in Provincetown.

"Surprises?" Jamie said.

"Eugene Kotowski served nine months for aggravated assault in 1987," Coffin said, "and Duffy Plotz has an outstanding arrest warrant for stalking his ex-wife."

Jamie looked over Coffin's shoulder. "Duffy Plotz, serial stalker. Who knew? The man's a vegetarian, for God's sake."

"The good news is, we can hold him awhile on the outstanding warrant," Coffin said.

"And Kotowski?" Lola said. "Did you know he had a record?"

Coffin scratched his head. "Well, no. Not exactly. But it doesn't surprise me."

"Me either," Lola said. "Not after the fish incident."

"Oh, shit," Jamie said, peering through the doorway into the living room. "I think there's a lobster under the couch." She opened the kitchen closet, took out a frazzled broom. "If I'm not back in ten minutes, call Jacques Cousteau."

Coffin leaned against the counter and sipped his wine. "Why do you suppose Louie would want to keep us away from REIC and the Moors project?"

"Does he?"

"Sure seems like it. He's got Boyle backing him up, too."

"Does Louie dabble in real estate, maybe?"

"He does more than dabble. He owns a ton of rental properties, and some commercial stuff, too."

"You're thinking he's involved in the Moors."

"Even money," Coffin said, glancing into the living room. Jamie was on all fours with the broom, trying to shoo the lobster out from under the couch. "You should have seen him today. He's a wreck."

"Afraid he's next on the people-to-whack list? Or afraid we'll find out something embarrassing about the Moors?"

"Either. Both. They want us to focus on Kotowski."

Lola refilled their glasses. "Makes sense, I guess. Kotowski does have a motive to kill Serena."

"But he went after Louie instead—with a fish. Not exactly murderous intent. Now Louie's pissed, and he wants Kotowski to go to jail."

Lola frowned. "So what do we do?"

"They want me to talk to Kotowski—I'll talk to Kotowski. Then we'll figure out what's going on with the Moors."

Jamie came in with the lobster and put it on the counter. "We'd better cook these guys before there's another jailbreak," she said.

"Not me," Lola said. "I can't stand putting them in the water. They flip around too much."

Coffin took the lid off the lobster pot. The water was boiling wildly. He picked up the lobsters and dipped them in, head first.

"See?" he said, putting the lid back on the pot. "First you boil their little brains. It's more humane that way."

To the local environmentalists, Conwell Marsh was not a marsh at all—it was a fragile wetland, vital to the preservation of Provincetown's unique ecology. To the homeowners who lived along its murky periphery, it was a foul smelling, mosquito-infested swamp. To its owner, Louie Silva, it was a potential gold mine: five acres of undeveloped land, just blocks from the center of town, which he had bought for almost nothing back in the eighties. All it required was filling, and the end result would be fifty new luxury condo units, each selling for a minimum of $600,000, which meant the whole project would gross well over $30,000,000. There were obstacles, of course—threats of litigation from the Mass EPA, a zoning board that was, for largely political reasons, reluctant to issue the necessary permits—but Louie Silva was a man who understood that the wheels of government sometimes needed to be greased; it was an unfortunate but inevitable part of the cost of doing business.

He climbed into his silver Mercedes and set his briefcase beside him on the passenger seat. The briefcase contained three fat manila envelopes: The slimmest envelope held $50,000 for the president of the zoning board; the middle envelope contained $100,000 for the administrator of the Mass EPA, who happened to be in town for the weekend with his boyfriend. The third envelope was oversized and stuffed with even more money—$250,000. It would go to a man named Lawrence Cooperman, an associate justice on the Massachusetts Land Court, the state judicial body that held jurisdiction over most legal matters pertaining to real estate. The first two were small-time—the Conwell development was just one piece of the puzzle—but the Cooperman deal was very, very big indeed.

He backed the Mercedes out onto Bradford Street and accelerated smoothly up the hill, heading toward Herring Cove. He would meet the gay EPA administrator there, then pop over to the zoning president's house later in the evening. Cooperman was paranoid: They'd arranged to meet on a secluded road in the woods near Wellfleet. Louie turned on the CD player, and Sinatra's voice came braying out of the Mercedes's top-of-the-line stereo system—that silly song about the little old ant who thought he could move a rubber-tree plant. Silva hummed along. At the end of Bradford Street, he turned right onto Route 6, past the Moors, the long span of the stone breakwater in his rearview mirror. And then a man's face was in the mirror, too, rising slowly up like a ghost from the backseat, and Silva, startled, swerved and almost lost control of the car, veering perilously close to the sandy embankment that sloped into the green, brackish waters of Bufflehead Pond.

"How's it going, Louie?" said the man in the backseat.

"Jesus fucking Christ," said Silva. "You scared the living shit out of me." He felt something cold and hard against his neck.

"Just drive, you little pus bag."

For a long time they didn't talk. They cracked the lobsters' shells, dipped the delicate flesh in melted butter. They ate and drank wine and licked the butter from their fingers. They picked at the salad and sucked the last bits of meat from the lobsters' spindly legs. They opened another bottle of wine.

"So what is it with the seafood thing?" Lola said, licking melted butter from her index finger. "I mean, I like fish and lobster as much as anybody, but it's practically all you eat, right, Frank? This from a guy who hates boats."

Coffin laughed. "I figure I'd better eat them before they eat me." He finished his wine and refilled his glass. "It's weird," he said. "All hell can break loose, but give me a lobster and a bottle of wine and I'm totally happy."

"Don't forget the two beautiful women," Jamie said.

Lola stretched, arching her back. Coffin caught himself staring at the curve of her breasts.

"Every white boy's fantasy," Lola said.

"Not to mention a damn fine avocado." Coffin speared the last, soft slice from the salad bowl.

"And a warm late-summer evening," Jamie said. "And Chet Baker on the record player."

"Exactly," Coffin said. "But shouldn't I feel guilty? Isn't it wrong to be happy when people are getting crucified?"

Jamie speared a romaine leaf with her fork and ate it. "Lest I forget you were raised Catholic," she said.

"I mean, I know Merkin was no prize, and Serena Hench was greedy and ruthless, but does that make it better somehow?" Coffin said. "And what about Duarte? He was just trying to get by."

"Well, he *was* building those horrible condos," Jamie said. "That makes him kind of evil, if you ask me."

"Then it's okay that I'm sitting here drinking wine among beautiful women and lobsters? Because maybe the victims had it coming?"

Jamie patted Coffin's arm. "My shrink would say it's okay not to feel terrible about not feeling terrible."

"Finish your wine and then go talk to Kotowski," Lola said. "You'll feel better if you pretend you're doing something useful."

"What," Coffin said, "no dessert?"

Chapter 24

Coffin waited in Jamie's Volvo, thirty yards from Kotowski's house, the harbor to his left, the breakwater and the salt marsh straight ahead. He'd been waiting almost an hour, watching the late-evening sky fade from magenta to black. Kotowski's house was still dark, his truck still gone. The stars glittered like broken glass in a parking lot. The harbor pulsed against the beach. A gull flew low, past Coffin's windshield, startling him a little.

Coffin was about to give up and go home when Kotowski pulled up and parked in the narrow yard. Kotowski got out of his truck, strode across the yard to his front door, unlocked it, and went inside.

Coffin waited until lights went on inside the house, then climbed out of the Volvo. He knocked on Kotowski's door.

"Who the fuck is it?" Kotowski yelled.

"Where the hell have you been?" Coffin said. "I've been waiting out here for a freaking hour."

The door swung open. Kotowski stood inside, grinning. "I was at Billy's, if it's any business of yours. You could have called."

"You shot your phone in 1982," Coffin said.

Kotowski waved Coffin in. They walked down a short flight of steps into the cavernous living room.

"Since when do you lock your door?" Coffin said.

"Since the real estate cabal and their goons started showing up at all hours and letting themselves in."

"What, no booby trap?"

"Thought about it. Figured I'd probably get you by mistake."

"Probably."

"Beer?" Kotowski opened his battered fridge and peered in. The smell of something rotten drifted out. "I've got Rolling Rock."

"Of course."

"I assume that the slightly charred piece-of-shit Dodge in front of my house belongs to you," Kotowski said once they'd unscrewed their beers and settled into the dusty armchairs.

Coffin nodded. "It does."

"Do you plan to remove it, eventually?"

"I do."

Kotowski sipped his beer. "And would you be the son of a bitch that stole my bicycle?"

"I am."

"The brakes don't work, you know."

"I know. I almost crashed into a UPS truck on Commercial Street."

"It's not chess night," Kotowski said. He stood and approached the half-finished painting on his big, paint-spattered easel. He folded his arms and squinted at it. "To what do I owe the honor of this visitation? Your shitheel cousin send you down here to bust my balls?"

"Bingo. They like you for two of the murders."

"I told you this would happen. You've become a tool of the real estate junta. You arrest me on false pretenses, they take my house."

"You never told me you had a record," Coffin said.

"Wasn't any of your business," Kotowski said. He pointed at the painting with his chin. "Brand-new. How do you like it?"

The painting was a self-portrait—gigantic Kotowski, naked, bearded, and splashed with gore, biting the head off of a much smaller figure holding a paintbrush and palette. Small dune-and-sunset paintings were hung in the background. The soon-to-be headless man's legs spasmed awkwardly. The paintbrush fell from his hand.

"Deeply disturbing," Coffin said. "What do you call it?"

"I don't know yet. It's a parody of Goya's *Saturn Devouring One of His Sons*. Any ideas?"

"*Self-Portrait with Snack? Art Imitates Lunch?*"

Kotowski blew a loud raspberry. "You'll have to try a little harder than that."

"I'll devote every waking moment to it," Coffin said.

Kotowski gazed raptly at the painting, rubbing his stubbly chin. "It needs more blood, don't you think? I mean, blood should be spraying out of the guy, right?"

"Definitely."

"Huh," Kotowski said. "Like you know anything." He turned from the painting, walked into the kitchen, and rummaged in the fridge. He came back with two more beers. He handed one to Coffin and flopped down into his armchair. "I don't see what my fifteen-year-old assault conviction has to do with serial murders in Provincetown," he said.

"In practice, nothing. In theory, it's starting to look like you have a pattern of attacking people."

"Two in fifteen years isn't much of a pattern."

"It's two more than most people have."

"They were both completely justified. Not that you're interested."

"I'm one gigantic ear."

"The guy fifteen years ago was an art dealer in New York. Supposedly reputable—friend of a friend. He had a hot new gallery in SoHo. Getting lots of press, very big deal. He likes my stuff, gives me a one-man show. Two years' worth of work. It's a huge success—the show sells out within a week."

"No wonder you beat the crap out of him."

"Do you want me to tell the story or not?"

"Sorry."

"The show comes down, the art gets shipped—I don't get paid. I'm not worried. The guy's got a major reputation; all the word of mouth is good. Two weeks, I give him a call. Don't worry, he says—as soon as he collects from all the buyers, he'll write me a big fat check. A month later, nothing. I start dropping by the gallery, but he's never there. I call him at home—answering machine. The guy has gone fucking invisible. One day I go to the gallery and the place is empty, locked up with a FOR RENT sign in the window. I hire a lawyer—we're gonna sue the guy, but we have to wait in line. Turns out he's a total cokehead and has pissed away millions of dollars on houses in the Hamptons and fancy cars and lingerie models, God knows what. *Every*body's suing the little bastard. The cops are after him. He goes into bankruptcy and disappears. No lawsuit, no money, no *nada*."

"So you were pissed."

"Pissed? I was fucking *furious*. I swore if I ever ran into him I'd rip his head off and cram it up his ass."

"So . . ."

"So one day, about two years later, I'm in this bar in Brooklyn. I go to take a leak, and guess who's standing at the next urinal?"

"Uh-oh."

"That's pretty much what *he* said. He almost drowned. Took three guys to get him out of the toilet."

"So he called the cops . . ."

"And the rest is history. Ancient."

"Did you try to kill him?"

"I was a navy SEAL, Coffin. If I'd wanted to kill him, he'd be dead."

"A SEAL? You?"

"Six years. Three tours in Nam. My unit was so fucking secret it didn't have a name."

Coffin's eyebrows went up. "You're full of surprises today."

"Whatever," Kotowski said, waving a hand. He belched softly, then took a swallow of beer. "I've been thinking."

"Uh-oh."

"I've been *thinking*," Kotowski said, scowling at Coffin, "about the whole scene at Town Hall the other day. My rage got the better of me, and that's not good. I'm damn near sixty years old—I need to find some serenity. I'm thinking of becoming a Taoist."

"What about therapy? Psychotropic drugs, maybe."

Kotowski snorted. "Therapy's for suckers," he said. Then he raised his beer bottle in a mock toast. "And I prefer my drugs in nonprescription form."

"What do you have to do to become a Taoist?"

"Nothing."

"Nothing? No burnt offerings or ritual mutilation?"

"Nope."

Coffin sipped his beer. "Then how do you know if you've become one?"

"There's no becoming. There's just being. If it's in your nature to be a Taoist, then you're a Taoist."

"Okay, fine. So what exactly do Taoists believe?"

"That things are the way they are because that's how it's supposed to be."

"That's it?"

"Yep."

"That's not a religion—it's just a giant excuse. What about war and famine and AIDS?"

"You're negative like that because it's in your nature. You can't help it, see?"

"But religion is supposed to help us understand things—it's supposed to comfort us when times are bad. Just saying things are the way they are because that's how they're supposed to be doesn't explain anything."

"And Western religions do? A God with a big white beard who lives in the sky and claims to love us but tortures and kills us by the millions? That helps you make sense of things?"

"What about *faith*? What about *believing* in something?"

"It's your nature to want to believe in things."

"Oh, for Christ's sake," Coffin said.

It was late when Coffin finally got home. Jamie and Lola were gone, and all the dishes were washed and put away. There was a note on the kitchen counter:

Dear Frank,
You're gone. It's late. We thought about taking a long, hot, sudsy shower together but decided it wouldn't be any fun without you. Kidding.
See you tomorrow?
XO
Jamie

Coffin drank a glass of water at the kitchen sink. The tap water tasted mossy and metallic. He sat on the porch swing and smoked a before-bed cigarette, listening to the crickets and the faint rush of traffic along Route 6. In the old days, according to Thoreau, when the wind was blowing right you could hear the Atlantic surf from the town center. Not anymore. The dunes and the densely built town blocked it; the small hubbub of thousands of human lives drowned it out. Now all you could hear was the *Tonight Show* on the neighbor's TV set. He finished the cigarette, flipped the glowing butt out into the yard, and went to bed.

Chapter 25

Why don't you go sit down, Frank? Why don't you come outside with me and get some air?"

"The other one," Coffin said. *His hands are shaking.* "The one in the bathroom."

"I don't think you should go in there, Frank. You really don't look so good. I think you should come outside with me and get some air."

But Coffin pulls away and walks down another short hallway to the bathroom. His legs seem too long, like he's walking on stilts—the floor keeps falling away in front of him. The bathroom door is open and at first he doesn't see the body, just the big clawfoot tub, the floor still tracked with dirty water. "Oh boy," Coffin hears himself say. "Oh boy. Oh boy." The tub is half full of gray water. A naked child, a girl maybe eight years old, rests just below the surface, her long blond hair streaming around her narrow shoulders, around her face, which is angelic, intact.

Oh boy. Oh boy.

Rashid comes in. Coffin is on his knees by the tub, clutching the drowned girl in his arms. Her head and arms flop as he cradles her against his chest. He keeps patting her back. "Oh boy," he says, over and over. "Oh boy. Oh boy. Oh boy."

"Frank, man," Rashid says, putting a hand on Coffin's shoulder. "Easy now. Easy now, Frank."

"Frank."

"No . . ."

"Frank."

"Lights. Bad."

"Frank," Lola said, "it's Louie Silva. They found him in the marsh. You need to get up."

Coffin opened his eyes, then closed them again. The lights in his bedroom were unbearably bright. Lola, in uniform, was shaking his arm.

"Okay," he said. "Enough with the shaking already. What time is it?"

"It's 5:00 A.M."

"Louie's dead?"

"Yes. I'm sorry, Frank."

"I think I'm naked," Coffin said, looking under the sheet.

"I'll wait in the car."

The Rescue Squad had already arrived. They stood around the ambulance in big rubber waders, smoking cigarettes.

Tony was wrapping everything in sight in yellow police tape.

"He's still out there, Frankie," Tony said. He was pale; his lips were pressed into a tight line. Louie was his first cousin. "It's pretty bad."

The roof of Louie's car was just visible, a gleaming silver dome emerging from the marsh's green, muck-clotted surface. There were tire tracks on the bank and a clear trail through the cattails and duckweed, leading out to the all but submerged Mercedes.

Coffin borrowed a pair of waders from one of the rescue boys; they were enormous, like rubber clown pants. He slogged into the marsh, fighting the edge-tangle of cattails and the deep muck on the bottom. His heart felt huge and heavy in his chest. He was light-headed, the walking-on-stilts sensation strangely complicated by the marsh's sucking goo.

The Mercedes's passenger compartment was half-filled with water; Louie's silver titanium briefcase floated lazily behind the passenger seat. Louie sat belted into the driver's seat, his head slumped forward. The inside of the windshield was streaked with blood. Louie's forehead was missing. Blood and brain matter covered his face. Gently, Coffin turned Louie's head to the right: There was a scorched entry wound in the back of his skull, just above the spinal juncture.

Coffin turned and vomited into the waist-deep water. "Fucking Christ," he said when he was done. He wiped his mouth on his sleeve. On an impulse, he reached into the car and fished out Louie's briefcase. Then he slogged back to the ambulance, stepped out of the ridiculous waders, and sat down heavily on the bank.

"I'm sorry, Frank," Lola said, sitting beside him.

"He's got three kids, you know," Coffin said. "Three girls." His mouth tasted sour; his eyes hurt.

Lola put an arm around his shoulders. Its weight surprised him.

The roof of Louie's car glowed like a crashed UFO in the aqueous half-light. Tony found them after a while and sat down next to Frank. Mosquitoes whined around them. For a long time, no one said anything. Then Vincent Mancini's black Lexus rolled to a stop on the dirt road.

"Shit," Coffin said. "The briefcase."

"I was waiting for the right moment to ask you about that," Lola said. "Are we removing evidence from a crime scene?"

"Yes."

Mancini and Pilchard climbed out of the Lexus.

"You two go and distract Mancini," Lola said, shoving the brief-case under her jacket. "Keep him busy till I get to the car."

"Well, well," said Mancini, standing next to Coffin's discarded waders. "I see the local constabulary has once again taken it upon themselves to fuck up a perfectly good crime scene."

"He was my cousin, Mancini."

"I don't care if he was your goddamn grandmother, Coffin. You and your Keystone Kops have got no business tracking up *my* crime scene."

"Or harassing witnesses," said Pilchard.

Mancini leaned toward Coffin. His cologne smelled like cedar shavings. "Detective Pilchard raises an interesting point, Coffin. You've been interviewing witnesses before we get to them. You're not supposed to do that."

"Jeeze, Frankie," Tony said. "The briefing—remember?"

"Professional curiosity," Coffin said. "We live here, you know." He saw Lola out of the corner of his eye, picking her way around the marsh, thirty yards from the car.

Mancini stuck out his chin. "Your *curiosity* is bordering on criminal misconduct, Detective. If you don't stop fucking up my crime scenes and tainting my witnesses, your next job in law en-forcement will be security guard at a 7-Eleven."

"That's a *very* nice suit," Coffin said, fingering Mancini's sleeve. "Is that rayon or what?"

"*Rayon?* It's wool, for God's sake. This is *Italian.*"

"If he gets fired," Tony said, "can he still collect unemployment?"

Pilchard scratched his head. "Fired or laid off?" he said. "If he's fired, it depends on *why* he was fired."

"For Christ's sake," Mancini snapped, snatching his sleeve out of Coffin's grasp. He pointed a manicured finger. "Keep away from my crime scenes and my witnesses, Coffin," he said. "You only get one warning."

Lola was standing next to the car. She waved, opened the driver's door, and got in.

"No more crime scenes," Coffin said, patting Mancini's shoulder. "It'll be my pleasure."

Tony bent close to Mancini's ear. "Dead people freak him out," he said as Coffin walked off, heading for Lola and the car.

"Hey, Frank," Tony called. "If you get fired, who gets your office?"

Chapter 26

"Cupcakes and a gun," Lola said. "Care to guess what's in the envelopes?"

"What the hell was he up to?" Coffin said. They were leaning over his desk in the dank basement office, peering into Louie's open briefcase. It contained three fat manila envelopes, a black and silver Montblanc pen, a yellow legal pad, a Glock nine-millimeter semiautomatic pistol, and a package of two cellophane-wrapped, cream-filled Hostess chocolate cupcakes.

Coffin wasn't used to wearing latex gloves. They made his hands feel sweaty and swollen. He reached into the briefcase and took out one of the manila envelopes. It was sealed. He slid a letter knife under the flap and looked inside, then passed it to Lola.

"Wahoo," she said. "Can we keep it?" She turned the envelope upside down, and five rubber-banded bundles of hundred-dollar bills flapped onto the oak desktop.

"If only," Coffin said, dumping ten bundles of hundreds out of the second big manila envelope.

"God, I love that sound," Lola said.

Coffin picked up a bundle of bills and riffled it with his thumb. It was nearly an inch thick. "Probably a hundred hundreds in each bundle," he said.

"Times fifteen is a hundred and fifty grand."

"Good Lord," Coffin said, peering into the third manila envelope, which was bigger than the other two and stuffed to the top. He dumped it, too, and counted the bundles. "Plus two hundred fifty thousand."

"What on earth was he doing with this much cash?"

"I smell bribes," Coffin said. "I'll bet Louie was on his way to buy a little influence."

"Jesus. What are we going to do with it? We can't exactly turn it over to Mancini."

"For now, it goes home with me. You never saw it. If it's Louie's, I'll give it to his wife."

"What if it's the town's?"

Coffin grinned. "I'll make an anonymous donation to the policeman's ball."

"You're doing this to protect Louie."

"His family. They're going to have a hard enough time as it is."

Lola picked up the legal pad. Several of its pages had been torn off. "Check it out," she said.

Coffin peered at the pad. The lined pages had nothing written on them. "What?" he said.

"What are you, blind?" Lola said. "Look at these indentations on the top page—you can sort of make out what was written on the page above this one."

Coffin held the pad under his nose, then at arm's length. "My, my. You're a regular Nancy Drew."

Lola laughed. "When I was in sixth grade, my best friend wanted to be Nancy Drew. I wanted to *do* Nancy Drew."

Coffin pointed at the legal pad. "Put your young eyes on that word and tell me what it says."

"Kotowski."

"Ha. Thought so. What's this below it?"

"Looks like capital *E*, capital *D*, then the word 'test' with a question mark. Who's E-D?"

"Beats me. What does it say under E-D?"

"Phipps. Circled a few times."

Coffin wiped a hand over his face. "Ed," he said. "Who the hell is Ed? Eddie Myers? Ed Ramos?"

"They could be initials. *E*-something, *D*-something."

"Early Detection?"

"Eggplant Dalmatian?"

"Emphatic Dropcloth?"

Coffin sat down in his desk chair. The sewer pipe rumbled overhead. "How much of a Nancy Drew fan are you really?"

"The biggest."

"Good. Because tonight we're going to break into Louie's office."

"Cool."

"If we get caught we're up shit creek, you know."

"So let's not get caught."

The phone buzzed, and Coffin picked it up.

"Get up here right away," Boyle said. "I've got some news for you, and you're not going to like it." The line clicked and went dead.

Coffin put the phone back in its cradle. His head ached. He wondered how much sleep he'd gotten—two hours? Three? Lola looked tired, too. "I've got to go talk to Boyle," Coffin said. "Why don't you take a break? Take a nap. Get something to eat."

"Are you sure? I'll come with you if you want me to."

"I'll be okay," Coffin said. "I mean, how much worse can it get?"

Chapter 27

S orry about your cousin, Coffin," Boyle said. He stood beside his office window, looking down at Commercial Street. "He was a decent guy."

"He would have sold his own mother for dog food, if the price was right," Coffin said, "but he was family."

"That's a hell of a way to talk," said Boyle, turning to glare at Coffin from beneath his beetling eyebrows.

"Yes, it is."

Boyle scowled and sat down in his leather chair. "All right— since we're apparently done with the eulogizing, let's cut to the chase. Two things, and you're not going to be happy about either of them. First, we had to release Plotz."

"Wonderful," Coffin said. "Perfect."

"His lawyer pointed out that the restraining order he was supposed to have violated was expired. Said lawyer also seems to think that you and Winters illegally pursued Mr. Plotz into his apartment and used excessive force in arresting him. Mr. Plotz is weighing the possibility of a formal complaint and a lawsuit against the town."

"Mr. Plotz shouldn't press his luck. Any progress on the pickup?"

"Nope. Unless Plotz is a complete idiot, he's either dumped it or had it repaired by now. Ready for the *bad* news?"

"You're enjoying this, aren't you?"

"That would just be sadistic, Coffin." Boyle smiled, leaned back in his chair, and laced his fingers on top of his speckled bald spot. "The bad news is that Mancini and that prick Pilchard have arrested your buddy Kotowski for all four murders. He's sitting downstairs in a holding cell, waiting to be transported down to Barnstable."

"Oh, for Christ's sake," Coffin said. "Those idiots."

"Yeah, you keep saying that. Mancini thinks it's a no-brainer."

"Then he's just the guy for the job. What a fucking moron."

"Come on, Coffin. Kotowski's the obvious call. The guy's a nut-case. He attacked Silva right here in this building, in front of Mancini and a dozen witnesses."

"He attacked him with a *fish*—not a gun. Not a knife. A fuck-ing *fish*. Serial killers don't attack people with fish."

"Okay—he also had a beef with the Hench woman, who was involved in the Moors project, which fits your own damn theory."

Coffin started to speak, but Boyle raised a hand, palm out. "Talk to the hand, Coffin. You're too close to this thing. You're not seeing it clearly. Mancini thinks there's an easy conviction here, and I happen to agree with him. Why don't you go home, take a couple of days off, and get your head clear. It's over, Coffin. Case closed."

"Is that what we're doing here?" Coffin said, standing up. "Go-ing for an easy conviction? And here I had this naive notion that we were trying to catch a serial killer."

"Of *course* Mancini's going for the conviction, Coffin. I mean, this is the biggest thing since Tony Costa chopped up those girls and buried 'em out in the woods in Truro."

Coffin paused in the doorway. "You've been reading up on local history, I see."

Boyle smirked. "I try," he said.

"Then you remember what Costa said after they sentenced him."

Boyle looked at Coffin blankly.

"*Keep digging,*" Coffin said.

Coffin rode Kotowski's bike to Wymynwerx, the two-story, cedar-shingled gym on Shank Painter Road where Jamie was teaching her two o'clock advanced class. Traffic was heavy; a carful of young women honked and laughed at his unsteady progress. Then, a few minutes later, a passing Winnebago almost clipped him with its bumper, forcing him into the ditch. By the time he got to the gym he was soaked in sweat.

Inside, Coffin nodded to the short, muscular girl behind the desk. She looked up from her magazine and nodded back but didn't smile.

Coffin poked his head into Jamie's class, a roomful of very thin women posed with hands and feet on their purple mats, butts high in the air. He caught Jamie's eye, and she winked at him. Coffin crooked a finger, and Jamie whispered to one of the women in the front row, who took over the class.

When they'd stepped out into the hallway, Coffin nodded at the roomful of women. "Downward-looking dog," he said.

Jamie hugged him hard, then kissed him on the lips. Coffin wasn't sure, but he thought he saw the girl behind the desk frown slightly out of the corner of his eye.

"Facing. Downward-*facing* dog," Jamie said, wiping sweat from her forehead with a white gym towel. "Horrible about Louie. Jesus."

"Thanks," Coffin said. "News travels fast."

Jamie hugged him again. "You okay?"

"No. I don't know. There's something else."

Jamie looked at him, head tilted a bit. The sun streamed through the gym's big front window, backlighting her hair.

"They let Plotz out of jail," Coffin said. "I don't want you staying by yourself."

"Duffy? That wimp? I can handle Duffy Plotz, Frank." She flexed her arm. "Feel that bicep."

"He had a *shrine,* Jamie, remember? Pictures of you all over his apartment. I didn't tell you this, but he'd sliced a couple of them up with razor blades. And now he's probably *really* pissed."

Jamie squinted. "Okay, slicing up the pictures *is* pretty creepy, but I'm not—"

"Look, I really need you not to argue with me about this—"

"Ask me again."

"There are dead people piling up all over town, for Christ's sake—"

"Frank. Just ask me again."

"—which is why you're moving in with me for a few days at least, till we figure out what to do about the son of a bitch." Coffin frowned. "What are you grinning at?"

"You have to ask me three times."

"What?"

"You've asked me to move in with you twice. Three is a magic number—I thought you knew that."

"Well, it's just until—"

"That's not asking."

"Will you move in with me?" Coffin said.

Jamie kissed him, slowly and with considerable concentration. "You know what?" she said when the kiss was over.

"Uh, no, ma'am."

"You'll be glad you asked. Yes indeed, I do believe you will."

When Coffin passed the girl behind the desk on his way out, she was intent on her magazine. He pushed the door open, and just before it swung shut behind him he heard her say, "Breeders. Ew."

The jail shared the second floor of Town Hall with the police dispatcher, the squad room, the day officer's desk, and the men's locker room. It had three cells in a row along an outside wall, and a small common area with a metal table and four metal chairs bolted to the floor. Each cell contained two cots one above the other, a small stainless steel sink, and a stainless-steel toilet. Kotowski was the only prisoner; he sat on the edge of his cot, dressed in an orange jumpsuit and rubber sandals, smoking a cigarette.

"Lawyers," Kotowski said. "One step up the evolutionary ladder from real estate developers. Several steps below spirochetes, tapeworms, and dung beetles. You know what Shakespeare said, don't you?"

"Well, you still need one," Coffin said. He stood outside Kotowski's cell, leaning against the bars. "Mancini thinks you're the next Tony Costa."

"Ha. I used to buy pot from Tony Costa. Very nice guy, as long as you weren't an eighteen-year-old girl."

"Costa died in prison, you know."

"Okay, I'll hire a lawyer. Whoever you recommend."

"Good. What else do you need?"

"Socks, underwear, toothpaste, toothbrush, a carton of cigarettes, some whiskey, and lots of pornography. Thought you'd never ask."

Coffin laughed. "You're only going to be here for a few hours, till they send somebody up from Barnstable to transport you."

"Okay, fine. Forget the socks and underwear."

"Anyone you want me to contact?"

"No, but you'd probably better stop by my house now and then and feed Spaz."

Coffin rubbed his chin. He hadn't shaved, and it was starting to get bristly. "Look," he said, "I'm not going to let you rot down there. We're going to find out who killed those people."

"Made a lot of progress, have you?"

"Well, no."

"So I won't hold my breath."

"Probably a good plan."

Kotowski waved a hand. "Hey, I did six months on Riker's Island, I can sit in Barnstable County till my bail hearing."

"Riker's, huh? Must have been tough."

"It's a shithole. It's out in the middle of the East River, you know—just downwind from this huge sewage treatment plant. God, it stank. Rats the size of schnauzers would pop up out of the toilets every now and then. One of my cellmates got bit on the sack and had to get a rabies shot."

"Jesus."

"But other than that it wasn't so bad. We had wicked competitive games of Scrabble."

"Oh, come on now—"

"No, seriously. A couple of those guys had memorized the entire Scrabble dictionary. They kicked *ass.*"

Coffin rode Kotowski's bike to the A&P and bought a toothbrush, a tube of toothpaste, and a carton of Camel filters. Next door, at Pete's Liquor, he bought a half-pint bottle of scotch. Then he pedaled back to Town Hall and delivered the goods to Kotowski, producing the scotch from his pocket when he was sure no one was looking.

"Thanks," Kotowski said, cracking open the bottle. "But where the hell's my porn?"

"What would people think," Coffin said, "if they saw me buying the latest issue of *Twinks in Chains*?"

"They'd think you finally came to your senses," Kotowski said, killing the whiskey in one long guzzle.

Chapter 28

Coffin was exhausted when he finally climbed off the bike and propped it against his front porch. There was a note from Jamie inside, on the kitchen counter:

Wild Man,
My stuff's in the bedroom. How about clearing out a drawer or two, now that we're roomies? Went to Orleans with Corrine to do laundry and buy fish, etc. Back by 8:00 or so.
XO
Jamie

Coffin dropped ice cubes into a glass and poured two fingers of scotch. He stood by the sink and drank the scotch while a scrum of tiny brown ants pushed a small piece of potato chip across the counter. Outside the window, the sunflowers drooped in the hum of late-afternoon heat.

When the scotch was gone, he refilled his glass, went into the living room, and sat down on his mother's uncomfortable sofa.

The answering machine blinked its red light at him from the end table.

He pushed the button and skipped through messages from reporters: ABC, Fox News, Channel 7. Serena's killing had been sensational; Louie's had driven the press into a frenzy. Coffin erased all the messages. The stuffed goat's head looked like it was about to say something insulting.

Coffin took the bottle of scotch out to the screen porch and sat down in the big wicker chair. He sat there a long time, watching the light slant and turn golden, then suffuse with red. He sipped scotch and listened to the slow crescendo of crickets out in the lowering dusk; more and more of them every night. Fall was coming. Soon the tourist hordes would perform their disappearing act and go back to their lives in Boston or Providence or New York or wherever, taking their noise and sunburns and various appetites with them, and leave the town empty and dark through the long winter—though even that was changing, Coffin thought. Soon the off-season would be a thing of the past. It was already shrinking, starting later and ending sooner, becoming less defined thanks to a string of mild winters (global warming was just fine with the B and B owners) and a concerted effort on the part of the selectmen to lure visitors to town for the holidays, which, in Provincetown, included Christmas—marketed as something called Holly Folly—and New Year's Eve, of course, and the long weekends of President's Day and Martin Luther King Day, and, most commercially viable of all, Valentine's Day. The growing popularity of telecommuting was a factor, too, as was all the new money generated by the high-tech boom and then the real estate boom. Twenty years ago, Labor Day had been like a movie about the Rapture that Coffin had seen once: The magic hour would strike, and suddenly Provincetown would be deserted, as though all the tourists had been sucked up to heaven by God's giant Shop-Vac. Now they lingered and lingered, staying on for Women's

Week and Leather Week and Bears Week and Tall Ships Week (officially Fantasia Fair, though no one called it that). And then for weeks after *that,* until the truly dismal rain and dark of November set in, little squads of Europeans and retirees would clog the narrow sidewalks with their big butts and elastic waistbands while pointing out the harbor, the tethered boats along the wharf, the Pilgrim Monument, and Commercial Street's hundred funky little shoppes (the Drag Strip, the Pleasure Chest, and, God help us, Poochie's— *Look at that! A bakery for dogs!*) as if they were the first civilized people to have discovered them. Coffin was pouring a third glass of scotch when a black Camaro pulled up in front of his house and Lola got out.

"Frank?" she said, peering in at him the way she might have looked at a grapefruit in the back of the fridge that had begun to liquefy. "You all right?"

"Fantastic," he said. "Want a drink?"

"God, yes." She opened the screen door and stepped onto the porch. She was wearing faded jeans with a small rip in the left knee, a black V-necked T-shirt, and black engineer boots. Her hair was pulled back in the usual ponytail. Coffin handed her the bottle. She took a swig, made a face, then took another swig. "Did we miss something, Frank?" she said.

"No," he said. "I don't think so. Aside from not actually catching the killer, anyway."

Lola sat down on the porch swing; its chains creaked a little. "We're not supposed to be working together anymore," she said. "Boyle told me I'm back on my regular shift."

"Good. Breaking into Louie's office is completely illegal. If we got caught, it'd end your career. I shouldn't have asked you to come along."

Lola grinned. "I told him I needed a couple of days off. He said I deserved it." She took another swig from the bottle of scotch.

"You're nuts if you think you're breaking into Louie's office without me, Frank," she said.

The moon was rising, egg shaped and off-balance in the violet sky. Coffin wondered if the coyotes were congregating in the cemetery, waiting for full dark to sing their feral song. He looked at his watch. Eight forty-five, and no Jamie.

"There's more bad news about your friend Kotowski," Lola said, looking out into the gathering dark. "The state police found a .44 Magnum slug embedded in the ceiling of Louie's car."

"Makes sense. You could have stuck your fist through the exit wound."

"They searched Kotowski's house; there was a .44 Mag Colt Python in his closet. They're checking the ballistics first thing tomorrow."

Coffin groaned. "Planted. Mancini's pulling out all the stops. A hundred to one, ballistics shows a perfect match."

They were silent for a few minutes. Coffin lit a cigarette. Then he said, "Do *you* think he did it?"

Lola's eyebrows drew together. "It's not impossible," she said, "even though he was with you the night of Duarte's murder. He could've used some kind of timing device. Or there could be two killers."

"Why not four?" Coffin said. "One for each corpse."

"Why couldn't there be two killers? Somebody saw an opportunity to settle a score, maybe, hoping the cops would assume all the murders were committed by the other guy. Maybe a copycat— somebody who wanted their fifteen minutes of fame."

"I just know Kotowski," Coffin said. "He's a crank, but he's not psychotic—and I've met a lot of psychotics. It's mostly instinct, I guess. I know how stupid that sounds."

Lola took a sip of whiskey from the bottle. "You hungry, Frank? Have you eaten anything?"

"I could eat. You?"

"Starving. What's in the fridge?"

"I think I have some cheese."

Lola stood and stretched. "Cheese," she said. "Great."

She walked into the kitchen. Coffin followed, fighting the urge to stare at her backside.

"There's *three* kinds of mustard in here," Lola said, peering into the fridge. "All about empty. A bottle of Bass Ale. And a scary little science project in the crisper. Look," she said, pulling out a hunk of smoked Gouda in a Ziploc Bag, "actual food. And the pièce de résistance—a jar of olives." She held the olives out triumphantly, then set them on the counter. "Sounds like dinner to me."

"There might be some Triscuits in the cupboard over the sink," Coffin said, checking his watch. "Where the hell is she?"

"She who? You expecting Jamie?"

"She was supposed to be back by eight. She's staying here for a while."

"Because of Plotz?" Lola said, putting the cheese and a handful of Triscuits on a plate.

Coffin opened the olives and spooned them into a bowl. "Jamie thinks I'm being paranoid, but that shrine of his gave me the serious creeps."

Lola shrugged. "Not to mention that trying-to-squish-you thing."

"Wait," Coffin said, when Lola sat down. "I just thought of something." He opened the cupboard above the sink and rummaged in the back for a moment before producing a small, flat can. "Sardines," he said. "In oil."

"Ew," Lola said. "Nasty."

Coffin put the sardines back in the cupboard. "For Kotoswki's cat," he said.

After they ate, Lola stood at the sink, rinsing her plate. "Am I crazy," she said, "or is somebody sitting in a blue pickup truck across the street?"

Coffin chewed an olive. "Plotz?" he said.

"Maybe. Hard to tell from this distance. Who else?"

"Let's find out," Coffin said. "You stay here—in front of the window, but don't look out. Pretend you're talking to me. I'm going out the back."

"Frank," Lola said, "maybe you should take a weapon."

Coffin dug in the hall closet and pulled the Colt out of its shoe box. He made sure the safety was on and tucked the pistol into his waistband.

"'Atta boy," Lola said.

Coffin slipped out the back door and circled the house, stepping through a weed-choked flowerbed. The yard hadn't been mowed in weeks; the grass was tall and going to seed. The stars were bright little rends in the night sky, lamplight behind a moth-holed curtain.

The man in the truck was slumped down, smoking a cigarette. As quietly as he could, Coffin duckwalked to the driver's door from the rear, keeping low, out of view of the side mirror. He could see Lola clearly through the kitchen window, her back to the street. He slipped the Colt from his belt and stood up, holding the pistol down at his side.

The man in the truck started, dropped his lit cigarette into his lap, fumbled, then recovered it. "Jesus Christ, Frankie," he said. "You scared the fuck out of me."

"Hello, Rudy. I thought maybe you were someone else."

"That's twice, you stealthy son of a bitch. You trying to give a guy a heart attack or what?"

"You could knock on the door, like a normal person."

Uncle Rudy gestured at Coffin's window. "I was waiting for Brunhilda to leave. Who's she talking to in there, anyway?"

"Nobody." Coffin put the Colt back in his waistband and leaned against the truck. He waved to Lola. She waved back, then moved away from the window.

"So, are you back?" Coffin said. "Or haven't you left yet?"

Rudy grinned. "You're pissed," he said. "Because of that stuff about Duarte and the drugs."

"Sure I'm pissed," Coffin said. "I had to look at Dogfish without any pants on. *And* I had to ride in a boat with that maniac Teddy Goulet. Who wouldn't be pissed?"

"Of all the things to have a phobia about, you had to pick boats. The son of a fisherman. Your dad never got over it."

"Thanks for bringing that up," Coffin said.

"I was just trying to change the subject," Rudy said. He took a flask from the glove compartment, drank from it, and offered it to Coffin. Coffin took a short sip, then another, longer swallow.

"Bad about Louie," Coffin said.

"Real bad. I'd love to get my hands on the son of a bitch that shot him."

"Me, too. As opposed to the guy they arrested."

Rudy laughed, then coughed and spat out the window. "Guy keeps a sign in his yard for ten years that says Louie's a son of a bitch. Then he goes and wallops him with a fish—not that Louie didn't deserve it. Then a few days later, Louie shows up dead. Who do you think they're going to arrest?"

"They planted a gun in Kotowski's house."

Rudy shrugged and took another drink from the flask. "Of course they did," he said, wiping his sleeve across his mouth. "Juries like it when there's evidence."

Coffin lit a cigarette. The smoke felt good in his lungs. "What was Louie up to, Rudy? What was he doing with a briefcase full of cash and a gun?"

"Damned if I know," Rudy said, "but you can bet your ass he was up to something."

Coffin turned and squinted at his uncle through a trail of cigarette smoke. "Where's *your* gun, Rudy? You carry a Glock, right?"

Rudy patted his jacket pocket. "Got it right here. Old Faithful."

"Let's see it."

Rudy scowled. "What the fuck. You don't believe me?"

"Nope."

"God damn it, I told you it's right here in my—" Rudy paused. He dug his big hand into his pocket. "Huh. I must've left it at Tony's."

"Why did Louie need your gun, Rudy?" Coffin said. "Who was he afraid of?"

Rudy snorted a laugh. "Hell—that's easy. The same crazy motherfucker everybody else is afraid of. And for good reason, as it turns out. What a stupid-ass question."

"Rudy." Coffin patted the big man's cheek. "Louie's dead. Whatever he was paying you to keep quiet about? He's not going to pay you any more. Right?"

Rudy snuffled. A single tear glistened on his cheek. He wiped it away. "I loved that little cocksucker like a brother," Rudy said.

Coffin nodded. "He was good people, considering what a slimeball he was."

They were silent a little while. Then Coffin said, "So why don't you help me catch the guy that killed him? We both know it wasn't Kotowski."

Rudy emptied the flask and stuffed it back in the glove compartment. "You're right," he said. "Who am I protecting?"

"Tell me abut REIC."

"They were working on a big real estate deal. The Project."

"Kotowski's house—is that it? What was Louie planning to do, tear it down and build condos?"

242 | Jon Loomis

"You're thinking way too small."

Coffin stood in silence for a minute. The crickets sawed around him. The air smelled like night and fog. "Well, there's the lot where the old A&P used to be—"

"Keep going."

"There's that swampy mess around Shank Painter Pond."

"And?"

"Across the highway, off the Province Lands Road?"

"You're barely scratching the surface."

"Jesus," Coffin said. "What else?"

Rudy opened the truck door, swung his legs out. "You name it. Half the town. They had a list of the properties they were after as long as your arm."

"They? Who's they? And where do I find this list?"

"They is all the dead people. Merkin, Duarte, Hench, and Louie. They were all partners."

"That's it? They're all dead?"

"Those are all the ones I know for sure, but I think there's at least one more."

Coffin had to stop himself from grabbing Rudy by the lapels. "Okay," he said. "Who's the one more?"

"That gay guy—the consultant. You know, the one with the great hair."

"Phipps? Jesus. That explains the attitude. What about this list—where do I find it?"

"It's in Louie's office somewhere. But the real smoking gun is the tapes."

"You're kidding me," Coffin said. "There are tapes?"

Rudy grinned. "Turns out Louie's office has been bugged for a couple of years now. The system kind of reactivated itself when I got back to town. I haven't listened to everything, but there's some very interesting material on those tapes. You're on a couple of them, too—funny stuff, Frankie."

"You bugged Louie's office? Your own cousin?"

Rudy chuckled. "First rule of politics," he said. "Whatever you've got on your enemies, make sure you've got twice as much on your friends. You should read Machiavelli."

Coffin rubbed his temples. His head felt too small for his brain suddenly. "So where are these tapes?"

"Safe deposit box. Fishermen's Bank."

"To which you have the key."

"The key is in a safe place," Rudy said.

"My mother's duck!" Coffin said. "Jesus—I *knew* there was something going on with that duck." His face darkened. "Who knows about that key besides you?"

"Nobody. Not even your mother—she thinks the duck's full of heroin."

"I don't get it," Coffin said, shaking his too-small head. "What's the percentage in buying up a bunch of existing properties? What were they going to do, tear down half the town and build *condos*? That's just crazy."

"Ah, Grasshoppa," Rudy said, doing a bad Chinese accent. "You are wise beyond your years, and yet you are foolish." He plunked a big hand onto Coffin's shoulder and squeezed. "Condo farms. Mc-Mansions. Hotels. Luxury rentals. The full catastrophe," he said.

"What if people decided not to sell?" Coffin said, squirming out of Rudy's grasp. "Like Kotowski. Wouldn't that screw everything up?"

"I don't know all the details." Rudy shrugged. "But Louie acted like they had it all figured out."

Coffin said nothing for a while. He smoked his cigarette almost down to the filter and flipped the butt toward a storm sewer grate.

"Why do you suppose the killer towed Louie's car into Conwell Marsh?"

Rudy shrugged. "Maybe 'cause Louie owned the goddamn thing. That'd be my guess."

"The marsh? He did?"

Rudy nodded. "Owned it for years. Dumbest fucking thing he ever did. About three days after he bought it, the state EPA declared it a fragile fucking wetland. I never laughed so hard in my life."

"Doesn't seem quite so funny now," Coffin said.

"No, it doesn't."

They were quiet for a minute; then Rudy nodded toward the house. "Does the Amazon princess like boys?"

"No. Sorry."

Rudy cocked an eyebrow. "You should be. And here I thought you were bangin' her."

"Hate to disappoint you."

"Ha. Bullshit," Rudy said. He leaned toward Coffin and poked him in the ribs with his forefinger. "You're going to go interrogate that consultant guy, aren't you?"

"Yes," Coffin said.

"I'm going with you."

"You absolutely are not coming with us. No."

"You might need some muscle, Frankie. I may be getting older, but I'm still pretty fucking scary."

"I've got a better idea," Coffin said, poking Rudy back. "Go get that goddamn duck of yours out of my mother's room. I can't believe you'd leave a thing like that with her."

"Are you kidding me?" Rudy laughed. "She was thrilled. Most exciting thing that's happened to her in years."

———

"It wasn't Plotz," Coffin said, stepping onto his screen porch. He took the Colt from his waistband and set it on an end table, next to a withered avocado plant.

Lola sat on the wooden swing, deep in shadow. "I saw," she said. "Who was that guy? He looked like an older version of Tony."

"His dad. Older, smarter, and a hell of a lot scarier." Coffin sat down in the crackling wicker chair. "But you didn't see him here. Okay?"

Lola nodded, blond ponytail bobbing. "Sure. None of my business."

"None of Mancini's business," Coffin said. He scratched his chin. "Know anything about real estate law?"

Lola pushed off with her heels and the porch swing glided slowly back and forth, creaking a bit on its two chains. "The basics," she said. "Three semesters of law school, remember?"

"Okay," Coffin said. "Tell me something: Let's say you want to buy my house, tear it down, and build a bunch of condos on the lot. But I don't want to sell. How do you get me to hand over the property?"

"Aside from offering you way more than the place is worth?"

"Let's say I won't sell at any price."

"I'd harass you. I'd buy the place next door and play loud music all night. I'd call animal control and bitch about your cat. I'd file all sorts of complaints with the health department and the building inspector and see if I couldn't get your place condemned."

"Let's say you tried that, and I whacked you with a fish until you said uncle."

Lola thought for a minute, then snapped her fingers. "I'd get my buddies in city government to eminent domain your ass. Try and stop me."

"Eminent domain," Coffin said. He slapped himself on the forehead. "ED."

"ED!" Lola clapped her hands. "The supreme court said it's okay to seize private property through eminent domain and turn it over to developers. *ED Test*—Kotowski was going to be the test case."

"Jesus Christ," Coffin said, sitting on the couch, stretching his legs out in front of him. "How could they get away with it? People would go nuts. There'd be protests and lawsuits out the ying-yang."

"They didn't care," Lola said. "They thought they had the angles covered."

Coffin looked at his watch. "Where the hell is Jamie?"

On cue, Jamie's Volvo chugged around the corner and pulled up in front of the house. Jamie climbed out and retrieved a bag of groceries from the backseat. "Who wants to carry in the laundry?" she said.

Grinning, Coffin walked to the car. "You brought food," he said, kissing Jamie on the cheek.

"Everything at the fish market was overpriced," Jamie said, "but I got some kalamata olives at Stop N Shop, and some great-looking Vermont cheddar."

After Jamie had poured a glass of wine and snacked on olives and cheese, Coffin told her that he and Lola had to go out for a while.

"It's not good that we're leaving you here by yourself," he said, "but I think it's more secure than your apartment." He locked the front door, turning the key in its old, corroded lock. Then he walked through the house, latching all the windows on the ground floor. "We'll go out the back. Make sure you lock the door after we leave," he said. "Keep the phone with you. If anything weird happens, call the police right away."

"You own a gun, right?" Jamie said.

"Of course I own a gun."

Jamie put her hand out. "So fork it over."

"Not so fast," Coffin said. "Have you even looked at a gun up close before?"

Jamie smiled. "My daddy loved three things in this life," she said. "Dogs, guns and Jack Daniel's whiskey. I've been shooting handguns since I was twelve. Bet I can shoot better'n you, Buffalo Bill."

Lola grinned. "Who can't?" she said.

Coffin retrieved his Colt from the porch. "It's an automatic," he said. "The safety's on."

Jamie took the pistol, popped the clip, and ejected a shell from the chamber. "Wow. Colt .45, World War II vintage. Nice piece. Blow a hole in you the size of a dinner plate. Where'd you get this thing?"

"It was my dad's."

Jamie hugged Coffin. "You're very sweet to worry," she said, "but give me a large-caliber handgun, and I can take care of myself just fine."

Chapter 29

It was almost midnight, and the upper floors of Town Hall were dark and deserted. Lola held a small flashlight while Coffin unlocked Louie's office door.

"Where'd you get the key?" Lola whispered.

"Master set," Coffin said, pushing the door open. "Picked them up when I was acting chief. Figured they might come in handy someday."

Coffin followed Lola into the office and shut the door behind them. "You do the file cabinet," Coffin said. "I'll get the desk."

"Can you see okay?" Lola said.

Coffin took a small leather case from his pocket and unzipped it. He took out a slender lock pick and set the case on the desk. "I'm fine—there's enough light from the street."

"Shit," Lola said. "It's locked."

"Hang on. Almost got it . . ." Coffin worked the pick in the desk's small lock for a few seconds, then pulled the upper drawer open.

"Wow, Frank," Lola said. "Hidden talents. Where'd you learn to do that?"

"Baltimore. My ex-wife had a nasty habit of changing the locks when she got mad at me. Hold the light right here."

Coffin slid the pick into the file cabinet's lock and wiggled it gently. " 'Atta baby," he said, withdrawing the pick. "All set."

Lola opened a file drawer. "My internal Nancy Drew is very impressed," Lola said.

"I'm just showing off," Coffin said. "You could pick these things with a paper clip."

"Remind me what I'm looking for exactly," Lola said, riffling through the files.

"Development, REIC, the Moors, the Project, and/or eminent domain," Coffin said, turning to the desk. "Well, now—what have we here?"

"Find something?"

"More cash. Lots of it. And something that looks like an account book." Coffin thumbed through the small blue book. "It appears to be a very meticulous record of the bribes Louie was handing out, with amounts, names, and dates. My, my."

"Anybody interesting?" Lola said.

"Oh, yeah. State EPA, a couple of judges—among about two dozen others. Interesting indeed."

"Dogs, Feral," Lola said, flipping through the files. "Decorations, Christmas; Development. Here we go." She pulled a thick file from the drawer and handed it to Coffin.

"Jesus," Coffin said, opening the file on the desk and flipping through its contents. "What *is* all this stuff?" He held up a document typed on letterhead. "Here, you speak legalese."

Lola peered at the letter in the small, bright circle cast by her flashlight. "It's a legal opinion," she said. "Fancy law firm in Boston.

Looks like a thumbs-up on eminent domain. 'It is our opinion that the invocation of eminent domain in order to undertake the selective redevelopment of Provincetown's blighted areas would not encounter significant legal impediments.' "

"Blighted areas," Coffin said. "The slums of Provincetown."

Lola held a finger to her lips. Someone in sneakers was walking down the hallway toward Louie's office. The sneakers made soft squelching sounds on the polished terrazzo.

"Fuck," Coffin hissed. He stuffed the Development folder into Louie's desk. There was no place to hide. Lola clicked off her flashlight and stationed herself beside the door, back flat against the wall. Coffin crouched behind the desk.

A wavering flashlight beam shone through the frosted glass in Louie's door. A key slid into the lock, and the doorknob turned. A man dressed entirely in black slipped into the office and shut the door softly behind him.

Lola took two steps away from the wall and kicked him hard in the crotch.

"Haaa—" the man said, doubling over and clutching his groin. "Aaaa, God—" His flashlight dropped to the floor and rolled under the desk.

"Get on your belly and put your hands behind your back," Lola said. "Or I'll kick you in the nads again."

The man looked up. In the light from the street Coffin could see his face. It was Brandon Phipps.

"You dyke bitch," Phipps said, straightening up. "I'm going to rip your f—"

Lola kicked him in the crotch again, and Phipps crumpled like a salted slug.

"Ow," Coffin said, wincing. "Man. My balls want to crawl up inside my chest cavity when you do that."

"Haaargh—" said Phipps, curled in the fetal position on the floor.

"Not much point in hitting men in the head," Lola said. "Y'all got these tiny brains and big, thick skulls." She rolled Phipps onto his belly. With a knee in his back, she pulled a pair of handcuffs from her belt and clicked them shut on his sturdy, well-toned wrists.

"So what brings you here at this time of night, Brandon?" Coffin said, half-sitting on Louie's desk. "You wouldn't be looking for large amounts of cash, would you? Or planning a little late-night document shredding, maybe?"

"Faakkk—" said Phipps, still trying to catch his breath.

"The black outfit's a very nice touch, by the way. And the flashlight. Stylish, but incriminating if you get caught."

"This is outrageous," Phipps spluttered. He coughed, then groaned. "You can't prove anything."

"Our word against yours, Brandon."

Lola set a booted foot on Phipps's head. Her heel rested on his cheek, the ball of her foot on his ear.

"All right," said Phipps. "What do you want?"

"A little conversation is all."

"Tell her to stop standing on my head."

"Let's talk about the Project first—then we'll see about your head."

"What project?" Phipps said.

Lola shifted her weight.

"Aarrr—" said Phipps. "All right—I heard things, but I wasn't involved."

Lola leaned harder.

"Aaarrrr!" Phipps said.

"He sounds like a pirate," Coffin said.

"Brandon Phipps, the gay blade," Lola said.

"Just because I'm well groomed doesn't mean I'm gay," Phipps said.

Lola frowned. "You're not gay? Really?"

252 | Jon Loomis

"You're not just involved," Coffin said. "You're a partner."

Lola leaned on Phipps's head.

"Not a full partner!" Phipps said. "I just worked for them! I was in charge of the visioning process!"

"Visioning process?" Coffin said.

"Right. My job was to finalize the optimal decisioning about which properties to target. It had to be done carefully, gradually, but also coherently—just buying up random properties wouldn't fully maximize the— Aaarrr!"

"Speak English," Lola said.

"What properties were you going after, exactly?"

"I don't know. Lots."

Coffin nodded, and Lola ground her heel on Phipps's cheek.

"Arrrr!" Phipps said. "Jesus! I'm not lying—I don't know off the top of my head. There were a lot. But there's a list."

Coffin raised his eyebrows. "A list," he said. "And where would we find that? It doesn't seem to be in Louie's file."

"I have it," Phipps said. "In my office. Filed under Real Estate Acquisitioning, Prospective. I'll go get it for you."

"No you won't," Coffin said. "Stay here and entertain Officer Winters with your pirate imitation. I'll get it."

Five minutes later, Coffin returned with the file. Lola took her foot off of Phipps's head. She removed the handcuffs and helped him into a sitting position against the wall.

"Thank you," Phipps said, a little breathlessly.

Coffin rifled through the file quickly, then pulled out the list. It was several pages long and stapled to a detailed map of Provincetown, liberally marked in green highlighter. Lola peered over his shoulder.

"My God," she said, pointing to an address on the list. "That's my building."

"My whole neighborhood," Coffin said, looking at the map. "Parts of the waterfront—there's Kotowski's house, and Souza's

Boatyard—Souza's not going to be too happy about that. Jesus—
the nursing home. A bunch of land across the highway, like Rudy
said. A big chunk of the cemetery . . ."

"Look," Lola pointed. "The Fine Art Center. And the lumber-
yard."

"A fourth of the town, at least," Coffin said. "Maybe a third."

Coffin prodded Phipps with his toe. "Who else is involved?"

"They're all dead," he said.

"That's not what I hear," Coffin said, nodding at Lola.

She took two steps toward Phipps.

"Okay, okay—there may still be one or two silent partners. From
out of town, like Merkin," Phipps said. "The local people were Silva,
Hench, and Duarte."

Lola frowned. "How'd a dead-end guy like Duarte get a piece of
the pie?"

Phipps shrugged. "He wasn't a full partner. He was a wage
slave, like me. He worked fast and he kept his mouth shut. He was
desperate for the money."

"You might be next on the developers-to-whack list, you know,"
Coffin said.

"I suppose it's possible," Phipps said, paling a bit beneath his tan.
His eyes narrowed. "Thank God that lunatic Kotowski's in jail."

Coffin gathered up the Project paperwork and stuffed it back in
its folder. "Maybe you're really dumb enough to believe Kotowski's the killer," he said. "Maybe not. Either way, if I were you,
I'd check under the bed before I went to sleep at night."

"We should caution Mr. Phipps not to leave town," Lola said.

Coffin stood. "Don't leave town," he said. "The state police will
want to talk to you, as soon as they're done chasing their tails."

Phipps touched the swelling bruise on his cheek. "I haven't
done anything illegal," he said, "and the killer's in jail. Why would
I want to leave town?"

"Phipps is going to bolt, isn't he?" Lola said as she and Coffin trotted down the stairs. "And there's nothing we can do about it."

Coffin grinned. "Oh ye of little faith. Let's stop by my office—I want to make a quick phone call."

Chapter 30

Jamie held her hand under the bathtub faucet. The cascading water was deliciously hot. She adjusted the mix a bit—she didn't want to scald herself—then poured in some organic bubble bath and watched it foam in Frank's big clawfoot tub. Downstairs, both doors were locked and the windows were latched. Frank's gun was on the bathroom counter, three feet away. She felt entirely safe. She took a sip of wine, slipped out of her yoga pants, top, and underwear. Because the tub was running, she didn't hear the small, sharp sound of glass breaking downstairs.

"You hungry?" Coffin said as they climbed into Lola's Camaro.

"Starved." Lola turned the key, and the engine roared to life.

Coffin looked at his watch. "Who's still serving at 12:53 A.M.?"

"E Pluribus," Lola said. "World's greasiest."

Coffin grimaced. "It'll be mobbed. How about Billy's?"

"The Ptomaine Palace?" Lola said. "Pretty scary, if you ask me."

"Oh, come on. It's a relic—practically the last remnant of old

Provincetown. It ought to have one of those historic markers out front."

"It's a dump. Do they have anything besides oysters?"

"Sure. Billy can fry up a burger for you, if you want, and the lobster rolls are good."

"Okay," Lola said, "but I'd better not regret this in the morning."

Standing at the window, Phipps watched Coffin and Lola climb into her ridiculous muscle car. After a minute or two the car's lights flicked on and they drove away.

Phipps sat in Louie's chair and picked up the phone. He dialed 9, then the number for Billy's Oyster Shack. The phone rang three times before Billy picked it up.

"They know," Phipps said, brushing the bruised side of his face with his fingertips.

"Who the fuck is they?" said Billy.

"Coffin and that what's-her-name. That dyke. They know about the Project. They have the files. The list of properties. Everything."

"That's just great," Billy said. "What the fuck. How'd they find out?"

"I don't know. That's not the point. The point is, you have to get rid of them. They have to disappear."

"Hold on," Billy said.

Phipps heard a clunk as he put the phone down. Then Billy shouted, "Closing time! Get the fuck out!" Phipps heard muffled grumbling in the background, and then Billy said, "It's closing time when I say it's closing time. Get the fuck out!" There was a brief silence before Billy picked up the phone again.

"Do they know about me?" he said.

"I don't know. I don't think so, but we need to make sure they don't find out."

"Who's going to tell them?" Billy said. "You?"

"Your place is on the list," Phipps said. "How long before they guess that the person responsible for the killings might be an angry homeowner—another nut like that Kotowski? All they have to do is go through the list and check everyone's alibi. Sooner or later, they come to you."

Another silence. "Well, what do you know," Billy said. "You'll never guess who just pulled into the parking lot."

"They have to disappear," Phipps said. "No bodies this time. If you do it right, we're home free."

"I can't believe you let them get their hands on that list," Billy said. There was a sound like glasses clinking together. "That was not a good thing to do."

"I couldn't help it," Phipps said. His chest felt tight. Beads of sweat had popped out on his forehead.

"You fucked up," Billy said. "Big time."

"But—" Phipps said. The line clicked and went dead.

The tub was wonderful—the water was deep and very hot. Jamie felt the muscles in her neck and back unkinking. She'd dimmed the lights and lit a candle. Her glass of chardonnay sat on the toilet seat, within arm's reach. The bathroom was wreathed in lavender-scented steam. Her apartment only had a shower stall—an amenities disaster of the first order. There could be no civilization, Jamie thought, without the occasional soak. She slid down in the tub until the water came up to her earlobes. She closed her eyes and sighed.

There was a sound. A faint creak from the staircase, beyond the closed bathroom door, at the end of the upstairs hallway. Jamie opened her eyes. It was the kind of sound old houses make on their own—a settling sound, a small groan of contentment or boredom. She closed her eyes and stretched her legs out under the water, and there was the sound again—in the hallway. She sat up.

"Frank?" she called. "Is that you?"

The bathroom door flew open. Jamie shrieked, covered her breasts with her arms, and tried to press herself flat against the tub's hard curve. Duffy Plotz stood in the doorway. Something slender and bright flicked open in his right hand. "Hi, honey," he said. "I'm home!"

Chapter 31

Billy's was empty. The stools had been turned upside down on top of the bar. Billy limped behind a push broom, his crooked body listing to starboard. When the screen door opened, he said "We're closed. Go home," without looking up from his work.

"Go home!" shrieked Captain Nickerson, swinging frantically in his cage.

"That's no way to treat the regulars," Coffin said, taking an upside-down stool from the bar, setting it on the floor, sitting down.

"Fuck the regulars," said Billy, grinning and leaning on his broom. "What brings you two out at this hour?"

"Starvation," Lola said.

"If we're not too late," Coffin said.

"Of course you're too late." Billy locked the door, turned out the overhead lights, and unplugged the neon beer signs in the front window. "But nothing's too big a pain in the ass for Province-town's finest. What'll it be?"

"Can I get a cheeseburger?" Lola said. "Onion and tomato?"

"Want it bloody or burnt?" Billy said. "I can't promise anything in between."

"Burnt."

"Frankie?"

"Shot of the monster," Coffin said, "and one for my friend here."

Billy retrieved the bottle of Old Loch Ness and poured two hefty shots.

"Not imbibing?" Coffin said.

"Let me cook the lady's burger," Billy said. "Then I'll have a drink with you." He disappeared into the kitchen.

Lola sipped her scotch. "Hoo-wah. That's potent."

Coffin told her the story about his grandfather's last run. Then he poured himself another shot.

"What do you think the odds are," Lola said, "that our killer lives in one of the highlighted sections of the map?"

"Overwhelming," Coffin said. "Unless it's Phipps, trying to cut himself a bigger piece of the pie."

Lola sipped her scotch, made a face. "You don't believe he was just working for a salary?"

"No way. If he knew about ED, they had no choice. They had to make him a partner, just to shut him up."

"Do you think he killed them?"

Coffin shrugged. "Maybe. He'd have to be crazy, or the greediest man in history. He was going to get extremely rich anyway, if things worked out."

"Maybe he didn't want to take a chance it *wouldn't* work out," Lola said. "Maybe he just wanted to take the partners' money and run."

"Maybe," Coffin said, "but does Phipps seem like a guy that would crucify someone?"

Lola shook her head. "I don't know. I mean, does anybody? Assuming they're not actually foaming at the mouth?"

"Show us your tits," muttered Captain Nickerson.

"This parrot obviously hangs around a lot of sensitive intellectual types," Lola said.

"It was my father's."

"Sorry," Lola said.

Coffin waved the apology away. "Ready?" he said, holding the bottle over Lola's glass.

She covered the glass with her hand. "I'm good," she said. "Shouldn't drink too much on an empty stomach. I already feel a little woozy."

Coffin nodded. "Me, too," he said, downing his shot. "But when don't I?" He fished a cigarette from the pack in his shirt pocket. He tried to light it, but the cigarette slipped from his fingers and fell on the bar. "Weird," he said, looking at his hands. "My fingers are kind of numb."

Billy came back from the kitchen and refilled Coffin's glass. "Food'll be out in a minute. Thought you quit," he said, holding a match while Coffin puffed at the cigarette.

"There's quitting, and then there's quitting," Coffin said.

"I feel funny," Lola said.

"Better drink up," Billy said, filling her glass with scotch. "It'll fix what ails you."

Coffin felt as though he were slowly rising out of his body. The room glowed a soft magenta. "I can't feel my legs," he said. The lit cigarette fell from his fingers.

"So," Billy said. "A priest, a rabbi, two lawyers, a midget, a lesbian, and a talking dog walk into a bar. Bartender says, 'What is this—a joke?'"

"I feel really weird," Lola said.

"I got another one," Billy said. "How many Republicans does it take to screw in a lightbulb?"

Coffin felt himself rising. The smoke-yellowed ceiling tiles warped into a long vertical tunnel, and Coffin levitated toward it. He looked back and saw his body sitting on its stool, next to Lola. Billy was talking.

"Nine. One to blame Clinton for not changing the lightbulb before it burned out. One to deregulate the lightbulb industry. One to claim that anyone who doesn't support changing the lightbulb is in league with the terrorists. One to go on *Meet the Press* and say that the lightbulb changers will be greeted as liberators. One to give Halliburton a billion-dollar contract to change the lightbulb. And three to explain to Bush that you don't really screw *in* the lightbulb."

"Weird . . ." whispered Lola.

"Frankie! Frankie! Frankie!" yelled Captain Nickerson.

Coffin felt himself being drawn into the tunnel. It was dark and very long, but at its end Coffin could see a brilliant magenta light. He felt as though he might have died—he wasn't sure he was breathing. The thought of his death did not alarm him. He was serene. He was the essence of being. He was love. He was godlike.

"Shit," Billy said. "That's only eight. I forgot one. I must be losing it." He waved a hand in front of Coffin's face. Coffin's eyes followed it for a moment, then drifted off.

"Whoa," Lola said. "The colors."

Billy shook his head, swabbing at the bar with the greasy rag. "I'll forget my own ass if things get any worse." He refilled Lola's glass, grinning with his big yellow teeth. "Drink up, honey," he said.

"No," Lola said.

"Now, be a good girl," Billy said, holding the glass to Lola's lips. "Drink up."

Lola clamped her lips shut, and the whiskey spilled down her chin.

"Fine," Billy said. "You want to do it the hard way, that's okay by me." He went into the kitchen. The back door opened. Lola tried to get up from the stool, but her feet got tangled and she and the stool fell sideways onto the floor. She struggled to her knees and was trying to pull herself upright with both hands on the bar when Billy returned, carrying a length of two-by-four.

"And where do you think *you're* going, young lady?" Billy said, swinging the two-by-four hard at Lola's head. It struck squarely and made a hollow cracking sound, like a bowling ball dropped onto a concrete floor. Lola collapsed, arms and legs sprawled out. Billy left again and came back a minute later, pushing a wheelbarrow.

Coffin's tunnel turned and looped, and then he felt himself falling headfirst into darkness, falling at great speed. He wanted to cry out but couldn't open his mouth—couldn't produce a sound. He was no longer godlike, no longer a shimmering column of pale magenta light. He looked back at his body, slumped on its bar stool; beside him, Billy was standing over Lola. Coffin felt hugely dizzy—his head had filled with buzzing snow. The room began to spin and warp, and then something very hard hit him in the nose.

The bathroom was small. Duffy Plotz seemed to take up most of it. There was only one door, opposite a small frosted-glass window that was twenty feet above the backyard.

"Jesus, Duffy," Jamie said, fanning herself with one hand. "You scared the crap out of me."

"Good," Duffy said. "I meant to."

"Well, nice going, then." Jamie tried not to look at the gun, gleaming dully on the countertop. She wondered how badly she'd be cut if she tried to grab it. The bright blade in Plotz's hand appeared to belong to an old-fashioned straight razor.

"You want me," Duffy said. "I know you do." He picked up the gun almost absently and stuck it in his belt.

Jamie looked up at him from the bathtub. Her heart was racing wildly. "Yes," she said. "Yes, I do. Why don't you take your clothes off and get in here with me?"

"No," Plotz said. "You get out. I want to look at you."

"Great," Jamie said. Her legs felt weak and quivery as she climbed out of the tub. "I was getting all pruney anyway." She stood on the bath mat, naked and dripping.

Plotz stared wide-eyed and said nothing.

"Look, I don't mean to break the spell or anything, but could you hand me a towel? I'm getting a little cold."

Duffy leaned to reach for a towel, and Jamie lunged against him, slamming her hip into his groin and grabbing his right wrist with both hands. Plotz grunted, stumbled back against the doorframe. He tried to slap her away with his free hand, but she twisted and ducked. Then she pulled the hand that held the razor close to her face and bit him as hard as she could.

Plotz screamed and dropped the bright blade. Jamie shoved him, pulled the gun from his belt, and ran down the hallway. She tasted blood in her mouth. She was still dripping wet, and the wooden floor was slick—if she fell, Plotz would be on her in an instant. She took the stairs as fast as she could, Plotz's big shoes clattering behind her.

"It's a damn shame it has to come to this, Frankie," Billy said, breathing hard as he shoved Coffin into the passenger seat of his pickup truck. "A damn shame. We go back a long ways, your family and me." He slammed the door and pushed the wheelbarrow back toward the restaurant. Coffin fell and fell down an endless hole, unable to speak or move.

Billy went into the restaurant and stood for a minute, looking at Lola and thinking. He bent down and pulled up the hem of her T-shirt. No gun in her waistband—but there was a pair of handcuffs. He checked her pockets and found the key. Then he pulled up her pant legs, and there it was—a .38-caliber snub-nose, tucked into her boot. He pulled the gun out, checked the safety, and stuck it in his pocket. He felt Lola's pulse at her neck—it seemed steady, a little fast. A trickle of blood oozed from her scalp. He rolled her over and handcuffed her wrists behind her back.

"Just to be on the safe side, honey pie," Billy said. He picked her up and heaved her into the wheelbarrow. She was surprisingly heavy.

Billy dumped the lady cop into the bed of the pickup, covered her with a ratty blue tarp, and pinned the corners of the tarp with concrete blocks. She lay very still. He flipped the wheelbarrow over and slid it into the truck, handles first, next to Lola. Then he went to the shed behind the restaurant and came back with a coil of thick nylon rope. He tossed the rope into the truck bed, slammed the tailgate shut, climbed into the cab, and started the engine.

"This hurts me, Frankie," Billy said, lighting a cigarette. "It truly does. I always liked you, and you know how I felt about your old man. But there's just a couple of loose ends, Frankie. And one of them's you." Billy turned left out of the parking lot, onto Shank Painter Road. The A&P and the liquor store were closed. The big asphalt parking lot was deserted.

Coffin was a point of energy in a vast, rotating universe of color and light. Other entities were there, too—pure fireflies of being, adrift in a metaphysical milky way. They were trying to communicate with him telepathically. They were trying to tell him something important.

There was hardly any traffic. Billy turned right onto Bradford Street and headed up the hill. Muscle Beach—the men's gym—was still open. Through the big front window, Billy could see a single devoted soul chugging away on a treadmill. Billy cranked the wheel at the top of the hill and made a left on Pleasant Street.

On the harbor side of Commercial, Pleasant Street became a

narrow alley between two shops, then petered out altogether, stopping at a rusting gate in a fence made of sheet metal and steel bars. Billy got out of the truck, keyed open the gate's heavy padlock, drove the truck through, got out again, closed the gate, and snapped the lock shut.

The moon was high. Souza's Boatyard was a maze of rusting engine blocks and the hulls of a half-dozen fishing boats, all in various stages of disrepair, all slowly subsiding into the earth. In the moonlight the place was ghostly; a chill ran down Billy's neck as he parked at the foot of a small, dilapidated wharf. He took a pint of whiskey from his pocket, uncapped it, and drank.

Jamie made the living room three steps ahead of Plotz, who stumbled and cursed as he chased her down the narrow staircase. She sprinted for the front door, past the leering goat's head, dodging through the dark living room with its maze of straight-backed chairs and occasional tables.

Plotz paused at the bottom of the stairs and tilted his head, as if he were listening.

The front door wouldn't open. The key was stuck in the stubborn old lock. "Fuck," Jamie said, desperately rattling the key. "Fuck!"

She turned; Plotz was barreling toward her, his face twisted with rage. She raised the gun and fired just as Plotz crashed into a spindly Victorian table occupied by two ceramic rabbits and a silver music box shaped like a toad. The gunshot was colossally loud in the low-ceilinged room. Half of the stuffed goat's face exploded into drifting hair and sawdust.

"You shot me!" Plotz said, sprawled in the wreckage of the table, the rabbits, and the toad. "You bitch!"

"No I didn't," Jamie said. Her ears were ringing. "But I wish I had. And I *will* shoot you, if you don't get the fuck out of here."

Plotz raised his hands, palms out. "Jesus Christ," he said. "Why are all the cute ones psycho?" He struggled to his feet.

Jamie pointed the gun at Plotz's head. "Less talking, more leaving."

Plotz slowly edged past her while she kept the gun aimed at his forehead. He unlocked the door, crossed the screen porch, and stepped onto the walk. She followed him, naked, out into the street, holding the gun in both hands. He climbed into his borrowed Toyota and started the engine. The beige sedan pulled away from the curb, then accelerated down the street. Jamie leveled the Colt and fired, punching a dime-sized hole in the trunk. Applause and raucous laughter erupted from a house across the street.

A group of women dressed in shorts and T-shirts stood on the big front porch, around a keg of beer.

"You go, girl," one of them called.

"Nice shootin', honey," said a heavyset redhead.

Jamie waved away the gunsmoke and dropped a little curtsy. Another round of cheering and applause broke out. "Want a beer?" one of the women said. "Want to take a hot tub?" said the redhead.

"Thanks," said Jamie, trotting back to Coffin's house. "Maybe some other time!"

It was nearly high tide. A forty-foot lobster boat was tied to a cleat near the end of the wharf, nose pointed out, rising and falling on the slight swell. It had a small, boxy pilot house near the bow and a low, open stern, designed to allow the strings of lobster pots to pay out, one after another, into the sea. On the starboard side, there was a tall winch for retrieving the catch.

Billy climbed out of the truck and dropped the tailgate. He moved the concrete blocks aside and looked under the tarp. The lesbo-cop was still breathing, but she was pale and lay very still.

He pulled the wheelbarrow out and flipped it right way up. He dragged Lola out of the truck and into the wheelbarrow and pushed her out onto the wharf. When he got to the boat, he tipped the wheelbarrow up and dumped her onto the deck. He made another trip back to the truck for the four concrete blocks and the rope. Then, on the third trip, he pulled Coffin out of the cab and into the wheelbarrow.

"It's a hell of a note, Frankie," he said, blowing hard as he wheeled Coffin down the sagging wharf. "I guess the Coffin jinx is the real deal. All your life you tried to avoid it, but here it is, jumping up to bite you in the ass." He dumped Coffin a few feet from Lola. Then he climbed in, untied the bow line from the cleat, and pushed the boat away from the wharf.

"Jesus Christ," Billy said, standing at the wheel in the small pilot house, trying to catch his breath. "This serial murder thing is killing me." He turned the key. The big inboard throbbed to life.

Lola felt the vibration of an engine. She heard its low mutter and the sound of rushing water. She opened her eyes. She was on a boat. Her vision blurred; she could just make out the pilot house and the man at the boat's wheel. A squat, broad-shouldered man. Billy. He took a bottle from his pocket, screwed off the cap, and took a long drink.

She lay on her right side. Her head throbbed; the pain centered at a point behind her ear. Her mouth tasted like she'd been chewing a latex glove. When she closed her eyes, she still saw swirls of color, but they were faint. She watched them awhile, then opened her eyes again. She turned her head a few degrees, afraid that Billy might notice even a slight movement. She could feel the cool stainless steel jaws of handcuffs circling her wrists, pinning her arms behind her back.

Three wire-mesh lobster pots were stacked behind her. Frank lay just beyond them, his eyes and mouth open. She couldn't tell whether he was breathing or not.

The boat turned, a long slow sweep. Lola heard the plastic honk of the Long Point foghorn. They were rounding the outer break-water, she realized—leaving the harbor. The boat straightened its course, then seemed to shift gears; the engine got louder, the bow lifted, and spray blew wet and cold across the deck.

Lola flexed her left hand. She made a fist, let it go. She closed her eyes and watched the colors slowly fade to black. She wasn't sure how much time passed before the engine stopped and the boat began to drift in relative silence—the only sounds were the wind and the waves slapping against the hull. Billy stepped out of the pilot house. Lola watched him loop the coil of rope around his shoulder, then pick up a concrete block in each hand. She closed her eyes, heart beating fast. He stopped at her feet.

"Just look at Sleepin' Beauty," he said. He poked her leg with his toe. "Still out like a light. I'm gonna take care of Frankie here, and then it's your turn for a swim, honey pie." He walked on, moving easily with the motion of the boat. Lola exhaled as quietly as she could.

Billy set the concrete blocks near the winch. Then he came for Coffin and dragged him across the spray-slicked deck. Billy un-coiled the rope and measured off a few arm-lengths. He took a Buck knife from his pocket, opened the blade, and sawed at the rope.

Lola flexed her wrists. The cuffs were fairly loose, which was good. She bent a little, trying to reach for the gun in her boot, but it was no good with her hands behind her back. The effort was exhausting—she rested a minute, breathing deeply. She'd seen more than one arrested suspect slide their handcuffed wrists under their butts and pull their feet through the loops of their arms, bringing their hands from back to front; as an MP, she once watched a young soldier hop through his own cuffed arms as if they were a jump rope and run away. She rolled onto her back, got her feet under her, and lifted her butt off the deck. It wasn't easy, sliding her wrists under her buttocks—her arms weren't that long, and the cuffs cut her flesh; she felt something wet running down her fingers and knew she was bleeding.

Billy was intent on his work. He looped one end of the cut length of rope several times through the center holes of the two concrete blocks before tying it off in a double square knot. Then he tied the other end around Coffin's ankles.

Lola's shoulders felt as though they might pop out of their sockets. She bit her lip against the pain. She curled her torso forward, flexed her shoulders down, and tried again, wiggling her butt and straining, and that did it—her hands were behind her knees. She pulled her feet through—her hands were in front!—and tugged at her pants leg. The .38 was gone. Billy had taken her gun.

"We got to do this the right way, Frankie," Billy said, raising his voice to make himself heard over the wind. "It's not just a matter of feeding your ass to the freakin' crustaceans. It's got to be aesthetically correct. We got to have a little ceremony. Somebody's got to say a few words, for Christ's sake." He bent over, hooking the winch line to the rope that connected Coffin to the concrete blocks. He worked the lever and the take-up wheel reversed, pulling the cable taut, slowly raising Coffin and the two blocks from the deck, letting him swing out on the winch's arm until he hung head down over the water, arms dangling.

"I dedicate the body of this man to the bottom of the sea," Billy shouted into the wind. "He's a good boy, and his old man was the salt of the freaking earth. There's worse fates than having lobsters eat your liver, although I'm fucked if I can think of any."

Lola scrambled to her feet, trying to stay out of Billy's peripheral vision. She kept low and directly behind him, moving slowly across the deck until she got within nine or ten feet. She could use both of her fists as a club, she thought, or jump on his back and use the cuffs as a crude garrote.

Billy spun around. "Mornin', honey pie!" he shouted. "Sleep well?"

Lola advanced another yard. Her vision was blurred, and she felt as though she were moving in slow motion, walking through a lake of glue.

Billy spread his arms as if he meant to embrace her. "You comin' to play with Uncle Billy, sweet cheeks? A little dance before you go swimming?" His hand dipped into his jacket pocket and came out with Lola's pistol. He grinned. "Why don't you sit down and keep still, like a good girl?"

Lola stepped on something and almost stumbled. She looked down. It was a four-foot gaff with a beautiful, gleaming hook. As she bent to pick it up, the gun cracked and a bullet whistled past her ear, punching into the bulkhead behind her. She grabbed the hook and dove to the right, sliding on her belly across the slick deck as the gun cracked again—Billy's second shot missing high, pinging off a broken lobster pot. She rolled onto her back and swung the gaff with both hands, cracking the top bone in Billy's forearm with the long handle. The gun squirted out of his hand and bounced off the gunwale, into the dark water.

"Now, God damn it," Billy said, shuffling backward a few steps, holding his forearm. "What you just did was extremely fucking impolite. Good thing I'm pumped full of hillbilly heroin, or that might have hurt old Uncle Billy."

"Let him down," Lola said, on her feet now, brandishing the hook.

"Let's see," Billy said, taking a few limping steps to his right. "Let Frankie down and go to jail, or chuck you both in the drink and go free. It's a tough one, I have to admit." He fished in his pocket with his left hand, pulled out the Buck knife, and flicked it open with a quick wrist snap. "But I think I'll take door number two, sweet cheeks."

Lola charged and swung the gaff hook at Billy's head. He ducked under its arc and slashed with the big knife. Lola stepped back. There was a long, diagonal slice in her T-shirt and a burning line of pain across her belly, from the point of her left hipbone almost to her right breast.

Billy laughed. "You may have the reach advantage," he said, "but old Uncle Billy's trouble in close."

I'm not gutted, Lola thought, touching her belly, feeling the shallow gash in her flesh. The pain was a rising, metallic taste in her mouth. *But next time, I might be.*

"Am I on a boat? I fucking hate boats!" Coffin shouted, swinging from the winch.

Billy turned, and Lola swung the gaff hook.

Billy's hands twitched. "That's no way to treat your old Uncle Billy," he said, his voice coming out watery and strange. The four-inch hook was buried in the back of his neck. The long handle wagged obscenely.

He took a step back, clawing at the gaff hook. He stumbled and fell against the winch, bumping the lever forward with his hip. The winch hiccupped and whirred, and Coffin plunged headfirst into the black water, the line paying out fast as he sank, a flurry of bubbles breaking the surface.

"That jinx of yours is a bitch, Frankie," Billy said, leaning heavily on the winch's steel frame, one hand reaching back, fingering the base of the steel hook that protruded from his neck. "Fuckin'-A—who knew a gaff hook in the neck would make you feel so weird? Talk about pins and needles—"

Lola kicked him hard in the ribs, then charged him, using her weight and the strength of her legs to deliver a mammoth shove. He toppled over the gunwale and into the ocean.

"Hang on, Frank," she said, grabbing at the winch's control lever. "Jesus Christ—hang on!"

The water glowed a deep, electric blue. It pressed Coffin's eardrums, streamed past his face. It was so cold it shut his mouth and stopped his lungs, so dense he couldn't see beyond the trail of magenta bubbles coming from his nose. There was still the bright universe of color, too, though it seemed less intense, his brain toggling back and forth between realities a thousand times a second. He felt he was being reborn, squirting through a watery birth canal. He saw his father—sinking, too, in his red armchair, hair waving like seaweed, crabs clambering one after another out of his mouth. Coffin's lungs ached. He could hear his heartbeat slowing in his chest.

Something tugged his ankles. The water stopped, then began to stream the other way, as though he were rising through it, or it was falling past him—up and down were meaningless, there was only space, darkness, the sensation of motion. He took a breath of water, and the colors dimmed—the glowing entities were long gone, taking their love and reassurance with them. He was alone and about to die. The water streamed through his clothes, his hair. And then the ocean spat him out, squeezed him from its womb and hung him, puking, in the world of air.

"God damn," Lola said, pulling Coffin into the boat. "Thought I'd lost you, Frank."

"You can't *do* this," said Brandon Phipps. A cold rain had begun to fall, and he was shivering. His right hand was cuffed to the handle of the Pilgrim Monument's locked steel door. A small Vuitton bag, embossed with the initials BRP and stuffed with cash—mostly tens and twenties—lay at his feet.

"The hell I can't," Rudy said. He was holding a very large pistol. A somewhat larger suitcase, similarly embossed and stacked to the brim with neatly wrapped bricks of hundred-dollar bills, lay in the bed of his pickup truck. "Now give me those pants."

Phipps unbelted his pants with one hand, let them drop, and stepped out of them. He bent awkwardly to pick them up. "Here," he said, holding them out.

Rudy took them, wadded them into a ball, and threw them as far as he could down High Pole Hill. The rain fell slow and cool. The Pilgrim Monument reared above them, its crenellated peak lost in fog.

"Nice underwear," Rudy said, waving the gun at Phipps's crotch. "What are those—boxer briefs?"

Phipps nodded miserably. "Calvin Klein," he said.

"Underpants for men who can't make up their minds," Rudy said. "I've always been most comfortable with boxers, myself." He put the gun in his jacket pocket and lit a cigarette. Then he walked across the monument's wide stone veranda, climbed into his blue Chevy pickup truck, and drove away.

Chapter 32

Coffin woke up from a long, troubled sleep and realized he was lying in a hospital bed, covered with blankets. He wasn't sure, at first, how he'd gotten there. He closed his eyes and remembered the ride to MacMillan Wharf on the lobster boat, Lola's T-shirt soaked in blood. He pressed the call button and asked the nurse for water, which she brought, then coffee, which she also brought, then a cigarette.

The nurse was a tall, pretty black woman named Estelle. She wagged a finger at Coffin. "You should quit, Mr. Coffin," she said.

"I have," Coffin said. "Lots of times." He asked if Lola was okay.

"She's fine. A bunch of stitches and a tetanus shot. We sent her home last night with some Vicodin."

"Why am I still here?"

"You were hypothermic. Plus, you had a *lot* of ketamine in your system. The ER doc wanted to keep an eye on you."

"What about Billy?"

"He's upstairs in the ICU," she said. "He's got some numbness on the right side of his body. Might have been the gaff hook, might have been a small stroke. We're treating him for both."

"I want to see him," Coffin said.

"You're supposed to stay in bed," Estelle said. "Until the doctor says you can get up."

"I feel fine," Coffin said. He felt a wave of nausea and dizziness as he swung his legs out from under the covers. "Fuck the doctor."

Estelle clucked her tongue. "Let me get a wheelchair. You can go, but you're not walking."

Billy lay handcuffed to his bed. He looked old and a little frail in his pale blue gown. Coffin knew better. A uniformed trooper sat in a hospital armchair beside the bed, reading a magazine.

"Detective Coffin to see the patient," Estelle said, pushing Coffin into the room.

The trooper stood up and shook Coffin's hand. "Nice work on the collar, Detective," he said.

"I had nothing to do with it," Coffin said. "Officer Winters had to save me from drowning."

"That's right," Billy said. "Frankie here was incapacitated."

"Mind waiting outside for a minute?" Coffin said.

The trooper frowned, thought for a minute. "The door stays open."

"Don't you get out of that wheelchair," Estelle said. "I mean it."

"Damn," Billy said when Estelle and the trooper had gone into the hallway. "Is that your nurse? Mine looks like a drill instructor."

"Is that you or the Viagra talking?"

Billy grinned. Then he looked down at his blanket. "I feel kind of bad about almost killing you, Frankie."

"You should," Coffin said.

"You gotta do what you gotta do. Once those dumb-asses arrested Kotowski, I was in the clear. Except for you."

"There's something I don't get," Coffin said.

"Just the one thing?"

"How'd you know about the Project? How'd you know about Merkin and Serena Hench?"

"Phipps. He came into my place about a month ago—wanted to buy it. I told him to go pound sand. Next thing I know, I've got the health inspector and the building inspector and the men's room inspector and every other goddamn inspector breathing down my neck—fining me for this, citing me for that, threatening to shut me down. So, not being a complete moron, I put one and one together."

"You went to see Mr. Phipps."

"I did. In private. Unlike our friend Kotowski."

"He told you everything."

"I was holding a very large knife to his throat at the time."

"Then he offered you a deal. He wanted to get rid of the other partners."

Billy nodded. "A big old bag of cash. He helped me set them up. He had it all figured out. Thought he did, anyway—I had a little list of my own, with his name at the bottom. The funny thing about all this is, you and the lesbo-cop saved his life. Got a cigarette?"

"They won't let me have any," Coffin said. "So you did it for the money? Killed four people?"

"Yes and no. It was a shitload of dough, and God knows they all deserved to die. What they were planning was morally offensive— legalized robbery, if you ask me. The way I see it, I'm a freakin' hero. I mean, I saved the damn town from those assholes—not that anybody around here would ever thank me, the worthless cocksuckers."

"It was a crackpot scheme," Coffin said. "It never would have worked."

"The hell it wouldn't," Billy said. "It's working all over the country. They were going to turn Provincetown into one big gated community—everything fake and tarted up like some kind of over-priced Disney World for rich queers. People like you and me wouldn't be welcome there. We couldn't afford it."

"That's one crazy white man," Estelle said, wheeling Coffin back to his room.

Coffin rubbed his chin. It was bristly and itched a little. "You were listening?"

"Of course."

"He's crazy," Coffin said, "but it's true—they were going to sell the whole town out from under us."

Estelle opened the door to Coffin's room and parked the wheel-chair beside the narrow bed. "Must be something in the water out there in P'town," she said. "Now let's get your butt back up in that bed."

Chapter 33

Jamie stood in the bedroom door, holding a breakfast tray. She wore cutoffs, a faded orange T-shirt, and an anklet made of red coral beads from Ecuador. "Look," she said. "Soup. Chicken noodle from a can—your favorite."

"And Jell-O," Coffin said. "Green, with the little oranges. Gee, thanks, honey."

"Wholesome, delicious hooves," Jamie said, smiling brightly. She put the tray over Coffin's lap and sat on the edge of the bed.

"Delightful," Coffin said.

"This is me being nurturing," Jamie said as she spread a white linen napkin across his chest. "What do you think?"

Coffin slurped soup. "You're doing a fine job," he said. "Very June Cleaver."

Jamie brushed a strand of Coffin's hair back from his forehead. "I'm not even faking it, really."

"Of course not."

They said nothing for a while. Sunlight streamed in through the bedroom window. Coffin ate soup. Jamie picked at the chenille bedspread.

"I'm thinking of getting rid of the taxidermy," Coffin said, nodding at the stuffed seagull on the wardrobe. "Tossing the goat, selling the rest of it on eBay, maybe. People collect it."

"Good God," Jamie said. "They do?"

Coffin speared a Jell-O cube with his fork and held it, jiggling, up to the light. The Jell-O seemed to glow from within, a mandarin orange segment suspended like a jewel in its green heart. He ate it.

"I don't know," Jamie said. "I kind of like them. I think you should get the goat repaired. Its eyes follow you around the room, you know—like a Velázquez painting."

"You sure? They're pretty creepy."

"But in a good way."

Coffin popped another cube of Jell-O into his mouth. "Delicious. The hospital doesn't do the fruit."

"It doesn't make sense," Jamie said, picking at the bedspread again.

"What doesn't?"

"Why didn't Billy just go to the cops—or the media? What is he, some kind of Libertarian?"

Coffin frowned. "He had prostate cancer a few years ago," he said. "They thought they got the tumor in time, but they didn't. It metastasized."

"That's not good," Jamie said.

"He says he's got a brain tumor the size of an avocado. Inoperable. Apparently it's making him pretty crazy."

Jamie dabbed at Coffin's mustache with the napkin. "Soup," she said.

"Sorry."

"I'm confused about Phipps, too," Jamie said.

"How he ended up handcuffed to the Pilgrim Monument, you mean?"

Jamie nodded.

Coffin grinned. "The Lord works in mysterious ways. As the Reverend Ron might have said."

"You have a little crush on her, don't you?"

"The nurse? Estelle? Absolutely."

"I was talking about Lola."

"Not at all," Coffin said.

"Liar." Jamie lay on her back beside him, looking up at the ceiling. "She's like a superhero or something, don't you think? I mean, when's the Lola Winters action figure coming out?"

Coffin grinned and shook his head. "Stuck a gaff hook in Billy, pulled me out of the drink, pulled *Billy* out of the drink, *and* drove the boat back to MacMillan Wharf, all while wearing handcuffs at the tail end of a ketamine trip. Make that the *Sergeant* Lola Winters action figure."

"Frank?"

"Yes?"

"How are you feeling?"

"Lucky. A little spacey from the drug, still. My ankles kind of hurt. . . ."

Jamie sat up, reached under the sheet. "How about Mr. Happy? How does he feel?"

"Suddenly much better, thanks," Coffin said, closing his eyes.

"Now that you've cheated death, don't you think that you should fully immerse yourself in life? I mean, you owe it to the universe."

"Oh, absolutely. . . ."

Jamie skinned off her shorts and pulled the sheet back. "My," she said. "They don't call him Mr. Happy for nothing."

"Hello," Coffin said. "You shaved. Everything."

"Waxed. Corinne and I went to the day spa in Chatham yesterday. It hurt like a motherfucker. It's kind of retro-cool; very 2002. I was going to surprise you."

"I'm very surprised."

"This would be a good time to say you like it."

"I like it."

She knelt at his hip, bent forward, took his erection into her mouth.

"Frank?" she said after a while.

"Yes?"

Jamie looked over her shoulder, chin cupped in her hand. "I might be ovulating," she said, raising her left eyebrow.

"Good," Coffin said.

"That's it?" Jamie said. She turned and sat up. "Good? That's all you've got to say?"

Coffin pulled her into his arms, kissed her, and rolled on top of her. "It's very good. It's *extremely* good."

Jamie opened and raised her legs, crossing her ankles behind Coffin's back. "You want to make a baby?" she said, looking into his eyes. "You've thought about this?"

"Yes." Coffin slid downward, kissing a warm trail from her throat to her clitoris.

"Remember what I said about wanting a boy?"

Coffin smiled. "Of course."

Jamie rolled onto her belly, raised her hips. She smiled. "Know what I call this pose?"

"Downward-looking yoga instructor?" Coffin said, kneeling behind her. Jamie's hair looked like spun gold, fanned across the bed.

"Downward-*facing* yoga instructor," Jamie said. "Goofball." She groaned a little as Coffin pushed into her, slowly, from behind.

———

Later, the afternoon light fading to dusk, Captain Nickerson climbed the bars of his cage in Coffin's living room. "Thar she blows!" he shrieked.

A week later, Coffin sat by his mother's bed, holding her hand while she stared at the television set.

"Dr. Phil," she snorted. "What a moron."

"He *is* kind of an idiot," Coffin said. "How can you watch this crap?"

"You know old Mrs. Sousa?" his mother said, flipping channels rapidly. "She's so daffy, she thinks she's on a goddamn cruise. They stopped trying to talk her out of it. The rest of us are stuck in this shithole, and she's on a cruise. Is that fair?"

Coffin touched the safe-deposit key in his pocket. "You don't have to be here, Ma," he said. "We could put you in a better place. Chatham, maybe. There's a really nice nursing home there. Would you like that?"

"Chatham? With a bunch of senile Republicans? Thanks for nothing."

Coffin tilted his head and looked at his mother. "How about Key West? Down by Uncle Rudy?"

"Ha!" his mother said. "Like you've got that kind of money."

"Maybe money's not a problem, Ma."

His mother stared at him for a moment, the room's fluorescent lights sparking her bright black eyes. "You don't have the balls," she said. She turned back to the television and flipped through several channels, stopping at a soap opera.

Coffin took a pamphlet out of his shirt pocket and unfolded it. "Look," he said. "Palm trees. They've got tennis courts and a pool."

"What the fuck would I do with tennis courts and a pool?" she said. "You only want me to go to Florida so you'll be rid of me, you little prick," she said. She pointed at the television screen. "Look at that girl, that dumb blond with the big tits. You'd like to fuck her, wouldn't you?"

"We've got company," Coffin said. He and Kotowski were walking slowly along Herring Cove beach, toward Hatch's Harbor. It was sunset, and the western sky was a shade of orange that Coffin couldn't name, streaked in fuchsia, dry-brushed with deep purple strips of cloud. Race Point lighthouse glowed pink in the backlight, foghorn honking its plastic bugle at precise intervals, even though there was no fog. The bay was dappled in color, sunset reflected and broken up in the mild chop, magenta on turquoise on quicksilver, kaleidoscopic. The small waves sloshed at their feet. In the distance, near the parking lot, a few tourists stood at the water's edge, but otherwise the beach was empty. The evening was surprisingly cold for early October.

"We do?" Kotowski said, leaning into the wind a little. He wore green rubber flip-flops and corduroys with patches on the knees.

Coffin pointed. A dark, wedge-shaped head bobbed in the water, ten yards out. "Harbor seal," he said. The seal watched them for a long moment with big, liquid eyes, then ducked under the waves.

They walked together awhile and didn't say anything. The waves sloshed. The foghorn honked. Forty or fifty gulls stood on the beach ahead of them, bellies gleaming pink, reflecting the sunset.

"So you're having a freaking baby," Kotowski said after a long silence. "One little brush with death and you run right out and spawn. How predictable. How embarrassingly unironic."

"She's only a month pregnant," Coffin said, cupping his Zippo against the wind as he paused to light a cigarette. "No guarantees. Besides, irony's passé. Haven't you heard?"

"So say the sentimentalist hicks," Kotowski said. "Babies are noisy little crap machines, Coffin. They eat, they piss, they shit, and they cry—that's pretty much it. They have all the personality of a sack of wet kitty litter. What the hell are you going to do with a *baby*?"

"You can try to make me feel bad about this all you want," Coffin said, "but you're wasting your time—and you're going to be an uncle, almost."

"What a disgusting development," said Kotowski. He turned on Coffin. "You used to be so full of interesting phobias and neuroses. You were practically psychotic. What happened to all of your anxiety about fatherhood? Your angst about how damaged you were? I feel like I hardly know you anymore."

"Oh, please," Coffin said. "I have a panic attack if I cut myself shaving, and I'm still having terrible nightmares. I'm much more mentally ill than you."

"Hmph," Kotowski said. "Nightmares. Big deal. I have pathologies that don't even have names yet." He picked up a flat stone and tossed it sidearm into the harbor. Instead of skipping, it disappeared into the water with a hollow *plonk*.

"The one about the dead children is the one that really gets me," Coffin said. "I dream about them all the time." He plonked a stone into the water, too, then managed to skip one a few times.

"The father killed those kids, right?"

"Right. He couldn't stand it that his wife and kids were living with another man. The boyfriend came home from work, found them all dead, and blew his own head off."

"Well, it's obvious, isn't it?"

"What's obvious?" Coffin said.

"The connection."

"If you say so."

"The father killed his kids—it's the worst thing a father can do," Kotowski said. "You dream about it because you're afraid that could be you. Or worse, in a way—you could be the boyfriend. Deep in your subconscious, you still think you're cursed."

"Nice try, Sigmund Fraud," Coffin said.

"Come on," Kotowski said. "It's perfect. Your father's all mixed up in it, and the girl was in the bathtub, which mirrors your thing about water."

"I don't have a thing about water. I have a thing about boats."

"Whatever," Kotowski said. "If I wasn't an artist, I'd have made a great shrink."

"Your patients would all sue you. You'd last about two days before you told them all to do the world a favor and commit suicide."

The two men walked slowly up the beach, skirting the flock of sleeping gulls. The sunset throbbed its lurid colors at them. A sleek head popped up in the water, just beyond the small breakers. The seal watched them for a long time, until they were blurry dots, arguing loudly in the distance.

Acknowledgments

Many thanks to Mark Wunderlich and James Cancienne, Justin Tussing, Daniel Hayes, Judith McGarry, and Anna Keesey, who read and gently critiqued earlier drafts of *High Season*. Thanks to Henry's grandparents—Gloria Loomis, Richard Goldin, and Alice Goldin—for your manifold generosities. To the board members and application committees of the Fine Arts Work Center in Provincetown and the Corporation of Yaddo—who did not, I'm pretty sure, intend to provide support for the early work on this book—checks are in the mail (but don't get too excited). Much gratitude also to Dr. Samuel Asirvatham, who fixed my heart rhythm and made this bigger, richer life a possibility. Thanks to Maria and Kelley for liking the book, and for all of your help in its final shaping. Stupendous love and devotion to Allyson Goldin Loomis, my editor-for-life and the real fiction writer in the family. There is no greater happiness than lounging with you in the Kolodnys' pool, sipping Citron on the rocks, and trying to figure out who done it.

DEC   2007